Politics 101

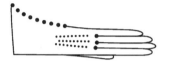

Politics 101

ANNA SMITH

CANTERBURY UNIVERSITY PRESS

UNIVERSITY OF
CANTERBURY
Te Whare Wānanga o Waitaha
CHRISTCHURCH NEW ZEALAND

First published in 2006 by
CANTERBURY UNIVERSITY PRESS
University of Canterbury
Private Bag 4800
Christchurch
NEW ZEALAND

www.cup.canterbury.ac.nz

ISBN 1-877257-41-9

A catalogue record for this book is available from
the National Library of New Zealand

Edited and designed by Rachel Scott
Printed through Bookbuilders, China
Cover concept by Julia Morison
Cover photograph by Brendan Lee
Author photograph by Alan Knowles

Canterbury University Press acknowleges a generous grant
in aid of publication from
Creative New Zealand

ARTS COUNCIL OF NEW ZEALAND *TOI AOTEAROA*

For Sarah and Frances,
who first saw the ties

I would like to thank my family for their long-standing encourage-ment of my writing. This book is above all for Jacob, Sarah, Frances and George and their partners, with my love.

I also owe thanks to the following:

To writers who generously read early drafts, especially Michael-anne Forster and her writing group; Michael Harlow, Owen Marshall and Carolyn Barnes.

In memory of Michael King, who did some research.

To critics Janet Wilson, Antoinette Wilson and Joan Curry.

To friends who love reading, Jane Nicholson, Jenny Lee and Charlotte Hardy.

To my siblings and parents, Jean and Bryan Smith.

To all those who listened and gave wise counsel.

And to Kirsten Rennie, who found a walnut shell.

To good colleagues, especially Annie Potts, Kate Kearns and Cynthia Hawes.

To Peter Hempenstall, Mary Gerram, Philip Taylor and Sarah Bevan for putting me right about things Australian. Needless to say, any errors of interpretation remain my own.

To the University of Canterbury, whose generous leave provi-sions made it possible for the final editing of the manuscript to be completed.

To the staff at the university's Fine Arts Library.

To Julia Morison, who designed the brilliant cover image.

To the anonymous readers who said 'yes'.

To political animals everywhere.

And finally, to Rachel Scott, Richard King and Kaye Godfrey, of Canterbury University Press, who ably brought this book from its rude, unprocessed state through to the beautiful object it is today.

Meg's story

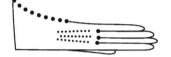

I was born on Black Friday in a brick house with a frosted stag on the door. My name is Margaret Shepherd, Meg to my friends, a diminutive my mother didn't stoop to until I reached middle age. I stand 5 feet 5 inches without shoes and last week at the doctor's I weighed 55 kilos, which if we were using numerology would add up to 2 (5+5+5+5 = 2[0]). Two has brought me nothing but trouble. Seeing every single one of my numbers is unlucky, it doesn't make much difference.

Not that I've always thought like that. I used to believe in bliss before I went to university, where everyone said bliss was unfashionable and if you wanted to grow up, you had to stop thinking that life was going to be kind to you. Ecstasy was for immature teenagers. What we should be doing, these people said, was trying to change the world and make it a better place, but not because you wanted to bring more of your friends into the circle of bliss. No, you had to do it because the human race needed to accept that we were like a disease and smelt bad. Jean-Paul Sartre called this the unhappy consciousness, and my lectures at university were full of ideas about how to get into an unhappy consciousness and stay there.

In those days, women went around wearing black skirts or voluminous dresses covered in flowers. Men wore jeans, and strange facial hair that made it look as if they hadn't bothered to wash when they got up. Once, I went to an encounter group where a man had hair growing all the way from his cheeks to his ears. It did not feel soft and silky as I had imagined, but crisp and dry, while his eyebrows, which were like lobsters' feelers, had an unpleasant, menacing quality.

I went to other encounter groups after that first one, and weekends for activists, and I slept the night on an urban marae. I marched with fellow students, bellowing out songs for peace. It certainly felt companionable standing in front of foreign embassy gates waving placards and throwing eggs at diplomats' cars. But as soon as I started talking about *inner happiness* and *real love*, the activists shuffled their feet.

'They're tired words, Meg,' said a man I wanted to impress. 'They've lost their currency. What young people are after now is social meaning – meaning that can be shared by a *collective*.'

I met a hippy on the street one day coming home from a noisy march on Parliament. He had bloodshot, pale blue eyes that made him look like a fish that had died a long time ago.

'Free love,' he said, 'that's cool. Why don't you come with me to Sweden? There's this great commune there. Girls do the meals, guys work in the gardens. Far out, man.'

The hippy hung around the city trying to get women to come to Sweden with him, but as far as I know, they never did.

'Look what happened to Katherine Mansfield. I mean, I only have to *see* a pear tree to get disillusioned.' Steph had black stockings and long dark hair she could almost sit on. It was massively dense with curls, and she sometimes wore it in a squashed roll on the side of her head. The weight of her hair used to make my neck exhausted. Seeing my own hair was as thin and feathery as the down on a duckling's behind and the colour of overcooked pastry, I took to staring at women better endowed than myself, and began a scrapbook of pieces of my friends' hair.

'You're so morbid, Meg. It's weird to steal people's hair,' one of them said when we were all having dinner one night, I can't remember who now, Gillian or Lou. I stole from Steph, the roll-wearer, later.

I didn't have a clue what a pear tree had to do with disillusion, or who Katherine Mansfield was, but I found out soon enough. Now my garden is full of pear trees, planted by myself. When I look out the window on certain nights in spring at the sheet of white stretching skywards, I know that the ironies life throws up take everyone by surprise, most especially the J.-P. Sartres and Katherine Mansfields of this world.

If you could describe the learning curve I took when I left home to go to the city, it would have looked like this:

passage the first: in which the heroine feels joy at her prospects

passage the second: the heroine builds a Happy City and makes some worldly friends

passage the third: an unexpected shock

passage the fourth: in which the classic reversal of fortune occurs and the heroine's downward slide begins

passage the fifth: disillusionment at every turn

passage the sixth: revenge

passage the seventh: bliss is restored and the heroine plants her orchard.

Note that not all points along the curve are equidistant. The first two appeared in a matter of weeks, whereas the fifth lasted more than two years, and even today breaks out when least expected.

Once foresworn, the path back to bliss is long and narrow; its end comes and goes with the seasons. I still never win Lotto, I'm just not a lucky person by nature. But if I were to see my old friends again as I am today, a middle-aged woman selling pears at the gate, I would be able to tell them that only last week the bone-density tests arrived back from the laboratory and the doctor shook his head and told me I was getting younger. Notionally, he said, I had the bones of a thirty-five-year-old woman, which, given my history, he said was a great surprise.

So nothing is predictable, I would say to my friends. Nothing lasts, not even the passage of time. Not even those seeds of disillusion we sowed when we were young.

It takes only an instant to slide from one state to another. I remember the first day when the city that had held out its arms to me slammed its doors in my face and I was shut out. Shut out from bliss, from inner happiness, from finding true love. I did my best not to notice, I pretended the waves were as high as ever and I was still riding their tops. What girl of eighteen set on dancing into life wants to know that when she's sitting pretty, fortune can pull her down faster than gravity?

Let me tell you how it happened. How one little thing, small as the knot in the end of a piece of thread, pushed me off my perch, and suddenly I found myself sliding faster and faster down waves steep as houses, watching my handful of treasures skitter away from me, bobbing towards a horizon I could no longer see.

I was noseying around the shops after lectures. I'd taken to rushing through my reading and going down into the city to explore, to catch the life wriggling there like a glittering fish on a hook.

The morning breathed on my face as it always did, pulling me down the ziggurat of steps to the shops. Before I knew it, I was dreaming in front of palaces of glass, smoke-coloured fragments of my face darting everywhere; feeling the slub of fabrics; weighing a green pepper in my hand, the exotic fruit so bright it looked like a globe of wax; watching the men in heavy coats asleep on benches. You know that feeling. You're restless, all over the place, but quiet as a lizard. You can feel the slow, slumbering currents of the earth under your feet, while inside you're sending flickering pieces of yourself into the atmosphere, a million per second. I circled the streets with the pigeons, scooped water from a fountain, mulled over old glass jars in an opportunity shop and brought adzuki beans and a porcelain bowl from the Chinese warehouse.

Then I saw him. Worn jacket, athletic walk, down-at-heel tan shoes. How could I help it if I remembered?

I called out across the cloud of pigeons and the traffic. He was disappearing into Cuba Street, being swallowed by the lunchtime crowds. The wind pulled the words out of my mouth, tossing them into the air. He turned around for a moment but his face was far away, too pale, melting into a sea of other faces.

I began to run, cold sweat trickling underneath my clothes. I ran past early newspaper hawkers and men who tried to give me little pink cards. I ran past students picketing a bookshop, and a group of men with shaved heads and yellow robes.

I knocked into a pile of boxes leaning from a doorway. People were beginning to look strangely at my drunken passage, this young woman with hair flying, shouting incoherently at the air. I lumbered along behind him, heavy-footed, with something bursting in my chest.

We drew level as a line of buses swept by at the lights at the end of Lambton Quay. I reached out a hand. As soon as I'd touched his shoulder, I knew it was too thin under the jacket, the fabric flapping where my father's bulging arms would have been.

'Oh.' Amazing what words come to the rescue when you've had a shock. My heart still flinging itself against my ribcage like a trapped sparrow, a mouth belonging to a stranger opened politely. The thin man gave a tepid smile, stepped away from the kerb. A horde of pedestrians poured past me, and I hated the flashing *Cross Now* letters for turning me into an orphan again.

All right, I confess. I did believe in bliss, but not because that's all I knew. He left us. My father left us when I was twelve. For years, I still went on believing in bliss, in happy families and in real love. I couldn't help knowing that the next day would be different.

It often was. Long, hot days walking down dusty roads picking wild apples; watching motionless cows, and white tufts of sheep needled into the hills as the sun set. Catching frogs in the swimming pool, hunting their spawn. And travelling down to Wellington, running into the future. I had an eager mouth, Mum said, hungry for change. To be a chief in my life, not an Indian.

So what if I had thought it was my father. So what?

I found myself wandering into Kirkcaldie and Stains. The windows were being dressed for autumn. There were desolate mounds of leaves waiting to be artfully scattered, and bits of mannequin lying half-dressed against chairs and dust-cloths.

My mother had been on a trip to Sydney and came back to Cambridge with photos of window displays from David Jones.

You should have seen the store, Margaret. It was a mass of flowers. Such luxury! I felt like a princess. You know, you should do a course in design, dear. You could be a talented window-dresser and it's a very respectable profession with a real tradition behind it.

The thought of window-dressing made me nauseous, to tell the truth. The dingy backdrops and little heaps of plaster dust that no one saw, crotchless men, and all that faded pink flesh waiting to be covered. Grotesque, Henry would have called it: grotesque, and very working class.

I crossed the store until I reached Haberdashery, the least dressed of Kirkcaldie and Stains displays. Pairs of socks and gloves and mittens for the winter season lay stacked against embroidery threads and tapestry kitsets. Forests of metal hoops waved from slopes of linens and calicoes and muslins. Minarets of glass phials waited to be filled with perfume or beads. Haberdashery was perpetually in chaos, its counters a wild collection of goods for odd parts of the body mixed in with cottons and sewing notions for the city's dressmakers and supplies for its handcraft artists.

All the nameless items the store could not find a home for elsewhere made their way over here. *What's this curious thing?* I can imagine the store manager saying to one of his assistants, holding out a set of needle-threaders and emery boards. *Take it over to Haberdashery, there's a good girl.* When you found something, you pulled it out triumphantly as if it were a rare treasure you had been searching for all your life.

I wasn't here today for supplies. Ordinarily I might have been. Hadn't Peach Grove Girls' given me the sewing prize? I'd cashed it in the next day for a Pink Floyd album. Still, that didn't mean I'd forgotten my needlework. I was an ace embroiderer, taught to fill a sampler by my grandmother on my seventh birthday.

It was a pair of cream gloves that finally caught my eye. There was just something about them, the way their purple stitching marked a shiny path of silk from wrist to fingertip like the trail left by a crawling snail, or a silkworm. Mum would have called them delicate. Dad would have laughed at her.

If I could have sat down and drawn a pair of hands, they would have had tiny mouths pinned to them. Tiny, hungry mouths.

When I was ten I had seen a picture of St Sebastian stuck with dozens of arrows, his eyes rolled back into his head, the palms of his hands trickling blood. Underneath it explained how 'suffering turned to sweet manna in the saint's mouth'.

Mum told me it was a lesson against masochism – against confusing pleasure and pain, Margaret. – Why is he a saint, then, Mum? – Hush, dear. Catholics have some very confused ideas.

Here I was on Tuesday afternoon in Wellington's largest department store, a thief with hungry hands, pierced like Sebastian, stuck through like my school needle-book, the one Mum had made out of cardboard from a Weet-Bix packet and covered in brown corduroy and charcoal flannel with 'Margaret Shepherd, Standard One' written in red pen on the inside.

The soft leather of the gloves gave off a faint brine smell of cured skin. I saw my mother stroking my cheek when I was sick with scarlet fever, bringing me drinks and ice blocks. And I saw Dad tickling my ear with Little Ned, buzzing the cream and purple stuffed elephant into my hair.

I pulled the gloves down over my fingers, stretching them as far as they would reach into the leather, noticing how the tips of the gloves collapsed inwards, empty and fleshless. My fingers were shorter than the standard size, a fact I knew to be true because I had been told before.

You haven't aristocratic hands, I'm afraid. Oh, dear me no, they're quite working class. And look at those lines on your palms. You know, if I wasn't a woman of faith I'd say you were going to lead a tortured life. But, as the world's greatest dramatist once wrote, our lives are our own fault; our stars don't make us underlings.

A plangent wave of fragrance from the perfume counters drifted over Haberdashery and mournfully circled my head, my palms prickled and prickled, Little Ned whispered in my ear.

I tweaked and straightened the gloves and marched out of the store. It was close to 5 p.m. Kirkcaldie and Stains was due to shut. I edged around the last-minute bargain-hunters, my shoes trailing leaves from the errant window display, and set out for the door.

As I approached the main exit, there was a commotion. Behind, a sound of voices knotted together, shouting. They were coming after me, baying slavering dogs only seconds away from plunging their fangs into my neck. The store intercom crackled: there would be a voice instructing me to stop. People were turning their heads. I hung back, dragging my feet, criminal eyes fixed on the polished mush-room floor.

When nothing happened, I wondered if someone could have been giving away free perfume samples. Mum told me that sort of thing happened at David Jones.

Sometimes they get stuck with perfume samples, Margaret. They come round with a wicker basket and spray perfume in the air and give out little bottles of it. You know, I've always thought you had a nose for fragrance. I could just see you working at a parfumier's in Paris.

It was some other thief they were after; they hadn't spotted me at all. I felt a mean gratitude for the diversion when I saw the guilty woman in a winter coat being propelled towards the back of the shop.

'She was filling her pocket with Belgian chocolates. Right under my bloody nose!' exclaimed an indignant shopper as they were herded towards the exit.

I took a furtive glimpse at the store detective before I left. She looked cool as the shadows that were falling directly down from the hills, filling the city with an inky-blue light and reminding me – *Meg, Klepto Girl!* – that it was time to go back to the hostel or I would be late for dinner.

Everyone steals. A psychologist will tell you that people who take things can be suffering from adjustment problems. Maybe their parents didn't give them enough pocket money or cookies, or they've just lost their jobs and it's Christmas. Or maybe they had kind parents but they like the challenge, the rush of it all. Besides, kids steal constantly: it's a part of growing up, of learning about boundaries, about where one person's property ends and another's begins.

So I reasoned to myself on the Newtown bus, wearing my cream leather gloves, which pulsed like the siren on *Z-Cars*. I was no differ-ent. I'd taken money from my mother's purse, picked Mrs Clark's strawberries when she was asleep. I'd even raided the local dairy for Fru Jus and choc bombs. Seeing a man who resembled my father had given me a shock and I'd temporarily flipped back to childhood. Simple.

I hadn't counted on repercussions. *Cast your bread upon the waters, Margaret, and it will come back to you.* Effects, a child learns, always follow causes.

That theft, small as the knot in a piece of cotton, small as a seed, started to sprout somewhere on a cluttered counter at the back of the universe. While the city ate and slept and went about its business, the seed poked down a snout of a root, and then sprouted a prickle of leaves. One day when I wasn't looking, it moved in. I think my first years away from home were spent in hacking at this giant invisible plant that had surreptitiously taken over my life and, in its turn, had begun stealing from *me*.

Meanwhile, dinner was getting cold. At the hostel, oblivious to my brush with crime, Gillian and Lou were waiting.

When I first met Gillian she reminded me of a hyperactive corgi, darting everywhere and crackling with energy. She'd been dating since we arrived, studying law and accounting so she could meet a suitable man to take home to her Hawke's Bay family, who were a cut above Lou's and mine.

'Meg! Where have you been?' she barked. 'We had dinner hours ago.' She lifted a bowl from a plate, pointed to a mound of sausages and mashed potatoes. 'Go on,' agitating the plate to bring it back to life, 'we saved them.'

'How was your day?' said Lou, whose father worked at a school in Greytown. Lou had freckles; brown hair that fell in strings. Already she'd swapped her skirts for loose muslin dresses and roman sandals. Last year she'd been a special youth representative at a United Nations conference in New York. She'd met members of the Black Panthers in Harlem, and the experience had changed her for ever. On the bedroom wall she shared with Gillian, there was a Che Guevara poster.

'I've been to Kirk's. What do you think of these gloves?'

'Nice,' said Lou.

'I thought you were short of money. Look at them – they don't even fit you properly.' Gillian scrutinised the purchase through narrowed eyes.

I adjusted my glasses. Since this afternoon they'd been pressing above my ears. 'They were on sale,' I said hastily.

'Yes, but you don't have to buy something just because it's on *sale*. My mother always says a bargain's a burden if it's bought in haste.'

Gillian was quick to suspect the health of spectacle-wearers. If she were responsible for colonising outer space, she certainly wouldn't permit short-sightedness. Physical weaknesses had to be weeded out. In this, she was merely being a clone of her ruthless ancestors, who had farmed in Hawke's Bay for three generations. The same toughness that made Mr Blaikie a wealthy rural accountant turned up in Gillian as an impatience for all forms of genetic failure.

'What of it?' I said rudely. 'I like them. Anyway, what about Lou?'

My politically savvy friend had never been distracted by clothes. Unimaginable to me, but there you are. Not to mention that she'd been crazy about *issues* from the time she could walk, thanks to her father, who used to coach her in politics when they were raking up the lawn. If Lou won a school prize, she would have bought the collected works of Karl Marx.

Politically speaking I was a dunce, but my dressmaking skills were fast acquiring a reputation at the Stella Maris Hostel (*It's such a lovely name, Margaret. I know we're not Catholics, but I can't help feeling you'll be happy in a hostel with a name like that*) and I had to agree with Gillian. If Lou wanted to keep up with us, her wardrobe required radical action.

Pigs might fly. She let me cut out a Viyella paisley dress for her once, but it looked so awful I rolled it into a ball and threw it in the back of the wardrobe. Lou favoured clothes with the dimensions of a tent. When she took up harriers three years later, the sight of her in shorts stunned everyone.

That year, I'd arrived in Wellington at the end of a summer so hot I'd worn a sleeveless cotton frock with a scooped-out neck and so short it barely reached mid-thigh. My legs were brown after weeks at the beach; my scanty hair had acquired golden lights mixed with the natural brown that my mother always said was a product of my Scottish ancestors. 'Celts,' she had said enviously, as if they were the last race swimming in her own blood. 'Even their hair is distinctive.'

The 1970s were exciting years to be in the capital. The harbour and its inhabited green shoulders plunging into the sea filled me with an unfamiliar sense of ownership, as if they were all there – the scenes, the people – for my personal delight. I claimed I was a Wellingtonian after a week in the city, and turned my face to the orange sun that tirelessly crossed the sky. Whoever would have thought a hot blob of sun could shine so much better in a new place? In those days I hardly remember clouds, just light, and high blue skies.

Life stretched out in front of me. Bright as the bulbils of ferry lights steaming around the point, each fresh day rose, shook itself, and danced in front of my face. It made my fingers itch. I picked up my scissors from the sewing kit, plunged them into yards of shiny material. Up from the cloth sprang a forest of figures waving at the sky. I made men and women carrying pipe-cleaner handbags and briefcases and umbrellas rushing along the street, dogs with collars, and quilted fish jumping through sequin-capped waves.

In my last year of school I had won the annual prize for Creative Needlework. My hands could turn a piece of cloth into a world. As far back as I could remember I'd won awards for embroidery and crewel work. I could run up a Voguish dress without a pattern, work a buttonhole by hand and effortlessly put a zipper in a pair of trousers.

The handcrafted city sat on the windowsill in the Stella Maris Hostel for Girls in Newtown. Every morning its optimism reminded me of the world I'd left behind. I'd jumped ship and run away to look for treasure, and now here were its first signs glimmering in the hostel bedroom. The wind hissed and blew in stinging waves against the panes. The dog with the pipe-cleaner collar put out his tongue as the little silk man ran for the bus. Everyone was looking for treasure.

When I saw the lists of books for my new university courses, I thought I'd found it.

'Students are advised to purchase Malory's *Le Morte d'Arthur*. It is recommended for French I that students read at least two of the following before term begins: Baudelaire, *Les Fleurs du Mal*; Stendhal, *Le Rouge et le Noir*; *L'Etranger* by Camus.'

Exotic, sophisticated names: passwords to a hidden inner world. If I could shrink to the size of my shiny figures, I would know where to find treasure. At least, that's what I thought at the beginning, leaning closer and closer to the tiny city of silk.

After Lou and Gillian had fallen asleep, I threw open the window. With the tepid heat of the bakery next door filling my nose, I picked up the gloves and pushed them down into the bottom of a suitcase.

Out in the night somewhere was my father with his baritone voice singing Vera Lynn and Schubert love songs, which always made my mother irritable. Everything about Dad had been an adventure. I used to wait for him outside the Riverina, that Cambridge hotel with the dirty cream stucco exterior and rotten fire escapes ending in mid-air. It disappeared twenty years ago, but when I was eleven and had my eyes glued to one of the windows while Dad sang and played billiards, it seemed the best place in the world. Once Mum thought I'd run away, but I'd only biked down to watch them. When she found out she gave me a skin-blistering hiding, a rare form of punishment in our family.

Now my father would be singing Vera Lynn in someone else's room.

I went to sleep slowly that night of the theft, the smell of yeasty bread still filling the room, the sounds of half-life all around me. The walls of Stella Maris were thin particleboard. Next door, Lou was snoring, Gillian's blankets rustling near my head.

I've found there is always a grace period after a shock — as if the faultlines drawn along a building's foundations by an earthquake temporarily vanish back into the stone, and your world goes to sleep again. It wasn't yet the hour for true disillusion, which skimmed away to my blind spot and stayed there, biding its time.

The next morning I woke ready for bliss again, rinsed and spark-ling. The day was glorious.

I stepped down from the cablecar, set off across the cricket field and up the hill to class. A new leather briefcase sliced an airy arc against my leg, my hair was on fire with the early sun, and my linen skirt danced and scraped against its lining. Ambience – was that the right word for it? Yes, I was full of the ambience of the morning. This autumn morning was stroking my skin alive, my body's portholes creaking open to the day's ambient warmth.

Lou had arranged to meet me for lunch. We unwrapped our brown-bread egg sandwiches and sat outside sunning our legs.

'Had a good lecture?'

'How anyone could call a mouse a *wee sleekit, cowrin' timrous beastie* beats me.' There wasn't much else I could say about English Lit. French disappointed me too: *Les Fleurs du Mal* possessed not a single flower, not even an evil-looking one. I had expected Venus flytraps or flowers that poisoned you if you ate them. Baudelaire, it turned out, was more interested in losing unhappy poets in the garden of his mind. 'What about yours?'

'Fantastic. Sociology is great. And Politics. All those things I did last year – they make so much more sense now.' Lou munched thoughtfully on her sandwich.

I suppose she was referring to her experience in New York. Imagine, a girl from the Wairarapa crossing Fifth Avenue! My grasp of geog-raphy was slight, but I did know something about America from Mum's *Woman's Days*, full of glossy pictures with models wearing gloves and a brassiere, and saying, 'I dreamed I took the bull by the horns in my Maidenform Bra.' New York was the Empire State, shops on Fifth, Grace Kelly handbags and long cars with tiny TVs in them.

'I heard you went to a lot of diplomatic parties.'

Lou waved her hand impatiently. 'It was bourgeois, all that eat-ing. They had fresh melons, Meg, *every day*.' She sank her teeth into an apple, broke it noisily on her teeth. 'The UN should be about working for peace, not cocktail parties. Which reminds me,' she said, wiping at the juice that was running down her chin, 'why don't you come with us to the next Stud Ass meeting?'

'Huh?'

'Students' Association.' Lou said the words patiently, as if she were teaching a child. 'It's an SRC – like a forum, you know? We discuss political issues.'

SRC? I was a child, then. 'Oh, I don't think it would interest me.' My politics were limited to fervent school speeches that were over and done in ten minutes.

'That's the *point*, Meg. You'll never know about politics and how it works until you come to a meeting.'

Meeting. The word had an ominous ring. Once, I'd looked at the rules of Mum's bridge club. There were resolutions, motions that lay on the table, motions substantive, procedural and foreshadowed. There were split votes, correct terms of address, minutes recorded as read. My mother spent more time writing up her meetings than she did actually playing bridge after Dad left.

Gillian was going to the meeting, she told us over dinner (coleslaw with tree-tomato – Lou; potato salad with dressing from a tin – Gillian; mince with a heaped tablespoon of mixed herbs, and lemon pudding, burnt – Meg), because her boyfriend Chris was spoiling for a fight with the commie intellectuals. The prospect of seeing a bunch of communists and radicals being slammed briskly against the wall by Gill's sporty boyfriend made me forget the cooking failures. I determined to make a new dress for the occasion. A new *summer* dress, despite the fact that it was now mid-March and the days were losing their warmth.

Later, my friends watched while I snipped triangles and rhomboids from the edges of a bolt of mattress ticking acquired in one of my op shop hunts. The scissors whirred, fingers dipped and flashed, deltas and peaks of cotton swayed under my hands: it was poetry moving over the cloth. The day before the meeting, I was still bent over the hostel's Singer, feeding in yards of striped fabric.

'Wow,' said Lou when I'd put it on. 'You look...'

'Out of this world,' finished Gill.

And we rode into town on the bus, me on the edge of my seat all the way in case the Vogue tailored dress might crush.

The Upper Common Room was overflowing with students.

'It's *stacked*,' whispered Lou, but how could you know whether 'stacked' referred to right- or left-wing supporters? A mass of university scarves and Aran jerseys had gathered at the back. These must be the Right. They were giants: big men and women with superior physiques, healthy scrubbed skin.

Sitting across the front were a lot of uncouth people who did not fit together under their clothes in the same way as the Right. Like Lou, the women wore dresses, beads and caftans, jeans and muslin shirts. In between, one or two students moved up and down with pens, clipboards, note-pads. Lou said they were *lobbying*.

The Left, I concluded, moved disjointedly – in the way your limbs might jerk into the air when someone struck your knee, as if they could not hold their separate parts together. You would need an entirely different dress pattern for a woman with spastic arms and legs. Mentally, I chalked out a loose-fitting caftan with an embroidered bird flying across the bodice.

At the front of the hall, the Students' Association Executive sat at a row of tables bearing water jugs, ashtrays, more notepaper and pens, and a tape recorder mounted next to a man with a luxuriant moustache and a black beret who chain-smoked throughout the meeting. A pale-skinned woman, awesomely beautiful, with lustrous red hair, took out a mother-of-pearl-inlaid case and offered it to the man with the moustache.

Their elaborate transaction hypnotised me. The man in the beret pulled back a wooden slide on the top of the case and a cigarette rocketed into the air. Crammed on top of individual springs, the cigarettes flung themselves out when released, slightly crumpled owing to their excessive length. The case had been designed for Damascus smokers, and it did not accommodate itself happily to Benson and Hedges, a bizarre fact that I happened to know because my father had had one exactly the same. It had been made in Palestine and he'd brought it back home with him after the war. Mum kept it on our living-room mantelpiece with the stuffed elephant Dad made in an army hospital after he was wounded in the war, and his RAF medal for reconnaissance work in North Africa.

'That's Diana Fahey,' said Lou, noticing my interest in the woman with the cigarette case. Lou, Gillian and I were sitting together, sandwiched between Right and Left factions. 'She's a radical. She votes against the rest of the Exec as often as she can.'

'Oh. Does that mean the Exec are conservative?'

'Oh, no. They're Left; it's just that Diana's more radical than any of them,' said Lou admiringly.

'Huh. She looks like a radical tart, if you ask me.' Gillian's mind could not put 'beautiful' and 'left-wing' in the same sentence.

Embarrassment at our reactionary friend's crude display was forestalled by the president's calling of the meeting to order. Apparently, it was stacked tonight because a controversial motion had arisen. Tabled at last month's meeting, the motion had been held over owing to an insufficient *quorum*, another word in my mother's minute book.

The radical Diana, whose looks must have assured her of numerous boyfriends, I calculated, drained the water jug, pushed back her chair.

President-elect Arthur Meyer pounded the desk with his fist and read out the motion: 'That the Students' Association show its solidarity towards the Palestine Liberation Organisation by donating $500 of its earmarked funds to Al Fatah.'

Somewhere in the hall an electrifying wind that announces the coming of a tropical storm stirred into life. Like some vast plain of restless beasts awaiting the disaster that drives everything before it, we all felt the storm's coming. Ears flicking, apprehensive down to our most invisible cells, we waited.

'Mr Chairman, for too long we've mouthed sentimental messages of support for the people of Palestine!' An angry hiss of lightning crackled around the room. 'Here's our opportunity to show them we identify with their struggle against Zionism and American imperialism!' A man with flickering eyes and a face like a rodent scuttled back to his seat.

A bearded man with a pile of newspapers against his seat spoke next: 'The Socialist Action League supports this motion, Mr Chairman,' he rumbled, 'and so should all people committed to bringing justice to this country!'

'As a m-member of the Women's Collective, I would like to show our s-solidarity with Palestinian women!' Another crash of lightning. The girl wore a scarf on her head and seemed to have a speech impediment, but the din of the opposition was so great that none of us could be sure.

This is great, I thought, mixing the cocktail of noise from the safety of my chair, swirling it down. This was a *real* meeting. I opened my skin to the deluge.

Storm, disaster, deluge – the words sound overblown, but in those days politics was the stage we'd been waiting for. Here we could let go. Every issue was momentous; every debate, we played to the death. Like the rest, I was on a total high. All that energy blasted us into space: we were like moon-walkers, masters of gravity. Politics was a high-speed transfusion – we certainly didn't need party drugs; it was the fission of collective energy that blew our minds. We could never get enough of it, and it never ran out.

Maybe we were repressed – that's what people said later, that our politicking was just a sublimation – but I don't think so. It forced us to own our rage and passions, and gave us a battlefield where we could play them out. It felt as if we had control of our own futures, that if we shouted louder, words and emotions would be powerful enough to knock down the whole of world capitalism, which we saw disappearing in one terrifying explosion.

People leapt shrieking from trauma to trauma, hurling speeches like missiles. In that wild climate of dramatic words and debates, my brave new dress felt out of place. It was self-indulgent, a relic of sewing classes in a country prep school. A hospital drama would be a more appropriate setting for this heroic struggle against evil. My butterfly mind summoned up waxed linoleum passages and creatures in white caps and gowns.

Nurse Shepherd wipes the sweat from Dr Kildare's brow after a life-threatening operation. There is blood on her white hospital gown, the instrument tray is a mess, but the patient is breathing.

Or a spy series, with 1940s wardrobes and Rita Hayworth hair:

One grey door opens in a line of grey doors and a woman walks into a cell. The door shuts behind her with a crash, and a key turns in the lock. Intrepid Odette Churchill says nothing as the Nazis pull out all her toenails. Winston's secrets are safe with her.

That came from one of my speeches. I used to sit in assembly and wonder what it would be like to stare down at a set of pulpy bleeding toes after the Nazis had finished with you. Did Odette Churchill's nails ever grow back, I wondered, and did she need special shoes?

Ignorant of the workings of the Palestine Liberation Organisation, I immersed myself in the chaos of feeling that night, remembering St Sebastian and tortured heroines everywhere, and waiting for each delicious thrust of argument, which seemed to have nothing to do with rational knowledge at all. It was not words, but a free-floating anarchy that swept us along. If some of us couldn't believe what others were saying, couldn't join in their fight to the death, at least we should be allowed to feel it.

A man from the conservative wing of the Student Christian Movement stood up. 'This motion is a piece of shit! We should be giving our political funds to help fight poverty *here*, not giving them to a bunch of Arabs. Look at the Sallies; they know more about suffering than any of us!'

'Mr Chairman, despite the round of catcalls and whistles given to our last speaker, I support his position. He's the only one who's said something reasonable!'

Right and Left, like rival sports teams, struggled for possession of the floor. I weighed up the merits of supporting Al Fatah, saw my head floating off on its own, trying to talk, spinning in the current of passion.

Lou, defiantly left-wing, spoke in favour, but her voice became lost in a hail of static from the microphone and an acid rain of foot-stamping from the Right.

'Sit down and shuddup, ya fat cow!'

'Can't hear! Can't hear!'

'Come closer and say that, sweetheart!'

'Order, order!'

'Fuck off, bitch!'

Lou retreated. Women from the Collective spat abuse back. En masse, the Collective was like a herd of wild horses. I spent a lot of time that first year at university deciding whether it was a good idea to be a horse or, indeed, some other beast. Student talk was full of animal words (pig, cock, cow, fox, sheep, bitch, goat, bird, chick, *vache* – this for the more European-minded of us), and you had to choose the right sort of animal to be or you would end up with no friends.

At the height of the storm, a young man with hair so blond it was white, and carrying clipboard and pen, took the floor.

'Friends,' he announced dramatically, raising his hands, 'Remember Palestine! Remember the Bay of Pigs! My Lai!'

The convulsions ceased. Back-biting dropped away. The new speaker addressed the crowd as if he were already a demagogue.

'Who's that?' I hissed to Lou.

'Ssshh! Henry Ballantyne.'

'Friends, these are examples of unspeakable atrocity. Atrocities committed by, or with the support of, the most powerful nation on earth. May I remind you of our commitment to condemning oppression and supporting self-determination everywhere!'

His timing was superb: the Right was running out of energy. Some of them had gone next door to watch a rugby replay on television; the rest sat waiting to vote.

When it finally came, Henry and his supporters won by thirty votes. There was uproar. The Student Exec, with Diana Fahey newly elected as their Women's VP, hurried off downstairs to celebrate a strategic victory for the Left in the cafe.

It was a time for review. At the heart of the maelstrom of bodies pushing frantically towards the door, a subtle form of accounting was taking place. For Gillian and me, two young country women ignorant of the ways of student politics, the meeting had been a baptism by fire. Each of us felt moved to make choices and decisions we had never dreamed of in the provinces: me taking a grudging step towards the Left while Gill, siding with Chris against communism and intellectuals and the growing tide of red staining the globe, stepped into the arms of the Right.

I see now that that was when bliss began packing its bags. It knew my numbers were coming up seriously unlucky; knew better than to stick around someone who was about to be dumped in trouble so big there wasn't even a name for it. And disillusion sneaked closer, whistling a sprightly tune from the side of its mouth.

Blame Lou's dress for what happened next. March had turned into April and we were sitting around the heater talking about what we'd all wear to a party and I saw her blue velvet dress hanging in our wardrobe. Midnight blue, with a deep neckline and soft gathered sleeves. She'd worn it once before and I'd caught myself wanting to touch it, run its prickle-soft nap through my fingers.

'Are you going to wear it?'

'Not tonight. I'm thinking maybe this top.' She held up a peasant blouse embroidered with red strawberries.

I've explained already that Lou wasn't into clothes, but she did have a few things packed away for times like these. Henry Ballantyne had invited us to his flat-warming party. Well, he'd asked Lou, who had asked Gillian and me to come along.

Gillian deliberated by consulting her weekend horoscope, knowing the party would be full of political debates driven by weedy men with no social prospects. 'Like a squiz?' she asked, handing over the newspaper.

I flapped her away. Who needed an oracle? I *wanted* to go. Henry's quick cunning, his worldliness and clever arguments had amazed me at the meeting, and I had to see more.

Lou pulled out the dress and laid it over the bed. 'Why don't you try it?' she said. Whether it was because she disapproved of my choice (pin-tucks with a Peter Pan collar) or felt sorry for me, I don't know, but I capered with excitement and held it up against me. *Hollywood.* A cool Corso activist looked out under a skirt cut from the night sky. In this gear she could take on the universe: student politicians, store detectives, her mother, anyone.

Flat Two, 17 Garden View Road, was in a two-storey villa buried in trees that looked on to the wooded slopes around the crest of Mt Victoria. Wearing my magic dress, I wavered up the steep path behind the others, aware of the cold bush smell, the quietness of the trees. A light snapped on, and Henry was greeting us at the door.

'We ran into each other at Corso a while back,' said Lou, introducing Gillian, who pretended to be bored, and me, wide-eyed and trying not to look naive. 'Henry's involved in student politics (*as if we didn't know*, I thought), and I've just joined his Aid and Development Group.'

The floor of the flat trembled with intellectual dialogue. I stumbled across a conversation that spread right across the lounge and into the hall. It seemed to be about compulsory military service, which I'd never heard of. I stared. Lou and Gillian had both deserted me. I found myself gawping at a striking woman with curling black hair, a gentle mouth and very dark, thick eyebrows.

'The anti-war movement's peaked, and Marshall knows it.' The woman tossed her hair, twisted a ringlet around her fingers. 'He's counting on public apathy.'

'For a change,' smirked a grey-haired man in a beret. 'Since when, Steph, have National ever wanted an intelligent constituency?'

'In that case,' interrupted Lou from the other side of the room, 'we're going to have to educate them ourselves.'

'Hear hear,' responded a dozen voices, and the initiative passed into the hall.

I had nothing to say. What good were my high-school speeches to me now?

Ladies and gentlemen, boys and girls, were it not for Captain Cook, these shores would never have been settled by our ancestors.

Ladies and gentlemen, the region must remember that its ultimate loyalties remain with all those nations that honour democracy.

'She's said nothing all evening. Wake up! What do *you* think?'

I turned around in my chair to see Diana Fahey leaning against the mantelpiece.

'Me?'

'Yes. It's Meg Shepherd, isn't it? Lou's told me about you,' said Diana tersely, giving her hair a *you're-surrounded-come-out-with-your-hands-up* kind of shake. 'What's your position?'

In one of those silences that sometimes fall on party spirits, I found everyone's eyes turning towards us.

The captive took a swig of wine, glanced uncertainly at the audience, cleared her throat.

Nothing came out at all. The pros and cons of the argument, like little neat packets of salt and pepper, had vanished from my head. Lou's dress was treacherously silent. My interrogator raised one eyebrow. Her mouth twitched. At any moment she would burst out laughing.

'Oh, I'm against conscription. Ahhh . . . Actually, I'm very against it.'

A small movement distracted me. A growing lightness filled the room. Henry Ballantyne had entered the lounge and was heading this way, a welcoming grin on his face.

Diana turned to hear another opinion. My dullness clunked apologetically to the floor.

'Glad you could join us, Meg.' Henry wore a navy guernsey, a blue-black open-necked shirt and dark blue jeans. I suppose the outfit chimed with his unusual eyes, which were the colour of blue hyacinths. Years later, Steph and I had an argument over their exact shade. I won. Steph always was colour-deprived, particularly with the more subtle shades.

Personally, I would have picked Henry Ballantyne for a fawn man, despite the eyes, but in all the time I knew him, his wardrobe consisted solely of blue-black the consistency of Salvation Army serge, and crisp denims that he pressed a crease into. That first time we met, however, I was too overawed to be critical. My inner bad-taste detector had unaccountably been switched off.

Henry settled himself on the arm of my chair. 'Well then, what's everyone talking about in here?'

The debate shifted and I threw him a look of gratitude – *thanks for saving me from being a fool, Henry* – as he perched swaying above me. *Thanks for saving me from Diana.*

In the fourth form, when we were drawing a cross-section of

the buttercup – *Watch those anthers on the ends of the stamens, girls; remember, they're little pollen sacs* – our biology teacher had told the whole class the story of my parents' courtship on the Limited. *Your father, Meg, sat on the arm of your mother's seat the whole way to Wellington. It was very romantic.* I sat in the science lab, the tiny yellow flower pared apart on a slide, and tried to imagine my father's red face held like a wild bloom above Mum's.

Now it was my turn for immortality – by which most of us, naturally, meant romance. And that was going to be easy, because it wouldn't take much to lick my parents' record.

Henry bent over me as my heart rocked in my ears.

'What do you think of our party?'

It was a sign. Someone out there listening to my confusion had sent a student politician to put me right.

I told him what it had been like coming from a house in Cambridge with a frosted stag on the front door to a city where everyone except me had heard of military service. I couldn't stop. I admitted to being an only child; I confessed that my father had left, and how my mother had become a Christadelphian. I lied about my Bursary marks and, worse, I told him how much I loved sewing.

To everything, Henry nodded sagely. Then, just before he got up to go, he whispered in my ear, 'Why don't we meet for a coffee next week and talk?' He inclined his head closer, idly stroking the velvet of Lou's dress. 'You know, I can't bear to think of you becoming a working-class drone. And,' he added sternly, so that a shiver trilled down my back, 'we'll have to rethink the sewing hobby. Sewing belongs to the petit bourgeoisie. You can do a lot better with your hands than that!'

When he'd gone, Gillian came over, bursting to know what we'd been talking about. How could she guess I'd found someone who understood me, who actually seemed to sympathise with my backwoods past, and who wanted to lead me through the mysterious undergrowth of student politics?

Lou was more guarded. 'Watch out,' she hissed. 'Henry Ballantyne is a Casanova. He's got a thing about first-years. He'll get you to trust him, and then use you.'

'*Use* me?'

'He'll drag you into his political schemes. You'll be doing his Gestetnering and typing if you're not careful.'

I looked up indignantly. People were beginning to leave.

'He says I have potential.'

Lou sighed. Gillian, who'd gone off to get our coats, pulled a face. 'We're missing our beauty sleep, girls,' she said. For the moment, that was the end of it.

Sometime during the next week, I met Henry at the cafe. I nearly didn't go. The whole thing was making me more nervous than I was letting on to Lou, who followed me around the hostel making endless cups of syrupy cocoa and warning me about what student politicians did to naive young women.

'Stop it – you're reminding me of my mother!' I said once in exasperation, as we settled down to yet another lecture over cocoa and arrowroot biscuits in the hostel kitchen.

'I don't want you to get hurt,' she said, spreading her arms helplessly.

Gillian was off washing her underwear and we were making sandwiches to take to university. Our packages of greaseproof-wrapped lunch looked small and vulnerable on the bench, and it was then that I almost changed my mind, worn down by all that maternal advice.

But I didn't. I met Henry the next day. It was just before Easter and I was busy eyeing up the row of hot-cross buns that had magically appeared in the cafe. He briskly patted a seat, opened his briefcase. 'Let's take a look at those courses, first,' he beamed.

What focus! It chastened and agitated me all at once; it made me forget my baser needs and ignore the cautionary tales I'd ever heard about careers advisers and the host of other well-meaning individuals who knew just what you should be doing with your life.

He'd even brought a calendar. We spent the next hour plotting my future, and he wrote the names of the courses in his diary. His pen moved energetically across one page, then another. By lunchtime

I had to agree that social sciences were the most relevant subjects for making things happen in the world, whereas French and English were antiquated tools of imperialism, ghostly shadows of an old world that had already disappeared.

'Meg, the study of literature has no place in a modern woman's pantheon. She should be filling her mind with political narratives. Critiques and methodologies: these are the humanist's tool-kit today.'

And he told me about the brilliant Geography professor who had given the best of his life to work for the Chinese, and was dying of throat cancer. Students still went to his classes and took notes from the words that came faintly from his diseased mouth. Whenever I saw the professor after that I gazed at him, fascinated: the first person I'd known who was fighting heroically against death and the corruptions of capitalism at the same time.

'Now,' Henry said, pushing across the subject plan. 'What's this nonsense about sewing?'

I thought better of mentioning my silk figures back at the hostel. They seemed childish this morning, like some clumsy enterprise for war widows. 'I'm a good dressmaker, that's all. As it happens,' with a last moment of assertion, 'I'm *very* good.'

'I don't doubt it,' he replied, casting an appraising look at my Vogue outfit, 'but you know, there's not a lot of room for sewing in student life. Most of us are too busy trying to change the world. Leave embroidery scissors to the goats, Meg. The ones who are never going to make a difference.'

Henry had a thing about sheep and goats. Later, on reflection, it seemed that now one, then the other, fell into disfavour. One minute you were a mindless goat, the next, as misled as a sheep. As I said, the quick-witted attempted to keep a step ahead of the downside of animal nomenclature. Some of us simply took longer to rise from the confusing stampede of hooves than others.

That afternoon I pushed my sewing kit under my bed. The goats could keep my embroidery scissors. A rush of gratitude swept through me as I remembered the athletic body swaying over my chair at the party. No way did I want to be stuck with being a goat.

The next day I dropped out of French and English and enrolled for Economics, Geography and Anthropology. In those days, changing your course six weeks after lectures had begun for the year wasn't such a big deal. Besides, I counted on Henry to bring me up to speed with whatever work I had missed.

A day later, I went over to Garden View Road to work on my first Economics essay. When I arrived, the house was empty except for Henry, who was eating his breakfast: two Weet-Bix covered in a mound of bran and sultanas topped with a sprinkling of brown sugar and whey.

Here I was, I reflected, plunging into life up to the armpits, seizing its vital germ, watching a student politician eat his breakfast.

His jaw cracked. His mouth moved briskly up and down. I could hear the gurgling of food arriving in his stomach and imagined the energy to be derived from such healthy eating: the speeches, the thought it could sustain.

My own morning sludge of cornflakes would have to go, I knew that then. I'd have to start visiting health-food shops and buying wholegrain food and knobbled vegetables covered in dirt.

I sat in the lounge and read out the assignment: *Discuss those aspects of Marxist economics that had the greatest impact on industrialisation in the Soviet Union after Stalin.*

Henry got up to make coffee and I listened to him moving things in the kitchen. A spoon clattered on the bench. I began to feel odd. The sun pouring in through the window gave a hard brilliance to his breakfast bowl. The noise of the birds outside beat violently on my ears; the smell of the coffee penetrated the room. If you could see it, I thought, it would be as thick as fog, rolling under the kitchen door and across the floor. The delicate shadow of a fantail needled across the glass. I was suddenly there and not there, sitting at the table picking at my skirt, and outside on the path looking in from the trees to a room where a girl from the country sat waiting among papers and books and dishes. The strange moment vanished as Henry came back with two mugs steaming with fresh coffee.

'Come on,' his amazing bright eyes bringing me to earth, 'write everything you know about Marx on this piece of paper.'

The list I came up with was impoverished, goatishly slight.

'Good God, that's piffling. Didn't you discuss these things at school?'

Provincialism stuck to me like a kind of leprosy. While he had been fighting against injustice in the Third World, I'd been making speeches about heroes of the British empire, or what Captain Cook found out about lime juice. My knowledge of politics was bizarre, residual. Whatever I knew, it was definitely *not* meaningful.

'Break a sheep's leg, Meg. We're going to have to work on you. You can't go around in a daydream. You've got to stand up and be counted!'

All this talk had a curious effect. Instead of wishing I'd listened to Lou's advice, I began to feel soothed by Henry's schemes to introduce me to the real world, to teach me to say 'fuck' and vote in student elections. I saw the whiteness of snow criss-crossed by lines and marks, by attitudes and positions, addresses and monuments. He was giving me the gift of his help, his energy.

When I left, an hour or so later, essay outline bristling with bullet points, I agreed that we'd meet next week to catch up. I strode to the library and took out the books he'd described: Weber and Emile Durkheim and Peter Berger; R. D. Laing on anti-psychiatry, and Levi-Strauss on the structures of myth. Their names belonged to a catalogue of imperial treasures secreted away in the Hidden City. Only the initiated knew the way there. Henry was showing *me, Meg Shepherd*, the way.

And I thought: I shall keep a diary. My life's far too disorganised and I'm always late for things. I'll take notes of everything I read and keep them in a special book. I'll write letters and file copies in clean manila folders. I'll change my signature at the bank, and I'll ask Lou if Henry has a girlfriend.

The rest of the day vanished. To be honest, I had no idea where it went. Lou and Gillian were in their dressing gowns eating pikelets when I came in, dazed and exhilarated.

'Guess what? Henry thinks I should major in Economics.'

Gillian rolled her eyes and licked the strawberry jam off the plate.

'I see,' said Lou.

'What do you mean, *I see*? Aren't you pleased?'

The bread factory began putting its late-night scent into the air. Lou's dressing-gown bulk folded itself on the edge of my bed, and the rest of the hostel lay in darkness.

'I don't trust him, and I know for sure that he's seducing you.'

True, I was finding it pretty difficult to separate the image of Henry and his navy guernsey from the pronouncements on ideology and economies of scale that were ready to fill my essay, but I wouldn't admit it. 'Rubbish. We've spent hours working together on my essay!' It had seemed like hours to me. Henry had a natural talent for giving you an hour of his time and making it feel like a week.

'There's another thing,' said Lou slowly.

'What's that?'

'Steph Jackson's doing English. If it's so bloody right wing, why's one of his best friends reading poetry?'

'You mean the woman at his party?' I had to ask. 'Are they . . . is she his girlfriend?' *Lover* stuck in my gullet.

'Probably. Everyone's heard about Henry Ballantyne's reputation.' Lou put the plates, licked clean of crumbs, on the top of the dressing table and began getting ready for bed. 'Although Steph is very bright.'

Henry's sceptical voice at the cafe buzzed in my ear. *Scribble away in private if you must, Meg, but young people should be agitating for a place in government, not fossicking around in literature.*

I couldn't help hoping that he found Steph Jackson's brightness an unattractive feature. She had to have some bad features; he would have been sure to have spotted them. Henry was very, *very* bright.

I wished then that I was more like Gillian. Where men were concerned, she had a distinct edge. Her nails were impeccably manicured, her underwear and nighties the envy of Stella Maris. We had never seen such fine lace, such *froth*. She had cami-knickers from Paris before they became fashionable, fine lawn peignoirs, Italian silk negligées. Her dressing table was draped with perfume bottles and pearls, and she was currently going steady with Chris Thompkins, a respectable young man from one of Wellington's bluestocking families.

'Chris and I have so much in common,' she sang. 'We do *every-thing* together and he's coming home with me at the end of term. I know he'll get on well with everyone. Mother's *dying* to meet him.'

Lou could see wedding bells ahead. When Gillian turned up with a polished trousseau box, I was amazed.

'I bought it from Kirk's. What do you think, Meg?' She knew Lou would dismiss the new glory box, which crowded out their tiny bedroom, as a sell-out. When I looked uncertainly at its lid, thinking of my own adventure in the store, she added archly, 'It will be your turn soon, don't worry.'

I did worry, but it was not a glory box I wanted. It was Henry, girlfriend-free and sitting on the arm of my chair while we wrote essays together.

So I set about captivating him in the time-honoured way: I determined to converse intelligently, to read everything left wing I could find, and to make impassioned speeches at SRCs. With Lou as coach, success would be mine.

For a while, the project went admirably. Lou got me along to all kinds of weird gatherings, believing I had finally embraced radical politics. I used to make sure she saw me methodically studying *Socialist Action*, until one morning she informed me quietly that the SAL was not a group I should be involved with. Too reactionary, she said.

'But I thought they were communists,' I complained.

'The problem with some groups is that they've got the wrong end of the stick,' she tried to explain patiently. 'Their ideology is old-guard, it's all wrong for the 1970s. The Maoists have got the right idea.'

I found a Mao badge and pinned it to my lapel. All I can remember of Mao today, apart from when the horrors of the Cultural Revolution came out, is that he cleaned his teeth in a mug of tea every day, which, as you can imagine, quickly turned them black.

And then, wonder of wonders, I went out on a date. I hadn't intended to: in my eyes I was already taken. However, to keep up happy relations with my flatmates, who had been nagging me to date someone, I finally agreed to go to a concert with a student from the Music Department. We'd bumped into each other in the library one day – the usual thing: it happened all the time, but mostly to other people, not me. Anyway, he'd asked me out on the spot and I couldn't think of a good enough excuse. Perversely, I also imagined that Henry might be jealous.

What a disaster. As my family never went to concerts, I had no idea it would be so informal. Pictures from opening nights at La Scala filled my head, so I hired – *hired*, can you imagine? – a silk evening gown that cut into my bottom and hardly gave me room to breathe. Ross Cameron, my date, nearly died laughing. Ross was a nice guy; I liked him, and his humour made me loosen up a bit and in the end I laughed too. But I did insist we sit at the back of the hall away from the crowd and the lights. Afterwards we shot out the door and down The Terrace steps, Ross still grinning, my shiny bottom bobbing unattractively.

We stayed friends, and later I was to call on Ross's talents at Gillian's wedding, but there was never any chemistry between us.

I went back to my books. Henry didn't call, and didn't call. One day, going through a particularly dark patch, I forgot to put on a pair of knickers. You know what my reasoning was when I felt the first blast of cold air attack my privates? What no one saw, no one bothered about. It wasn't the closest I came to insanity, but that's a pretty way-out kind of thinking.

The only occasion Henry made time to meet was after I'd told him I'd got around to finishing Andre Gundar Frank. Not every man's idea of a lure, but it worked for me.

Anyone who knew the book could guess what happened next. We got stuck into the politics of underdevelopment in Latin America. Except that for some reason I completely forgot everything I'd swotted; I couldn't even pronounce *latifundia* properly. Henry was full of scorn. As the conversation lurched on like some rackety bus on a dangerous mountain road, he finally burst out, 'For Christ's sake, Meg, you're wasting my time! I've got things on my plate you can't even imagine. Come back when you've actually learnt something; maybe then we can have a useful conversation.'

Useless Meg Shepherd slunk away to the library.

I spent the rest of the morning with my nose to the window watching boats beetling across the harbour. Small schooners were tightly packed into the wharf like a row of gleaming shellfish hauled from the sea. Cars passed on the roads, remote and slow.

And I saw my desires as fragile skiffs, one moment bright-eyed and nimble, skimming free; the next, upended and collapsed under the crushing weight of the water.

Lou, who had been watching me more closely than I knew over those months, told me Henry was busy planning a Youth Summit for the following year. When we finally met next, just after exams, he casually suggested I apply, an invitation I brooded on over the Christmas break in Cambridge.

'I'm thinking of going to a conference.'

'That's nice, dear.' My mother was lying down on the sofa with a mug of tea.

'What do you think?'

She waited a moment. 'You know I've always thought you should be a journalist. There was that lovely article about James K. Baxter's poetry I cut out for you. That's how *you* could be writing.'

Like Henry, she found my obsession with sewing a mystery. 'There's no money in it,' she always said. 'A Youth Summit? It sounds a nice idea.' Her Boxing Day brightened. 'You could write something up for the paper. People are very interested in a confident young woman's opinions.'

I pulled out my father's old typewriter and wrote a long, frustrated letter to Wellington.

I spent the rest of the summer working in the kitchen at the Riverina, reading the books that Henry had recommended in lunchhours. If there were moments when my attention slipped from that new world, nobody knew. My mother believed I'd become an activist, and got some books on great statesmen of the world out of the library for me. I took long walks around the lake on my days off, thinking curiously about the way life was changing. Less than a year ago, I'd been bent over the sewing machine running up a new wardrobe for university. Now I went to meetings and rallies that gave me no time to think about anything else. The stolen gloves, still buried in one of my cases left behind in Wellington, belonged to the discarded skin of some other unhappy girl. A verdant forest of new language was taking its place, choking older thoughts, making them seem common. There were new seeds sprouting behind my eyes. I could hear the noise of their growing, and waited eagerly for the harvest.

In the meantime, I pottered restlessly in our kitchen perfecting my baking skills and sculpting bizarre arrangements of vegetables.

'Why don't you take up chefing?' Mum had suggested one evening after dinner as we sat down to a cake covered in a multi-coloured dome of butter-icing roses.

'What, you mean like Gran?'

'You could go to Otago and do Home Ec.'

'No thanks.'

'What about polytech, then? The hospitality industry is crying out for young chefs. Who knows, you might even go to Paris. Wouldn't that be exciting?'

'I'll think about it.'

'Good girl.'

When I returned to university, I was glad to escape the sound of Mum's improving voice, which had dogged me all holidays. In the end I had written an article for the newspaper, but the editor had turned it down. 'Dear Miss Shepherd,' he wrote, 'We regret that we find your essay on student activism too polemical to reproduce. *The Times* is a family paper with family values.'

The forest thickened and spread its borders. I couldn't wait to take the train south.

As I walked through the campus in early March, there outside the Student Union was the poster advertising Henry's conference. HUI, it said in red and black lettering. 'Do you believe we can build a better world? Enrol for our Youth Summit. The National Board of Youth invites *you* into the global village of the future.'

I looked up the Maori word in the dictionary. *Hui*, it said: *to put* or add together; to congregate; to meet; to double up; assembly or group; to take as plunder; to capture; to be affected with cramp; to twitch (in an ominous way). You had to take the word seriously. It suggested the potential for mana, another new word.

Meg Kingi had rippling black hair with a sheen of blue like a pigeon's back, and a moko on her chin. Precious jade decorated her arms and neck, and a feather cloak fell to her feet. She was pressing noses with white and black leaders, radiating mana, giving wise counsel, appearing on television striding in front of her tribe.

I didn't stop to wonder why Meg Kingi looked so much like Steph Jackson.

No, hui satisfied my exploding fantasy life because it contained just the right degree of challenge to seem dangerous. The newspaper had labelled me polemical. Well, I'd show them, show them all what I thought of their *family* values. A student conference was a great idea. Henry was right: we had plenty to say.

Lou and Gillian and I found ourselves a flat in Kelburn at the beginning of the new term. No one wanted to go solo; none of us had made better friends. All three of us began to grow up that year (or down, in my case, but I wasn't to know that yet), and the atmospheric changes in the flat as time went on were both subtle and distinct.

One evening Gillian went out with Chris and didn't come home. Lou had excused herself after dinner, leaving me to clean up. I wandered emptily from the dirty kitchen to the lounge, which was spread with books from the interminable reading list Henry was always on about. If I tried to stuff any more existentialism into my head, it would burst. What was the point of all this reading when I never saw anyone to talk to? The hopes of endless discussions with him, busier than ever with conference organising, were fading. We'd had a couple of exciting conversations not long after lectures began, just enough to convince me the plan to upgrade my mind was working, but I hadn't seen him since.

I threw *La Nausée* across the room in a rage. It was after midnight. The room watched. All its objects were brutish, grossly material. The chairs with their thick wooden legs, the worn ugly sofa, the table silent, refusing to see the way I saw. It didn't bother the world out there whether you lived or died. What was the point of an unhappy consciousness if nobody saw you, or *engagement* if you had nobody to be engaged *with*? Sartre had lovers, he had Simone de Beauvoir, he had the press. Here I was at home alone in a dark place, with no one.

The door clicked and banged.

'Are you still up? It's so late.'

'Had a good meeting?'

'Fantastic. We got so much done, you wouldn't believe it.'

At least, I thought later when Lou had gone to sleep, Gillian would never accuse me of political ineptness. Gillian's idea of engagement began and ended at the squash courts these days. Right now she would be rolling in bed with Chris, giggling and throwing her lace camisole on the floor.

It's pure silk. Mother bought it for me in Rome. What do you think, Meg?

'You need to get out,' she'd say to me. 'Put yourself about. And why have you stopped sewing? You could do with some new clothes.'

'I've got too much to do right now. One day I'll get around to it.'

'You'd better, or Chris will fix you up with a blind date! And don't forget, you can always borrow my camisole if you're stuck.'

A month later I got a call from Steph Jackson, who told me I was going to the Youth Summit. There was a pause. Henry's excited voice breezed down the phone: 'Meg! You're coming to our Summit! That's fantastic! Congratulations on being selected – we've had applications from all over the country.'

My nerves jangled. Surely he must have informed the selection committee of my inadequate background?

'It's your *potential* we're interested in, Meg,' Henry had told me gravely. 'We believe you have a lot to offer. Your speeches at school, your debates – it's all there. It just needs direction. Our hui will provide it.'

Potential, potential, potential, I carolled to myself.

'Thank you so much,' I said. 'It's an honour.'

'Oh, by the way, we're a bit short on committee members. Steph and I were wondering if you could give us a hand helping to make the conference happen?'

You bet I could. 'Sure,' I said. 'I'd love to.'

'You know, I can't imagine what you would find to talk about with Henry Ballantyne,' said Gillian when I told my flatmates about the Summit. 'Isn't he rather sophisticated for you?'

'I'm not dating him! I'm helping him with a conference!'

To Gillian, it was the same thing. 'If you're so keen to go out with someone, why don't you find a man more your style? Henry Ballantyne's way out of your league.'

At least she didn't say 'class'.

Lou looked up from her work, frowning.

'What's wrong?' I said. 'I'm finally doing something useful.'

'I thought the Youth Summit was supposed to be for experienced activists. Henry wants to use it to lobby government.'

'I've been on marches.'

'Yes, but anyone can go on a march. You haven't joined the Women's Collective, have you?'

The Women's Collective was a jab out of left field; she'd never mentioned it before.

'I don't get the feeling you're an activist. I could be wrong, but I think your mind's on other things.'

Lou was an activist, a committed one, complete with Che Guevara poster hanging faithfully above her bed. Why hadn't she applied?

'I've told you before. I don't trust Henry, that's why. He's talented, I'll give him that, but he's the cleverest manipulator I've seen. Watch out: he'll destroy you in the end.'

And that's when it really began: when madness struck in the full light of day. I decided I wanted to be destroyed. If that's what helping Henry with the Summit meant, then yes, I wanted it all. I watched the bubbles coming out of Lou's mouth and swam quietly away.

Outside, the late afternoon sun curdled and settled on the trees for a last lick before it fell behind the dark hills. Some lower drifts of cloud gathered, driven by the wind like smoke across the face of the sky, fleeing before an apocalyptic angel. I tossed my hair. I wouldn't be surprised if it was going to rain.

Lou wasn't home the morning I stole her dress. I'd been having trouble with eye-strain and was running late for a Geography lab. My double crêpe collar, rolled and cut on the cross, wasn't sitting properly. I slipped into her bedroom to borrow the mirror.

The room reeked of Lane's Emulsion and Irish Moss cough syrup. Lou's mirror winked and glimmered on the wall, rainbowed in the early light drizzling through the window. The carpet rose up around my toes and I felt myself sinking into a pile that felt soft as bush moss. My throbbing feet sank further.

The house was a dreaming boat taking me out to sea, Lou and Gillian distant specks on the shore. I went forward to the wheel-house where an erect figure was spinning the gigantic disc. I saw the hands that gripped the wheel's golden wooden knobs. 'Wait for me!' I cried out to the silent house.

A mournful yowl settled down in my chest. The ship and its captain vanished. I stepped into the wardrobe and buried myself in the clothes. They smelt of grassy herbs, and the blistering stench of fresh mothballs, scattered in those days to guard woollens. I crouched among the shoes and bags, pulling down muslin shirts, a brushed Viyella paisley skirt, and finally, the velvet dress that made Lou look like a vivid stitch of blue holding the sky together.

'What am I doing?' I said. 'What am I doing?'

The midnight blue velvet dress slipped from its hanger, lay snug against my skin for a moment, then buried itself in my bag. It would stay there for the rest of the day, swinging against the small of my back in the Geography lab, knocking against my legs in the bus. It was my talisman: midnight-blue to ward off the evil eye, blue for spirituality, for wisdom; a blue world wrinkled to the size of a nut in my briefcase.

It threw itself protectively against my hip when I bumped into Diana Fahey outside the Student Union. Half an hour late for the lab, I saw her eyes inspecting me as I climbed nonchalantly up the hill. I tried to turn her into an insignificant speck, except my shoe caught in my bellbottom trouser cuff, sprawling me on the path, books and folders careening over the grass.

Worse, something very odd was happening to my sight. Lying there with my head on one side, I watched as the crevices of the path rose to meet me, stereoscopically enlarged. Imperfections in the asphalt turned into a grainy moon landscape; cracks became serpentine rivers, snaking greasily in front of my nose. A familiar hand touched my shoulder.

'Here, you should be more careful. That path's slippery when it's been raining.'

Raining? I hadn't taken in the drenched ground, the cool air. Diana was finishing a piece of apple strudel. I stared at the brilliant egg-wash coating the chewed pastry, the plump sultanas taut with orange juice or brandy; imagined her incisors fanging through the floor of the strudel, leaving only the sparest of crumbs clinging to her mouth.

'Meg Shepherd! Hey, you flat with Lou, don't you?'

'Sure.' Some flatmate: I'd just stolen her best dress. What was wrong with me?

'Would you tell her there's a Collective meeting on Friday? Our phone's been cut off.'

When I arrived at last to do my Geography lab, I was not at all surprised to find the class working in pairs. Each equipped with a stereoscopic lens mounted on legs, they had to match up two aerial photographs. When aligned correctly, you could see the landscape in 3-D. It was all to do with changing the focal length of your eyes, a lab instructor said once.

My way of doing it was more primitive. I screwed up my eyes and imagined my vision coming from the middle of my forehead, the product of a cunning extra eye that knew instinctively how to manipulate the photographic images into one single landscape. Words like 'focal length' meant nothing. It was that extra eye that did the trick. Out of the asymmetrical pair with their indistinct lumps and hollows, their odd-angled sharps and flats, would come another world, one I found my way to through instinct.

I always found the transition from two to three dimensions astonishing, a quiet miracle. Scientists must walk over miracles every day. I saw them crunching indifferently across theorems and equations and delicate pieces of equipment that littered the quad. Well, I was going to make sure I remarked on miracles. I stretched out my hand and caressed the cold metal with my skin, blew a puff of steam onto the thick glass of the lens.

On a good day, I could see fence-lines knotted with barbs of wire stretching over the pallid greyness of hills and along creek-beds. Stands of pine and macrocarpa with black brush limbs marking off paddocks, a stippling of houses in darker shades of grey and black.

Today my eyes were on strike. I couldn't marry the images at all, the photographs lying sullenly on the bench keeping their secrets. I could no more make my special world appear now than I could erase Diana's growing friendship with Lou. And yes, I was jealous, I confess. A normal person would not need to undergo the humiliation of a failed Geography lab to know they were jealous, but in those days it took me a while to figure things out. My friend had someone – I didn't.

Nurtured by jealousy, the madness put out more shoots, and disillusion became such a sneaky beast that it played its tune loudest when I least expected it. I felt myself losing what little charge I'd had over my life, while each step took me further and further away from the place of bliss.

'Lou,' I said that night over dinner, 'I saw Diana today.'

'I never liked her,' growled Gillian. 'What's she up to now?'

'What did she say?' Lou put down her spoon. Gillian had cleaned the silver in the weekend and our faces winked at us like gibbous moons.

'Their phone's out. She said to tell you there's a Collective meeting on Friday.'

'Thanks.' Lou bent over her plate.

Gillian had made baked chops in a sweet and sour sauce. I traced the crust of gravy baked onto the side of the dish. It looked like an imprint from a nuclear holocaust: human distress cooked into a piece of pottery. Nuclear war was terrifying. The speed of the attack, the waste, the abandoned projects, feelings trailing brokenly over the burnt earth.

'Why don't you come with me, Meg?'

I scraped fiercely at the stuck gravy. Lou was looking all doe-eyed.

'You can count me out!' said Gillian. 'Chris and I are taking the day off. We're going to a ball in Hastings.'

'Oh, for God's sake, can't you ever take politics seriously?' I threw the spoon down. My nerves were jangling again; I could feel my eyes inflamed in their sockets.

'You don't *have* to go with her,' snapped Gillian. 'In my opinion all these meetings aren't doing you any good at all.'

My voice came out sharper than I intended. 'Not everyone wants to live your sort of life!'

'What's wrong with my life? It's a damn sight healthier than yours. The way you mooch around the place is getting on my nerves. You know what?' Gillian stood with her hands on her hips. 'You should get yourself some contact lenses and come to the ball with me.'

'Bugger off,' I said rudely. 'I'm going to the Collective.'

The day before the Women's Collective meeting I went to an address by a visiting professor from London. Our Anthropology lecturer had told us Professor Laing was a world-famous psychiatrist who had written a number of highly regarded books on human relationships. We should allow the professor to challenge our values, he'd said.

Values: the word bloomed like a weed in those days. You could have either the right ones, or the wrong ones. But I had none. Not really. Those brave words to Gillian over dinner had totally lacked substance, and we all knew it. Plainly, I ought to find some values before other people found out.

I'd forgotten that Laing and anti-psychiatry had been on Henry's reading list.

The theatre was crowded. Unfamiliar people from the city sat in the aisles and in tangled rows on the floor; journalists milled at the back. A little man was led into the room by the vice-chancellor, who had assumed his regal robes to honour this colourful messenger from the international community of scholars. As the VC introduced the distinguished guest, Professor Laing stood twisting his face into the most extraordinary contortions until it began to resemble an agitated piece of string. The audience writhed in sympathy. I couldn't take my eyes off him.

'The origin of human bondage lies in the family,' he grimaced. 'The family teaches us to become subjects of fantasy. This is because its members learn to evade the truth of their being. Dishonesty over our own identity leads us to fantasise about the truth of other people.'

Was I fantasising over Henry? If I saw myself truthfully, would I then see Henry more clearly? And would I tell the Shepherd family story differently?

The mouth of the visiting speaker was behaving aberrantly, opening into a zero and flattening into a squashed eight on its side, a horrible kind of infinity shape. I thought of my mother at home sitting on the sofa while the house fell to pieces around her. And I thought of my father, gone for ever. For ever, for ever, for ever.

'The arch-criminal Genet,' stuttered the professor, 'stole from others. Things, yes, but most importantly, he stole roles. These roles and personae blurred into each other like melting sweets. As that great existentialist Jean-Paul Sartre said, the thief is a man eaten up by his own dream.'

How could you be eaten by your own dream? And why melting sweets? Later I saw, but back then the idea totally stumped me. To tell the truth, Laing's wisdom was unpalatable to so many of us that his theories fell on very stony ground indeed. Maybe it was the same everywhere he went, I don't know, but listen to this – you'll see what I mean:

Ladies and gentlemen, we fall into illusion – or, shall I say, elusion – because someone originally stole from us something of our own truth. If Eve was the first criminal, it is only true inasmuch as to steal is endemic to the human condition. The western family has made a prison of the natural cycles of appropriation and exchange, give and take. It has created a series of knots with which we scourge ourselves.

People shifted in their seats. The references to criminality and masochism rang strangely in the hallowed Philosophy lecture theatre. I saw clumps of worms indifferently chewing books with purple cotton binding into ragged pages. The vice-chancellor coughed and adjusted his robes, which had slipped off his shoulder. I looked around for Lou, only to find the theatre full of people I'd never seen before.

A flock of insidious *nots* reverberated around the room. Professor Laing was concluding his talk.

'Let me leave you with one final *k-not* to illuminate the substance of our discussion this morning. The ordinary person today, and that includes all of you here,' and he could have been pointing at me with his shaking chin, 'lives an impoverished, shrivelled existence. Your *not* of experience leads you to allow your innocence to be plundered. And so you steal, because you have lost your rightful sense of entitlement.'

A cavernous silence. The professor smiled through his string mouth. Then, a scattering of applause and a buzz of conversation broke out as the VC led his errant guest away.

Walking up the hill, I didn't know what to make of the strange address. The knot idea, for instance – did I have knots? None of my friends seemed to, but then, people didn't talk about their lives as curiously as Professor Laing had. And no one, ever, had pulled such bizarre facial expressions. How could you trust a man like that?

I disappeared into my bedroom, locked the door, dragged Lou's dress out of my bag. I felt under the bed for the abandoned sewing kit and picked out an ivory-handled knife, one blade capped with a small red plastic drop, the other curved and sharp. My palm opened and closed like the wings of a moth. A moth weighing its options on a slender twig. Then up and down, up and down went the blade. Up and down, up and down went Lou's wrist making tree-tomato coleslaw, up and down stirring the cocoa and mashing egg for our hostel lunches.

I slashed open the seams of the dress, watched the blue threads trailing over my bed. I picked up the scissors and sliced into the soft pile, over and over. At the end of an hour, I packed my bag again, locked my room, greeted Gillian calmly, and caught the bus to the library.

On the bed sat an exquisite patchwork pillow. Blue strips of variable length framed a central block of blue squares alternating with hexagons cut from an old sheet of my mother's. In the centre of each hexagon, as if they were embroidered French knots, I had glued crushed pieces of white button. The effect was startling.

Now, before you lose patience with the slack kind of heroine that I am – a woman who steals from her best friend and, worse, scalpels her dress – have a care. My tale's not done. What did I say about the path from disillusion, way back at the beginning? Why, it hasn't even taken off yet. One or two gestures, one or two threads in place to that effect, but not the whole thing: I wasn't ready for it just then. How could I be? This is a story about thievery and found objects, about loss and recovery, as much as it is about animals. Wait, as the forbidden, world-famous dramatist used to say. Lend me your reading ears, for what waits on *us*.

May: nearly winter, my second in Wellington. I'd purchased a heavy duffel-coat from the army surplus store, and whenever I put it on I felt like a spy. Which conveniently matched the furtive expression I wore as I told my friends I was moving in to Henry Ballantyne's flat.

I shifted in at the weekend. I'd sprung it on Lou after we'd come home from the Collective, Diana's cigarette case lying asleep in my coat pocket. I'd stolen it from her during the ecstatic celebration that ended the meeting on abortion. *Stolen from a student politician!* Okay, Lou was a politician too, but she was my friend; Diana most definitely wasn't.

'I'm moving out. Tomorrow. Henry's asked me to go flatting with them.'

Lou couldn't believe it. It sounded extreme, even to me.

'Meg, why? We were getting on so well. And *Henry*! You know what I think about him.'

'You're always busy these days. Let's face it, we don't see that much of each other.' I kept my eyes on Che Guevara. A tragedy he'd lost his life so young; I wondered if the Americans really were responsible. Lou was so paranoid about the US, it was becoming a real bore. I bet Guevara was shot by anarchist mercenaries who didn't know shit from shave, as Henry would say.

'It's so convenient here. Mt Vic's miles away. Won't you miss being this close to varsity?'

'The walk will do me good.' Which was a lie. I hated walking: it chafed my thighs, even wearing tights.

'Gill will miss you, too.'

I found that I would also miss Gillian, her worldly presence and advice, her transparent lack of inner agony.

'I won't be able to see you as often,' added Lou. 'And he'll change you.'

My tongue and my hands: three instruments of destruction. 'I just want the stimulation,' I answered. 'A mixed flat would be nice for a change.'

She flushed.

'I'll be in touch,' wanting no time to examine the wreckage I was leaving behind.

When I arrived with my boxes, Garden View Road was deserted. I lay down on my bed and looked out the window. It was noon, but the bedroom felt freezing. The sun had left this side of the house in shade, although the trees outside were still bright with heat, and I couldn't help remembering the warm nights spent in Cambridge sitting out under our umbrella tree. My new bed was unexpectedly lumpy.

I carefully extracted three objects from the pockets of my duffel-coat. Two of them I put on the mantelpiece in my room, one each side, for luck. I hung the third from the curtain rail. It spun and swayed on its string. There were dozens of Megs in its shining sides: upside down, distorted. I stroked it. The hard water bead spun away and flashed behind me.

I closed the door and went for a walk.

Alone in the room, three mute objects surveyed the huddle of bags. A cigarette case inlaid with mother-of-pearl, Dad's RAF medal, and a crystal, taken from Mum's desk, stood like watching ghosts.

That night, I lay on my bed with my mother's tear-marked face wandering through the rooms of the sleeping flat and Dad's steady hands looping the loop in my dreams.

Whenever I came to remember the sequence of what happened next, I couldn't.

Some time later – it could have been as late as June: the dates are all mixed up now – Henry heard me crashing around the kitchen trying to find the teapot.

'Meg, haven't seen you for days. Hope you're liking living here.' He noticed my face. 'Hey, what's up?'

'Someone's asked me out.'

'Break a sheep's leg. Who's the lucky guy?'

I mumbled the name of a man in my Geography lab.

Henry took out his handkerchief and considered me sceptically.

'You know, you look very drained. I think you're in shock. Here, I'll do that. You need to lie down. I'll bring in a cup of tea.'

I did, though, remember the pain of the penetration, as if I'd been kicked by a rugby ball. And later, too, I realised that my body had not opened like a flower as I had imagined it would. I lay rigid on my lumpy bed, bruised to the kernel of my deepest part.

What had happened after that? Did he hold me? Roll over and go to sleep? Perhaps he buttoned his trousers and bounded out of the room, ready for more Gestetnering? Another blank.

I did recall watching the crystal marking off the hours, turning on its string and gathering the growing dark into its glassy eye. Dad's medal and the inlaid case sat sadly on the mantelpiece as I put on my gown and went off to the bathroom to clean up. By morning, the pain was gone.

After dinner that evening, I ran myself a bath. It had been a difficult day. My bones ached with exhaustion. Diana's angry face had been pursuing me, demanding to know where her cigarette case was. 'It's an antique from Damascus!' shouted the face.

The bedroom was cold as a fridge. I turned on the light and saw the folded piece of paper sitting on my bed. It was a poem. From Henry.

Shy Pocahontas paddles her trembling bark on the rushing stream . . . her face is the moon on the water to me, my sweet, stream maiden.

He did love me. He'd written a poem. To the shy, beautiful Pocahontas.

I slipped my feet, pretty as a deer's, into the bathroom, poured out a glug of sandalwood bath oil. I watched my nipples disappear into the steam, saw two bark canoes paddling in unison down a soft-flowing river.

In the middle of listening to Hiawatha's love song, I heard a door slam, voices. There was the sound of drawers opening, an animated conversation. Steph laughed, so did Henry.

Wreathed in sandalwood bubbles, I lay in the rocking river. Steph was making a moaning noise. The walls were paper-thin and my ears put on angel wings, mounting through the steamy air, passing under the door and into the next room, where they flapped faintly on the back of Henry's towelling robe. Then he was groaning too.

'Oh, Henry, Henry,' says Steph.

'I love you, I love you,' he shouts, and it is all over.

My wounded ears repaired themselves to my head. I pulled out the plug.

An hour later – *an hour!* – there was a tap on my door, and Henry's head appeared, a shining orb rising from the firmament of the hall.

'Mind if I come in?'

Such a loud knocking set up against my ribs, I felt convinced he could hear it, however, he seemed oblivious to my percussive chest.

'Haven't seen you for a while. That was a very meaningful time we had the other day . . .'

Yesterday, Henry, it was only yesterday.

'. . . I keep on thinking about it.'

Meaningful? What was that? I could hear my mother snorting in contempt.

'Did you get my poem?'

How could I not have got it? 'Yes, thanks. It was very . . . mean-ingful.'

His ear let him down badly. 'I put a lot of time into it. You're a special person.'

'What about Steph?'

'Well,' he said cautiously, 'of course Steph and I are close. But there's no reason why I can't be intimate with you as well.' He reached out a hand and brushed my overcooked pastry hair back from my face. 'You're beautiful, Meg.'

Intimate. Beautiful. I swallowed and looked down at my feet. The dainty feet of Pocahontas looked back. My skin stirred, and woke up. I smiled shyly at Hiawatha. Time dropped from my shoulders like a heavy garment, my bird hands flew to his shirt. We fell slowly backwards.

I could see the gold flecks in his eyes as big as flames in their twin hyacinth-blue beds. I felt a tug from deep inside my belly; he was unwinding me into his eyes. My cells of blood and water rushed to the gate of my skin, begging to go to him. I shut my eyes and concentrated on his hands. They had pulled off my jeans and were stroking my thighs. Sounds of pleasure were coming from my mouth. My whole body was galloping away, melting into the sheets, sticky and tingling under his touch.

Henry was less noisy, deadly of intent. He pushed himself into me and came almost at once. We lay panting and sweaty on the cold bed.

'Thank you. That was lovely,' said the sad mouth of Pocahontas.

He stroked my back and looked the window.

'Fuck a duck! It's late! I'm due at Steph's at seven-thirty. Got to go. Sorry. Let's talk some time soon.'

He rolled off the bed, stepped into his pants. I lay watching him, puzzled. Was this love? Could a man really love two women at once?

The next morning I found out. Before I left for university, he called me into his room.

'Got a minute, Meg?'

I stood against the bookcase and ran my finger slowly over the spines of his library.

'I told Steph about us last night.'

'Oh.'

'Well, we do believe in being honest with each other.'

'What did she say?'

'She was pretty upset. Now, don't get alarmed. I've had a think, and no question, we've got to keep on seeing each other. Not here, of course.' He patted my hand reassuringly. 'A friend's family have a bach in Coromandel. We can spend a few days there later in the year, if you like.'

The books were cold lizards under my fingertips.

'Meg? How about it?'

I nodded dumbly.

'Good girl.' He squeezed my buttocks and grabbed his briefcase. 'Busy day, today. You?'

'Oh, yes, I'm thinking I might –'

'That's great. Well, see you later then.'

The front door crashed inwards as he vanished down the path.

Coming out with my books, I was startled to see one of our flat-mates still at home.

'Hi,' said Ruth, 'What's going on?' She was carrying a box full of African violets.

'Not much,' scraping my shoes in the mud outside the kitchen door. 'Where're you going?'

'I'm shifting out. Just packing up a few plants before work. Henry's been pressuring me for weeks to move so Steph can live here.'

'Steph?'

'Yes, you know, his partner in crime, ha ha. Help me with these, will you?'

I grasped another tray of furry-leaved violets.

'Steph's a great cook. She's a vego nut but don't worry, there'll always be meat with Henry around.' She disappeared outside.

So they were going to flat together. Henry was somehow planning to have it off with both of us, night after night, under the same roof.

I walked angrily into Ruth's room and examined her bed. I moved to the kitchen, opened the kitchen drawer, took out a bone-handled paring knife. It was very sharp. It sat in the palm of my hand like a tiger's tooth. My fingers closed around the bone and sliced off one, then two of the African violet leaves.

On my thirteenth birthday my father had given me a year's subscription to *Finding Out*. One weekend, bored by the weather, I'd found a list of instructions for building a terrarium. The meaning of the word lingered. *A terrarium denotes a sealed transparent globe or similar container in which plants are grown; a glass case in which small land animals are kept under observation.*

No one had ever given me a doll with a long golden ponytail and a pink tutu: I think both my parents thought such things were pure foolishness. I grieved like any kid would, even though I'd always accepted that present-giving in the Shepherd family was a non-event. It didn't matter, after all. With the gift of the *Finding Outs*, my father had actually given me the instructions to make something far better than Barbie in Tutuland. I turned eagerly to my new, secret world of revolt.

At the back of the sink cupboard I discovered a big old glass light-globe that had come apart. I filled one half with earth, inserted the stolen leaves and a bird skeleton found in the garden, sat the other hemisphere on top. The right name arrived as the globe sat in the sun. *Terrorium*. Terror, not terra would be its ground. I studied the perfection of the terrorium, and smiled.

From that moment on, my daytime madness began to tip over into a more steely determination. I wouldn't say that my numbers had changed, or that bliss was back, but I was going to be avenged, and, what's more, I was going to make something of it. My hands were going to take all this hurt and rage and thievery and turn them into something remarkable, something terrifying, even.

With Ruth gone, the flat was totally still. On a roll, I wandered down the hall and opened Henry's door. He was an impeccable keeper of records, using sheets of blue carbon paper for all his correspondence. He'd probably kept a copy of the Pocahontas poem.

His files were in a locked cupboard but I knew where the key was. The lock made the sound of silk slipping; the cupboard swung open. A gush of stale air hit my nostrils: a mix of dust, dirty socks and something indefinable decaying. The files were there, two rows of teeth gleaming up at me from the back of the cupboard. I pulled out a pile and sat down. There were records on every imaginable transaction a clever, politically astute young man might engage in. Files labelled *Reading: pending; Reading: complete; Press clippings: Environment, Vol. 1; Press clippings: Development, Vols 1–4; Correspondence: Academic; Correspondence: Family; Correspondence: Personal.* Personal. That's what I was. The file was bulging. There appeared to be subdivisions, with separate labels and dates. I marvelled at the rigour of his mind, his sheer energy. I just read letters and threw them away.

I passed labels that read *Diana, Virginia, Veronica, Meg, Steph.* Surely not Thomas's Veronica? And who was Virginia? I turned to the *Steph* file. It was a mistake. 'Dearest Steph,' I read. 'Darling, I can't wait to see you . . .' 'Dearest one . . .' He did have a way with words. Some of his writing was very . . . intimate.

I could see his hands holding his expensive Parker pen, white around the fingertips where the blood stopped with his grip, smooth as bone, purposeful, never stained with ink. Henry, the scholar lover. *Dear, dearer, dearest.* The carbon script turned to bile in my mouth, a cruel alphabet soup. I hurried the letters back into their file, locked the cupboard.

Then I turned to his wardrobe. I had never felt so focused, so sure of what I had to do.

A set of shining ties fluttered into the air as the door unlatched. I paused, contemplating two whole rows of them swinging gently on their loop of wire. Beautiful ties, gleaming like stones washed by a river. Ochre, rust, cadmium blue, steel grey, moss green; patterned with stripes and diamonds and eyes like the scales of a fish. Woven ties, silk ties, cotton ties; ties made from leather and ties made from crimplene. There must have been close to four dozen. I hadn't realised he was so fond of them.

I chose carefully, pulling each tie out and studying it under the light. After selecting ten, I snibbed the wardrobe door and went back to my room. He was an unshakeable egotist, and it served him right.

I saw him walking up the path, dumping his briefcase on the bed. Would he count his ties? When he opened his wardrobe, would the rows seem depleted? Interfered with? Would he storm into my room demanding to know why I had done something so foolish, so *completely insane*? I rolled each tie into a careful ball and tucked them into a box of blankets waiting under the bed for winter. All those beautiful coils flowering undetected in the dark. Later, I'd know what to do with them.

He didn't immediately notice the loss of his ties. When he did, he blamed his fifteen-year-old brother, who had just taken out a girl for the first time.

Henry and I continued to sleep together when his energies permitted. I still wanted him. But it was furtive and shameful, all that writhing around late at night at the back of lecture theatres, knowing I was an extra in his life.

I took comfort in the secret that was noiselessly growing behind glass in my bedroom: the blue pillow on my bed, the cigarette case and the flower ties. And I pulled out the old stolen treasure from Kirkcaldie's, cut off the fingers, and turned them into glove puppets.

Steph moved in shortly afterwards – *Dear Steph, dear Veronica, dear, dear Meg.* I had one more task left to do.

One morning I dressed late and crept into her room. A jar of flowers stood on a small side table near the bed, incense sticks brown as bulrush cones lay in a heap near the flowers. She had a lamp with a homemade shade. Someone had pressed ferns and leaves and glued them to parchment, which had then been covered with heavy cellophane. I noticed the crude blotches of glue, the unevenness of the seams. I imagined Steph lying in bed reading, her hair dark on the pillow, the speckled persimmon-coloured light filtering through the buckled shade, leaving her in a sloping pool.

A pottery bowl as big as a woman's belly and filled with dried petals was placed on the floor. A green crackle-glaze jug and a collection of ivory objects arranged on a plate sat on an old brass hearth trunk with a ship imprinted on its side. The air smelt rich and complicated.

Then I saw the thing I'd come to find. I went over to the chest and knelt down until I could see my face disfigured in the brass ship on the side of the trunk. The ivory objects were tiny, perfectly made. There were people and animals: a man, a woman, two children, a horse, a dog, a lion and a stork, each one supported by a minute jade pedestal. I imagined my breath covering the figures with wet drops. Runnels of salt coursed towards their precisely marked feet growing out of the jade. I breathed a sigh on a slip of a woman no more than an inch long who was combing her hair. Everything about her was fine and complete, from each separate glossy strand of hair on her head to her delicate half-moon toenails. A woman with no flaws. I harvested the precious shoot of ivory and jade and slid it into my pocket.

In the evening it fell out of my coat onto the bed and lay on my bedcover like a heavy, gleaming seed. The next day I planted the seed woman in the soft bed of the terrorium floor, driving the jade pedestal under the earth. I imagined the seed asleep in the dark, slowly growing roots and turning into something else.

All week I thought of the woman combing her hair in her glass garden room. The hair falling like a silk ear of corn, the perfect husk of a body, feet deep in the earth, minute fingers gripped around the ivory comb. I remembered the story of the beautiful maiden murdered by her lover, whose fingernails and hair kept on growing until they pushed up through the ground.

And I thought of the miniature world of life and death in front of me, and knew that it was only perfect because it was protected by the skin of glass that surrounded it. The stolen violets and ferns grew because of a surface of sand that had been ground, then melted at unimaginably hot temperatures and spun out, bubbling and globular, to cool. It was all this marvellous work that supported and sustained the terrorium's defiant existence.

The persistence, the mutiny of life was extraordinary. Steph would never find me out. Ever since I'd moved in, I'd used a padlock on my door. Not only that; my terrorium regularly enveloped itself in a parasol of humidity as the violet leaves breathed out their insurrectionary dreams on the glass walls. Secrets and dreams now could sprout and grow huge; and so they did, as if I had angrily wrested permission from the universe to expand. The shadow of the monstrous leaves taking over the bedroom filled me with awe.

It was to be the first of many worlds put together through theft and salvage. Projects crowded my head after that terrible year. At the beginning, it was just quilts covered in needlepoint and appliqué, then a more ambitious version of that first Happy City I'd made. Call it therapy if you wish, or crafts gone mad – whatever name I came up with never truly reflected the residual criminality, the cabbalistic vision that I had developed, thanks to my adventures with student politics and student politicians.

Once, stung by my lover's cruelty, I made my first pair of earrings. It was just after the disastrous hui. Miraculously, at the Summit I'd managed to keep up a façade of loyalty. Nasty, maybe, but Steph had temporarily been given the push, and I felt obligated to support Henry. He had no idea I was coming to despise him, especially seeing I had backed his leadership at Takaka so wholeheartedly. It made it easier for me, I'm ashamed to say, that Steph had also let him down.

When we had all cooled off, Steph and I agreed to join forces on a final holiday, a consolation prize for both of us. We were too tired to protest that we were going to Coromandel, Henry's ancient hide-out.

The two of us had been inspecting Huka Falls, walking slowly back to the car, scuffing the damp grass. Henry was shaking out the map in the glovebox onto his lap and studying the tracings of colour and line ferociously.

'Just because you got away with your miserable game at the hui,' he ground out to Steph, 'doesn't mean to say we've forgotten.'

She looked shocked. She still loved him, I'm sure of it. I saw that the whole of the Waikato plains lay crushed against the rib of mountains running down the east coast, as his thumb pressed and pressed into the paper. The town of Cambridge – dull, disloyal, disappointing – was erased in a smear of printer's ink. Tokoroa fell through a tear and drifted off through the black vastness of space. Finally his hands clamped together and gave the map a Chinese burn.

Steph had had a psycho episode at the Summit, and went around telling everyone her name was Janet Seed and she lived in Tokoroa. Now I watched Janet Seed trying to tug Steph out through the car window. I could see her with her black clothes floating above the charged atmosphere of earth, holding a copy of *Scented Gardens for the Blind* against her chest. Tokoroa and the frosted timberlands circled alongside willing her to join. We looked down at the map again. It was twisted into foreign shapes as if there had been a devastating earthquake. All that remained legible was the faithful blue of the sea, its coolness closing like a velvet glove over our hot pumping hearts.

Immediately we arrived in Coromandel, Henry went exploring, Steph grimly set about making lunch, while I had a brainwave. I walked down to the camp store and bought two identical maps of the North Island. I glued them back to back and spent the rest of the morning folding and cutting. The resulting paper pompoms, coloured in the AA's cartographical palette, were quirky but functional. I attached them to a defunct pair of earrings, tried them on. Steph, rival no longer, looked at me.

Close up, you could see the line of the Waikato River forging to the sea, the lush dairy plains, the furrowed Kaimais, the shining black thread of coast travelling somewhere between Gisborne and Coromandel. Tokoroa and the rest of the Volcanic Plateau lay invisible, defiant, hugging the centre of my spheres.

'What the hell are those?' Henry arrived back for lunch short of breath.

'Pompoms.'

'Crafts,' he shrugged. 'You should join the Country Women's Institute. They do that stuff all the time.'

I was glad to move out of Garden View Road that summer. I made it up with Lou, too, after I had a vision of her cushion with trailing blue threads sitting shame-faced on my bed.

I didn't steal from friends any more, but I did comb op shops and city dumps after that for *objets trouvés*.

When Lou got herself together, after Diana left, she finished

Sociology and began a degree in Art History. For a few years she ran a gallery space for the Women's Collective in a renovated warehouse on the Quay. I think she'd been converted when she saw her dress cut up and turned into a piece of art. Of course, I was her first exhibitor.

I suppose I should say something about this: my first solo show in December of 1974. It did turn out to be important, for a number of reasons.

I'd decided it was time to admit to what I'd been doing behind the padlocked door. I knew Steph was just dying to find out, although she would never have broken into my room. Over one's private space, she was very respectful. Unlike me.

The apology to Lou had made it easier to come out as a salvage artist. Which was, I guess, putting a nice gloss on the origins of my art. Anyway, one of the exhibits was a denim-covered book filled with a collage of Henry's letters, a handful of which I'd stolen from his correspondence file. It looked marvellous. Tragically comic, or comically tragic, the critics said. Despite quibbling over terminology, most agreed it was a step forward for women's art. Actually, my favourite piece was the Perspex galaxy, but I've since learnt that what critics choose to pay attention to is most often for perverse reasons of their own.

To cut a long story short, Steph took one furious look at my work at the exhibition opening and lunged at me as I was chatting with friends. It was a new experience, being the centre of attention, and I was savouring every moment. When Steph felled me, I had a moment of complete blankness. I couldn't remember what we were both doing tangled up on the floor together, or who would want to attack someone at an exhibition. Fortunately, the *Evening Post* photographer had just left. A photo of a brawl on the front page would have definitely been a bad way to begin my professional career.

You'd think it would have been Henry who was piqued. He probably was, privately, but Steph was the one who lost control, a fact that showed me how much she still cared for him.

I've spent the rest of my time as an artist exploring the darker side of love, where a found object is always preceded by its loss. Since mine has been a particularly successful career, I am ever grateful to Henry Ballantyne and Steph Jackson for schooling me in the priceless worth of losing one thing, only to find another.

The other *objet trouvé* I ran into just weeks before my first exhibition was a biology student called Simon Wong. He occupied himself in his spare time by propagating illegal plants and growing them in the ceiling of his flats. Like me, he never read the newspaper, and had had a miserable time in encounter groups, so we were ideally suited.

Over dinner at a birthday barbecue organised by Gillian and Chris, he told me he'd gone to Henry's old school in Wanganui as a boarder. They'd never liked each other. Simon had hung out in the science lab and Henry didn't have time for boys who wanted to perform experiments. Right from the third form, Henry had been organising United Nations clubs and Corso action groups.

I bent over the dish of pears in wine, imagining the earnestness of a third-former with shining white hair, a leader ahead of his time, declaiming from the school platform.

Friends, staff, members of the board, we are here to remember the tremendous task given to young people today. If our country wishes to take advantage of the events stirring our world, leaders of the future must be encouraged to plant the seeds of their endeavours at every opportunity.

And I saw my own schoolgirl self, dressed in Peach Grove Girls' school uniform, sitting in the sewing room with my friends, stitching an elaborate ruffle on a gingham skirt. The news came on, announcing the Cyprus crisis. Someone switched it off, laughing.

It was too late to go back to the languor and safety of the sewing room, I knew that. I had to live my life forward. Over the summer, Lou would be leaving the gallery in my hands and going to China with the China Friendship Society; Gillian would be wallpapering their house and preparing a layette. As for me, when Lou returned, I would enrol in design at polytech.

At last I was leaving university, setting a field as vast as a continent between me and the towers of learning where I'd spent so much time sleeping while politicians fought. One day when I'd cleared my mind of their static, I would turn on the news again, and this time I would listen.

Gillian's dish of pears lay swimming in amber, fragrant with cinnamon and speckled with dots from a vanilla pod.

My boyfriend had forgotten about Henry. He was laughing, admiring the cake, blowing out the surprise candles. Lou was leaning back in her chair dreaming about Diana, while Gillian wore the calm of a crescent moon suspended between the delicate spinarets of motherhood.

I dipped my silver spoon into the dish and caught a passing glimpse of my face, fat-cheeked and fully present, before it disappeared beneath the juice and rose, dripping with pinkish fruit, into the circle of light.

Simon and I are still together. (There's a limit to how many found objects you want to lose.) We laugh now, at the silliness – and the cruelties – of our student days in Wellington. Just to show he has no hard feelings, he helped me plant a pear orchard a few years ago when our kids were old enough to allow us a little time to ourselves. I'd told him years ago that the pear tree was not a symbol of disaffection at all, but a wonderfully fecund sign of life.

Although I'd lost contact with Steph, I still remember her mournful face when she told me how she was related to Katherine Mansfield on her mother's side, and how their family history was full of stories of unfaithful husbands and unhappy wives who knew down to their last metacarpal that bliss was the biggest of all myths. I thought at the time that she must have been right: Henry was hurting me and I'd lost all will to fight back.

When I crafted those pompoms at Coromandel and felt the fierce thrill of rebellion, though, I knew she was wrong, I knew pears were a lot more mysterious than she allowed: that they released their secrets to you only when you were ready to listen.

I remember just before the exhibition when Simon and I were on our second date, seeing a pair of birds tenderly piping on a pear tree. The birds fluttered into a knot and thrashed wildly together, disturbing the tree's leafy poise. Professor Laing had been able to see knots. What was it about him and his strange lecture on the family? 'The thief is a man eaten up by his own dream,' he'd said. My appetite for stealing things had devoured me, had allowed others to devour me. Meg, the Keeper of Lost Things; mother of emptiness and vertigo, of all lost children spinning above the earth; Klepto Girl, harbour for stolen treasure, lover of devourers, of politicians eaten by their own dreams.

People steal, the professor said, because they have lost their rightful sense of entitlement. Someone had stolen their birthright. So who had stolen from me? My mother? My father? And did that mean that someone else had stolen from them when they were children?

The cycle of stealing could go on and on to infinity, a fallen circle of bark and leaf, falsely green that inverted the natural cycle Steph had celebrated in her background papers for the hui's environment workshop.

And then I thought: people choose to deplete themselves and each other, and it is no one's fault. *I gave up my name myself, my house was unguarded. Henry took away my name and I let him.* I saw my hands holding a pen and copying his signature, and I cried then, but Simon, who instinctively seemed to know what I needed, was tremendously comforting.

'Come on, sweet,' he said over the remains of our fondue, 'let's go to the nursery. Pear trees are on special. We can put one in a pot till we get our own place.'

Henry's story

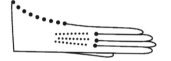

Personal Diary, Vol. 4, 1971
This book belongs to Henry Benjamin Ballantyne. If found, please return to: 263 Days Bay Road, Eastbourne, OR 17 Garden View Road, Mt Victoria, Wellington.

It is unlikely that this diary will be lost. Still, one never knows. I like to be prepared for all outcomes.

January
Christmas celebrations finally over. Dad retired to his study to finish the cave weta population project. Mum in garden. Garth across the road at the beach, I think. He's been a pain in the arse all holidays. Mum got out my old Meccano set for him the other day, and the little creep immediately snapped a construction spanner in half. Impossible to replace, but that's what you get when you pander to children.

Books for Christmas include: *The Naked Ape*, a new botany one on natives by Professor Richards (one of Dad's colleagues), and *The Feminine Mystique* by a woman I have never heard of. (Mum worried about my female friends. Naively assumed *The Feminine Mystique* would be able to enlighten me. I took one look and tossed it. I could tell her a thing or two about feminism, but it would pass clean through that pea-sized brain of hers.)

Christmas the usual droll parade of Dad passing a hand across his forehead and declaiming on the meaninglessness of all ceremonies, and Mum cooking an atrocious amount of food that sat around unconsumed gathering *toxins*. Mum and Garth pulled crackers in the lounge, Dad fell into bed in black-dog mood, I took myself on a refreshing solitary walk around the bay. A few families scattered about picnicking, but easily avoided. The light on the water an unctuous tribute to the sentiment that lards human interaction at this time of the year. Doubtless, Peter Berger would view the season of good cheer as a commendable opportunity to study family relationships. Sadly, I find it difficult to retain the necessary objectivity. Berger a great sociologist, but even he has his limits.

On Boxing Day the atmosphere lifted. Mum went off to her croquet cronies after lunch, and Dad and I discussed the forthcoming year. Like, what courses would I be doing, and why didn't I forget Sociology and get back into the sciences. I explained for the tenth time that Political Science is a highly employable subject, but of course the bastard didn't listen. Pointless to launch into a discussion on the politics of education, or anything else pertaining to Real Life, but I'm used to this stand-off with the old man, and it was good policy to be seen to be making an effort to communicate. After all, they still pay the bills.

I called June around 7 p.m. Found it something of an exercise in self-control enduring forty-eight hours without being in touch with any of my friends. She was delighted to hear from me, eager to meet. Of course she knew Steph was away and we needed to be discreet. June's one of those unrepressed women who enjoy making love wherever they can find a spot on which to lie. We wandered up the hill and had sex under the solanums. A native shrub with purple flower, yellow centre. Maori call it poroporo, which is *not* a transliteration of purple, I keep telling people. According to Prof. Richards, the berry used in manufacture of hormones! June picked the twigs from my hair and we descended.

Garth bug-eyed, beginning to be curious about sex. If he's lucky, Mum will rescue him from his adolescent misery with another well-chosen pamphlet on wet dreams and teen pregnancies from her Marriage Guidance counsellor friend Pam. Pam knows about as much as a cud-chewing cow when it comes to fucking, but have no intention of enlightening Garth myself.

June mounted her bike, disappeared around the bend. She

looked like a moth fluttering into the dark. The moment inspired me so I hived off to my room and wrote a poem to Steph. All up, the encounter with June rather functional, I'm afraid. I riffle through my little green book for an alternative. Irritated this has become a necessity rather than the pleasurable diversion it usually is.

Steph's insistence she spend the first two weeks of hols in Christchurch with her family an act of bad faith. I explain about the woman in the café who leaves her hand in a man's and continues to talk philosophy. Sartre knew she wanted the man more than the conversation. So: bad faith because she can't admit it. Steph unimpressed. I consider whether she needs replacing, but decide against it. She's hardly mind-blowing in bed, but supportive and intelligent, good-humoured, and can keep up with me in any conversation I throw her way.

Last year we made a big splash presenting a joint Pols seminar on 'The social structures of poverty in Latin America'. Full marks for her research, particularly those tabulations that clinched our case. There's no doubt about it, the rich nations are getting richer. We have begun an aid lobby, and so far our committee has gathered an impressive amount of local support. We take the campaign nationwide this year. I was delighted to hear Steph and myself referred to by one of Corso's directors as 'the bright flowers of their generation'.

I am beginning to be consulted by people here. 'What do you young people want, Henry?' demanded an old duck at the Red Cross AGM just before Christmas. My prizegiving speech at my old college in Wanganui was on 'Facing up to the generation gap'! The youth question has been big in Europe and the States for some time and it's here as well now. An exciting era for all of us. More to come on that score, I'm sure of it.

5 January 1971   Copy to file *Correspondence: Personal*
Dear Steph,
How goes it in sunny New Brighton? I trust your cello arrived in one piece and you are getting some good practice in. Expect you'll be doing the picnic and swimming thing with your family too. Do say hi to Teddy and Lydia. And tell Lydia I liked her recent exhibition. It

began just after you left. The seas I thought very good, although, as you know, painting's never interested me as much as photography. I suppose that sister of yours will be riding her horse and over-grooming it as usual. Why does Teddy let her have one? Jumping's such a bourgeois sport.

As you can see, not much is happening here. The usual ghastly Christmas day, and now the house is silent. Dad ensconced in his study churning out more research on the fate of cave wetas. Mum shopping in town. Garth has disappeared somewhere, thank God. He's becoming a right pain. I had a friend over the other day, and he took to following us. Very irritating. Can't wait for school to begin.

Actually, I'm thinking of moving out next month and going flatting. I know Mum is pretty resigned to your staying over on the odd night, but I'm sick of having to take to the hills for extended privacy. If I treat the old man with some respect between now and February, I'll be able to get them to support me. What do you think? We could end up living together after all!

Honestly, Steph, I've got a feeling this is going to be a big year for us. The movement isn't going to go away. I see young people everywhere speaking out, getting involved. I'm not yet convinced we should move into the streets, but we need to make our lobbying more effective, give it a broader base, so government can see we mean business. I've put off the meeting on development till you get back. I really count on your support and, as you know, right now with the city practically empty and the students away, I'm missing you a hell of a lot. One night I watched a girl cycling away into the dark, her white shirt shining long after the rest of her had disappeared. She reminded me of you.

I know you enjoy my poems, so here's another.

Love ignites, spins
Roman Candle flowers
in radiant brevity, then
overcome by the
unexpected
breath of chill air

falls
like a spent star.
Can it be worth
anything at all,
this brief leaping
to flame
that leaves less
than an imprint
of its presence behind?

Much love,
Henry

P.S. Had those pictures I took in Coromandel developed. Some most impressive early morning and late afternoon shots. You can take a look when you get back. Correction, *if* you come back.

Reading this month
The Naked Ape by Desmond Morris
In a nutshell, Morris argues that human behaviour is fundamentally primitive. He refuses to pander to the bourgeois need to put man, the human being, at the centre of the universe. Right on! Morris correctly begins with the assumption that man belongs to the animal kingdom. I couldn't agree more. We are apes; our habits are those of animals driven by biological necessity. Steph should read this. I think the word *love* vastly overrated. Animals pair bond when necessary, but their copulation is free of sentiment.

My favourite writer to date also makes the intriguing discovery that breasts are copies of buttocks, lips, of labia! I knew it. Originally, when man went on all fours, buttocks and labia were signals for copulation, but an upright posture required a secondary set of erogenous zones on the chest and mouth. So much for all those ignorants who confine sex to regions below the belt. Not that my nipples tingle when Steph kisses me. Note to self: pay closer attention to hers.

Certainly didn't know that 70 per cent of Americans employ the missionary position. In future, Steph and I will resist this bourgeois impulse and experiment more freely.

Invitation to Sociology by Peter Berger
I met Berger in Sociology last year, but he's good enough to come back to. One of the most challenging sociologists around. Aware of the movement, alert to the need for change; serious-minded and analytical. Keeps his writing objective.

He says the sociologist must disturb complacency. I liked this: 'The sociologist is the man who must listen to gossip despite himself, who is tempted to look through keyholes, to read other people's mail, to open cabinets.' We *are* professional Peeping Toms, our own lives grist to the mill of research. Yes! As Berger concludes, Sociology is a passion, a demon that possesses one. Exciting stuff. Botany and Zoo leave me cold. This is where it's all at right now. The human sciences. I can see the sociologist and the political scientist being in the vanguard of the transformation of consciousness our generation will ignite.

16 January 1971   Copy to file *Correspondence: Personal*
Dear Steph,
Thanks for yours of 8 Jan. You say you've been reading *The Female Eunuch*. Personally, feminism doesn't grab me, but I guess if you want to discuss it I'll have to gen myself up. Be prepared for a fiery exchange. Mum gave me a strange book for Christmas by a woman called Betty Friedan. I've never heard of her. Have you? Obviously Mum hadn't the faintest clue what Friedan was on about. I think she hoped *The Feminine Mystique* would give me a more sympathetic insight into women's lives.

Hah! Thanks to Desmond Morris, I know quite enough already. I think you ought to take a look at his book *The Naked Ape* when you get back. Plus, there's a big file of press clippings building up. Political stuff, mostly. Some articles on youth protest. I told you, it's going to be a busy year.
Best love,
H.

Personal Diary, Vol. 4, 1971

February

Ran into Diana Fahey freshly arrived from Sydney, at a demonstration in front of the US embassy yesterday. An abortion march the week before that. The woman's everywhere. Skin pale as a vampire's, thin lips and surprisingly luscious red hair. She was wearing a beret. Honestly, the night was hot as Hades, and they're all wearing Mao caps and Guevara berets. Sometimes you wonder at the Left's commitment levels.

I'm told she's standing for Women's Vice President, and will probably cruise in. I don't like the sound of that. She could be dangerous, especially if she's as radical as people say. I'll have to sit her down one of these days and see which side she's on. It would be good to have Steph there; Fahey looks hard to handle. One of the first women I haven't wanted to fuck. Must make effort to inquire into her background.

The long-awaited development meeting takes place, with Steph and a new member, a first-year called Lou Waters. Not much to look at but she sounds promising. Very onto the same issues we are: poverty, the reluctance of rich nations to gift aid without strings to the Third World. Those old Corso collectors would turn in their graves if they knew the politicisation that's going on. The committee's been chaired up till this month by a pro from Internal Affairs. Good enough sort. Pipe-smoking, tall and rangy, admired by the Old Guard. I'd say conservative masquerading as liberal. Steph and I lobbied like crazy right up until the meeting started for a new chairman. I want this lobby to go places and the Internal Affairs pro isn't the guy. We were joined by the Waters girl, who dumbfounded us by her passionate speech about the growing interest of the world's youth in the problems of poverty. She pleaded that the committee make a pledge for better representation of young people – young people who would take Corso into the future, into a better world etc. The Old Guard looked shaken. That kind of rhetoric, even if somewhat insubstantial, is hard to resist. In the end, the chairman had the sense to step down and we were spared a public blood-letting. We may not have had a sufficient mandate for outright victory, so our strategy, spearheaded by Lou Waters (I must look into her background: she's a potential ally), won the day.

Steph and I experienced a spectacular session in bed, quite the best since she returned from that possessive family of hers. I gave her orgasm after orgasm. She seemed to vibrate like a top until I wondered if things weren't getting rather out of control. As they always do, her breasts slid in the direction of her armpits like a pair of poached eggs. 'Oh, Henry, Henry,' she said. It doesn't look much written there on the page, but a woman's submission has a powerful effect on the male.

Amazing the variety of the female form. (June's breasts are more fibrous and pert.) Steph has a sparse crop of pubic hair, but makes up for it on the rest of her body, which is thickly covered by a soft down that drives me crazy when I am in the right mood. I am grateful that she is one of those women who scorn the idea of using perfume. She also has a tendency to under-wash, which is fine by me. I adore all her smells. As Desmond Morris says, why refrigerate a room and then light a fire in it?

Well, Hamish found out some information for me about Diana Fahey. And, indirectly, the Waters girl. Diana, he tells me, is an Australian with Irish connections, exact natal whereabouts unknown. She began a degree at Melbourne, then moved to Sydney with the Moorhouse set. Sexual liberationist, I suppose. Germaine Greer's name cropped up again. I see I'm going to have to dip into *The Female Eunuch* after all. So she's radical, all right. Associated with the Red Letters, Hamish said, the hard-nosed violent activists that as yet, thank God, have hardly penetrated these shores. Useful man, Hamish. He's totally wasted doing Psychology. I can't abide the subject. Steph's current crush on Jung drives me spare.

Now I come to the discovery of the day. I think I'm in the middle of a revelation. I've been casting around for some time for a project that would be satisfying, give me something to get behind. The ubiquitous Hamish happened to run into a friend of his from Auckland recently – a hippy drop-out by the name of Steve Runcie. Steve, I learned, as Hamish and yours truly sat in the cafe with him, had only last year returned from a United Nations conference in New

York. I regarded him sceptically. I failed to see how such an apolitical specimen could possibly have been voting on motions and resolutions with a simultaneous translator hissing into his ear, and the air conditioning of the UN blasting away, without being noticed for the phoney he so clearly is. But not at all. Runcie assured me hazily, his beard falling into his coffee, 'Man, it was a *representative* gathering. Young people having a say in world history. We socked it to the UN. There was a riot: parties, drugs. We saw *Hair*.'

Hamish looked away. I tried not to reveal my contempt for this apology of a spokesman for youth. Apparently, the National Youth Board are trying to co-opt him into sharing his experiences with young people by running a summit here. This is when my revelation began. I have one or two contacts on the board. Why not inveigle my way into Runcie's confidence (which, judging by his permanent drug-induced euphoria, should not be difficult) and use the platform myself? Join the summit organising committee? They're right – it *is* time for this country's youth to gather and show some muscle. And I want to be there when they do.

To cap it all off, I discovered that Runcie was in league with Lou Waters, the girl I'd met at Corso. If Steve had been the representative hippy sent by our country, Waters was its schoolgirl. A seventeen-year-old from Greytown at the World Assembly of Youth in New York! That explains the passionate speech. She's been travelling up and down the country speaking at school prizegivings and Country Women's Institute afternoon teas. Rapt audiences follow her every word. I found this gem (Steph came across it, actually, doing her weekly sifting through press releases) in the *Te Puke Times*:

> Man has come a long way. He has learnt to battle with nature and to control his environment – he is able to settle arid deserts and the polar wastes. But he has made small progress in improving human relationships.
>
> In a shrinking world, we must abandon all forms of hostility and intolerance. We must aim for tolerance and co-operation to find the key to a complete and meaningful existence.

We'll have to knock some of that out of her head if she's to work with us.

Reading this month

The Harrad Experiment by Robert H. Rimmer

This caused a sensation in America when first published. The most forward-thinking approach to sex and relationships I have seen. A fictitious co-ed college given over to an experiment encouraging multiple partners. Book full of sexual encounters. Interesting information not found in *Naked Ape*.

Physical education conducted in the nude!!! Imagine all those breasts bouncing in front of your nose when you're attempting a press-up!! Everyone had to keep a personal diary, a habit of which I approve. Characters actually began showing each other their writing. Not so keen. In their case, communal reading and group meetings produced spontaneous and natural approach to sex and sleeping partners. Jealousy surmounted through rational discussion. College directors proved through their teaching that you can love many people in a lifetime. And fuck plenty more. Certainly in agreement. Mind-blowing. Must show this to Steph.

Personal Diary, Vol. 4, 1971

March

New living arrangements sound, despite reservations about flatmates. Found a place in Mt Victoria – not close to varsity but affords pleasant views of bush and harbour. Have a two-in-one arrangement. Smaller alcove facing north for bed, very sunny, opening into larger room off hall for spare bed, desks, Gestetner and books. Dim, but am not averse to working under lights. With Steph's help, the arrangement is quickly habitable. We make love for the first time in the afternoon. Our bodies enjoy the last heat before the sun drops behind the hills. A curious, rapid fall into gloom up here, unlike the bay. (Possible poem?)

Three flatmates, one pending. Veronica and Thomas, both in mid-twenties, all but married, and their bourgeois behaviour proves it. Veronica a social worker. *Social worker!* Thomas tutoring in English Department. Carries a rolled black umbrella at all times. I believe writing a thesis on Alexander Pope. Close-cropped bullet head with the body of someone who eats too many cheap, fatty cuts of meat.

Will have to restrict his access to kitty. Even vegelinks would be preferable to mince. Veronica: tolerable appearance, brownish curls, long eyelashes, hazel eyes – scorching, however, not soft. Tread carefully.

Ruth, the third inhabitant and longest stayer, therefore some deference required. Hippyish. Bright clothes, permanently jingling with bells. Wears bright orange colour on toenails, which are attached to amazingly long feet. A plant fanatic, so a lot is forgiven. I note kitchen and bathroom windows lined with healthy African violets, my mother's favourite house plant. Alas, in my mother's case, the leaves alternately rot and desiccate with her monthly cycle.

Ruth studying Indonesian, works part time at Asian Imports and always bringing home weird stuff to eat. A fearsome Chinese chopper in the knife drawer. Has an equally hippy musician boyfriend but, thank God, not living together. Question: do they get high on pot? If so, will voice strongest disapproval.

Am now sitting at desk after unusual stir-fry dish cooked by Ruth. Veronica and Thomas at movies, Ruth listening to music in room, Steph not yet arrived. Preparing for first SRC of year. A crucial motion on Al Fatah coming up. We need to be seen to be supporting this. Will add ballast to the development lobby. Must call Aid and Development Group members and get them to speak. Make advice terse, persuasive.

April

SRC according to plan. Also Exec election. Arthur Meyer president, of course, and Diana Fahey, the newcomer, Women's VP. The Waters girl proving an asset in her enthusiasm and sharpness. A troubling lack of social finesse, but then what can you expect from someone from the Wairarapa? Waters introduced me to a friend. Quiet, enigmatic first-year. Attractive, if rather too much flesh on legs, and no bosom to speak of. Hails from Cambridge. Not a political bone in her body, I suspect. All the same, will keep an eye on her. She told me she was taking French and English. I lost my composure at that point. Could not bear to see her go the way of Thomas – or Steph. Arranged at party (most significant intellectual gathering of the term) to go over her course of study. There ought to be something else she can do. By the sound of it, she has a terrifying mother who writes poetry. *Verse* is what she probably means. Meg Shepherd. Must write name in appointment diary immediately.

May

Weather cooling off. A new guernsey purchased from Kirk's. My old one emerged in a tangled heap from Steph's twin-tub and is beyond repair. Steph's upbringing has obviously been too bohemian for her to have absorbed the finer details of fabric care. Her clothing sourced from op shops, which means indifference to laundry fast becoming a habit.

Am meeting with National Youth Board reps this pm. Heard from Hamish that Runcie has lost interest in co-operating with National Youth Board, and retired to a commune on Waiheke Island. His loss my gain. Will hit them with my growing mandate to speak for youth of this country. Doubtless they will have seen my recent profile in the *Evening Post*:

> Student speaks up for young people. Henry Ballantyne, third-year Political Science student from Victoria University, and chairman of the Corso Aid and Development Group, stated today that the 'now' generation were more in touch with world affairs than their parents. In an address to the Wellington branch of the United Nations Organisation, Mr Ballantyne claimed that youth were keenly aware that their world is tomorrow's world. 'Unless we pay attention, we will not have a habitable world tomorrow,' he said. He named the fight to preserve the environment, race relations and the low level of aid to Third World countries as major issues facing New Zealand today.

If properly conceived, we can showcase the cream of our generation's talent at the summit next year. Press would be interested.

20 August 1971   Copy to file *Correspondence: Personal*
Dear Meg,
I hope you are finding the holidays a worthwhile break. Most of us take the chance to catch up on reading. So, I would recommend the following: *The Naked Ape* by Desmond Morris (his comments on man's animality you'll find instructive, and useful for quelling the

conservatism of your anti-evolutionist mother. Though how anyone can believe in a seven-day Creation beats me hollow. Also study the chapter on sex. Quite the best introduction to that subject I've come across.) Next, *The Social Construction of Reality* by Peter Berger. You've met Berger before in your Soc. lectures, but they don't hit you with the heavy Berger stuff until next year. In the meantime, try this. It's hard, but you'll be ahead of your Stage Two class if you can master it. Read especially the stuff on roles and masks. Waikato library will have both of these.

And, by the way, mutatis mutandis means 'making the necessary changes', not mute but mutating.

I occasionally write poetry. What do you think of this one?

If to breathe thoughts to the drifting air
were to give them planes in space,
who knows what proportions
these obsessions may take – perhaps
ringed stones of fire, a
palpable witness to inward desire,
without speech but giving voice
in unheard waves of song
that fret the high surfaces of cloud
in attenuated tracery
with a quiet and discernible
bliss.

Best wishes,
Henry

Personal Diary, Vol. 4, 1971
November
A retrospective, I'm afraid. Lost the plot over September and October swotting for finals. Tore strips off Meg for being obtuse; she seems to have no capacity for independent thought! Almost missed Pols terms. Had to push assignment under door at last minute, which seems to have done the trick.

Exams the usual pain, although my photographic memory came in handy with the Latin American political stuff. Argued that political reform a waste of time unless it was conceived in tandem with green technology and social revolution. Think my radical approach means I've missed out on a Senior Scholarship. No matter.

Made great strides with Youth Board since I last wrote. They were delighted to involve me on their youth summit organising committee. With other members showing a range of degrees of apathy, most of the thinking has been left to me. Waters and I had a couple of meetings, but clear I couldn't co-opt her on to the organising committee. Totally weighed down by scruples and doctrinaire beliefs that don't budge an inch, no matter what you throw against them. *And* I've a suspicion she's not normal physically. I don't get a hint of any of those feromes (check sp.) women are supposed to put out in the presence of a young sexually active male.

Fortunately, after one confrontation too many with yours truly, Waters closeted herself away in Women's Lib group. Her weak spot is that she's too easily undermined by criticism. Women are, usually. I haven't come across one who didn't buckle under fire. Except for Diana Fahey.

Which reminds me, I got her into the sack one night after a particularly stimulating exchange on the evils of exams. Both slightly plastered, thus not a great success. As I'd suspected, Steph finds her a threat without reason.

Back to summit. Out of respect for better race relations, we've decided on a catchy title: *Hui '72: Youth, Politics, Passion.* Hans Batchelor's secured funding from government and non-government agencies. Diana and Steph have joined the committee; will encourage Meg – as long as she keeps up – to apply. The spirit of co-operation is genuinely encouraging. We're set for an amazing year.

13 January 1972   Copy to file *Correspondence: Personal*
Dear Meg,
Our flat is quieter than a church at present. Flatmates all away. Did you go anywhere? How is your mother? You say she's going on a refresher course next week. I hope her absence will give you a feeling

of relief. It cannot possibly do you good arguing about religion all day. You should be meeting people your own age from Waikato. I don't actually think much of the politicos up there (fairly Maoist, I believe, and too heavily committed to the anti-war movement to attend to any of the hundreds of other issues that are crying out for attention), but there you are. I've written to Doug Franks. He'll be in touch if there's anything on. Don't be shy and refuse to go.

Now, in the way of reading, I'm recommending a book called *The Harrad Experiment*. It'll blow you away. It's brilliant. This is the kind of stuff you need to be getting your teeth into. Find it in the library.

All the best,

Affectionately,

H.

Personal Diary, Vol. 5, 1972

This book belongs to Henry Benjamin Ballantyne. If found, please return to 17 Garden View Road, Mt Victoria, Wellington.

January/February

Frustrating summer. Flatmates absent for much of January so I rattle around alone, but preferable to watching Garth systematically destroy Meccano. Home a madhouse with Dad's book on cave wetas late to printer and Mum I think going through *menopause*.

Difficult time with Steph. Becoming unpleasantly clingy. Impossible to get away with anyone else, though had hoped to see more of Veronica. Thomas over in Noumea for a final fling before their impending marriage. Can't think of anything more ghastly at present. Steph's state taken me by surprise. Normally an independent woman, supremely talented on cello. Plays away for hours at exercises and scales. Has temporarily moved in, although I shall encourage her to leave when term begins if this keeps up.

Finally penetrated Veronica's icy reserve just prior to Christmas. A delicious body. Nipples tasted like cranberry juice, creamy skin smelling of attar of roses. How she can hitch herself to an oaf like Thomas, I can't imagine.

Diana has vanished. Probably, given her shady background, to

Australia. There's something troubling about that woman. Need to make greater effort at investigating. Since Hamish, all further inquiries drawn a blank. She maintains an effortless fund of information about numerous topics, but I've a hunch we haven't seen the real Fahey yet. If, in fact, there is such a person. Certainly in my case, borrowing the words of St Paul, whose wisdom was drummed into me weekly at Divinity, 'I am all things to all men.' Women generally find this flexible approach to persona too demanding.

5 February 1972   Copy to file *Correspondence: Hui*

Hans Batchelor,
National Youth Board,
P.O. Box 449, Wellington

Dear Hans,

Trust your summer was enjoyable. What did you make of the New Year's Honours List? One or two surprises, I must say. I think the old man was disappointed not to get a mention.

Seriously though, Hans, I think we need to move fast on pre-summit publicity. The committee wants us to canvass as wide a cross-section of the population as we can manage. Presumably we'll have access to the NYB's mailing lists, although we'll want to move beyond those into the community itself. Straight into the horse's mouth. Let's do a mail-out to schools, hospitals, maraes, trade unions, university campuses of course, and polytechs. We could also use a press release or two. Why don't we meet soon (what are you like Tuesday next?) and nut out an all-purpose statement that could be PA'd. Television will come on board later.

Talk again shortly,

Best wishes,
Henry Ballantyne
Chairman, Hui Committee

Personal Diary, Vol. 5, 1972
March
Following lengthy phone calls join Diana Fahey for a meeting in

cemetery. Adjoin to pancake parlour, which looked suspiciously like pick-up joint to me. An impossible woman to pin down. Smart, though and a useful ally, so long as we can get a handle on her Red Letters gang.

Steph departed for own flat at the end of Feb. Really, will have to straighten things out with her, or relationship a no go. Been meeting occasionally with that woman from Cambridge, Meg Shepherd. She came back looking pale and sickly from the summer vacation with her dreadful mother. Cheerful enough to chat to, and seems to have finally got on top of her reading. Didn't mention *The Harrad Experiment*. May have been premature.

As I'd hoped, she saw our hui poster and applied. I'd been building her up for this all year. Consider her ripe for development, political if not sexual. Much untapped talent and the joy is, she's such an unclaimed field. As far as I can tell, no one else has watered there before. An ex-boyfriend is dragged into the conversation occasionally, but less often these days. Women who can't leave their pasts behind bore me silly. Steph has no inkling of my interest and was able to be quite civil on informing Meg of her selection. Naturally, I spoke warmly of her abilities to the committee, who took my advice without batting an eye. Underplayed my hand so as not to disturb Steph. Feel I'm going to need her loyalty more than ever this year.

April

Diana now living with a group of women from the Collective. All lesbians! I must say I always suspected her rigid preference for trousers was not natural. I blame a cook by the name of Jessie she's currently hugger-mugger with. If Fahey's going to be of use, I'll have to wean her away from all that stuff. Find myself resorting to terms like 'opiate' and 'false consciousness' to underscore my point, but so far am making no headway.

Which is why I'm slow to embrace the enthusiasm for gay rights currently infatuating the rest of the Left. It's leading them away from issues that really matter. Government probably delighted. Attended a conference on homosexual issues last year and was alarmed at the growing sense of division among the protest movement over this one. Strange sexual proclivities are all very well, but keep the bedroom out of politics, I say.

The same goes for female rights, which I have heard more and more about recently. Perhaps this could account for Steph's summer behaviour? On balance, I doubt it. Steph still loves me, I know that for a fact, while Germaine Greer and her ilk do not approve of men at all. (And why Fahey would expect me to believe that ridiculous nonsense over pancakes about Greer being a relative of hers, I have no idea. Didn't fall for it, as she well knew.)

To cut a long story short, invited Meg Shepherd to dinner at the flat. We needed another flatmate. Steph moving in at present not a good idea. *Ms* Shepherd, although she does not seem a feminist, may prove the ideal substitute. Quiet, self-effacing, eager to absorb new ideas. Her reactionary past can be slipped from her shoulders like a tired banana skin.

Speaking of which, I have become involved in yet another lobby group, this time to press government into paying higher prices for Fijian bananas. The Americans have totally compromised the banana industry in Honduras. Here's a chance for New Zealand to take a more proactive stance in the Pacific. Unfortunately, Fijian bananas regularly spotty, and of poorer quality than South American imports. Will have to change market expectations. What we need are consumers preferring sugar to starch. (Reminder: for Development Group to look into? Contact nutritionist?)

Meg turned up at flat for dinner with her hair in a knot, a piece of jasmine pinned above her ear. I took one look and collapsed into laughter. 'Where have you sailed in from? The Islands?' That girl needs kid gloves. I probably still had bananas on my mind. They come across to New Zealand in ancient boats and fester too long in the hold before the wharfies finally get to them. This country's ports are in a sorry state. Despite my commitment to the Left, I do not support the stranglehold the unions have on the waterfront.

Ruth labouring in kitchen cooking another mystery dish. The flat smelled hideous, like an old midden. It turned out the pungent odour belonged to a substance called trasi, a rotten-shrimp paste allowed to ferment for years. Asians said to use it in stir-fries.

Veronica and Thomas in attendance, their wedding weeks away. A night of gossip on latest scandalous project exercising the minds of Wellington's public servants: the proposal to extend the motorway through city and out to Hutt.

'I can't think why the council is allowing it to go through.' Veronica chewed and talked at the same time. 'They say, you know, that the project committee have been bribed up to their eyeballs. And that that bitch Moira Williams is sleeping with the mayor.' Seemed oblivious to the shreds of pork dangling from her incisors.

'Come on, Pickles. You know that's just a rumour,' said Thomas, rubbing his girlfriend's knee and wiping mouth with serviette at the same time.

Pickles, I ask you. Meg quiet as a mouse. Ruth politely invited her to comment.

'Well, I think . . .' she started out.

I'd had enough. 'Oh, don't ask her, she wouldn't know if there was a nuclear war on.'

But no, Ms Shepherd plunged on courageously. 'What's the point of a motorway ending up in Cook Strait?'

Suppose I should have been more encouraging, but banana business had quite exhausted me.

I placed my fork down firmly. 'Growth is inevitable; even a Labour supporter like myself thinks so. A better motorway will handle more traffic.' Then had a bright idea. 'Wellington will be the entrepôt of the country. I find that an inspiring notion.'

'You're an idiot, Henry! If the bloody council were really concerned about the city, they'd let us have money for night shelters. I'm seeing more poverty than ever.'

Veronica's scorching side making an appearance. Spent a moment wishing for Steph's company. Alas, she was out at a cello lesson. In any case, best not socially introduce her to Meg just yet.

'Last week,' continued Veronica, 'I met a student who ate catfood because he couldn't afford the student cafe! It's disgusting!'

And so on. Discussion wilted soon after. Retired with Meg to room. She sat sedately on bed, inspected surrounds. Gestetner, books in bookcase, striped towel slung over chair and towelling robe hanging from door. Can't be much to look at. However, she seemed fascinated.

'So what about it?'

'About what?' she said innocently.

'Coming in with us.'

An enigmatic stare into the distance.

Okay, *ne touche pas le chat.* 'Let us know by the end of the week,' I said helpfully.

Concluded evening with poem. Steph read aloud some Mexican poet last weekend. Challenged me to have a go at his style. A good imitation, I think:

Meanwhile the day winds down
to a predictable burnt-out end
with no prospect of the hills
dropping their clothes at my feet
and leaping to swim in the sea.
Light struggles to dance
with wings on the surfaces
of a city dull with words.
My cranium does not sprout
gardens of harps
or rivers that rustle and sing.
Beyond the Sunday roast – sullen opacities.
The edges of the weekend unfold, rise up to enclose me
in their frayed boredom
and I drown in a dreary sea of habitual sensation.

Personal Diary, Vol. 5, 1972

May

Meg moved in this morning. A load off mind, as we have been short on kitty and I've had to resort to soybean recipes from Steph. The soybean is tasteless and indigestible, no matter how long you boil it. Will have to watch kitty is not depleted when Veronica & Thomas leave. That may then be the time to ask Steph to join us. If all goes well with Meg.

Our new flatmate seems to have a pathetically small amount of worldly goods. Hardly any books to speak of. A strange girl. She's put a padlock on room. Perhaps violent father? Unless, of course, she's reverted to sewing in private. I did advise her to drop that peculiar hobby; it'll certainly get in the way of her education. Only petit bourgeoisie and effete aristocrats engage in needlework. Meg definitely belongs to the former category. (Checked her background and discovered it to be deficient, socially speaking.) Have doubts about decision to get to know her better. Later, I found her making cocoa in kitchen dressed in red dressing gown with gold collar (unusual, purchased in Cambridge!), and appearing more normal. Feeling of relief. Reminder: go carefully with enigmatic women.

Broken caliphont episode precedes what turned out to be important meeting with Fahey. Avoid all personal subjects. Concentrate on hui, under cover of which I make further attempt to size her up. Political inclinations definitely Left, but how far? A hard woman to read. Only see her in trousers these days. Wonder how many other males have been permitted inside them?

Discussion at one point turns into coaching session, with her triumphantly pulling books I haven't yet read from my shelves, as if life weren't busy enough already.

'Aha! Paulo Freire and Ivan Illich. Look, you've got to dip into these writers.'

'Well, I damn well won't study them just because the Left says so. I'm an intellectual first. I'll read a writer because he challenges me, not because he's the current god of radicals.'

'You'd like him.'

'Who?'

'Freire. He talks about humanism.'

Detect amused tone entering Fahey's voice.

'He says real humanism trusts in the people. One day they'll wake up and throw off the myths they've been fed by their masters.'

'We've all been fed myths, Diana. Look at our colleagues. Look at the apathetic masses. I can't see how face-to-face communication will fix them. Even the most naive politician knows dialogue can bloody well blow up in your face!' Felt admitting to continuing belief in intelligent manipulation of masses to be untimely, as debate now becoming heated.

'Intellectuals have to throw in their lot with radical activists or they're as guilty as the fucking institution they're trying to change!'

Fahey stalking up and down my room as if she owned it. Relieved rest of flat out minding their own business.

'Look at Latin America. Intellectuals are coming down out of their ivory towers and living lives of sacrifice.'

I sigh. Want to lead conversation in direction of hui, but don't dare for now. Too much at stake. Listen while she schools me on another waffler.

'When the revolution comes, we'll line you up against the wall like everyone else.'

'Steady on, there. That's a bit rich. I mean, if we're being frank, who could guarantee your credentials?'

'What's that supposed to mean?'

Ferocious looks all round.

'Well, you've just marched over here from God knows what Aussie organisation, and charmed the crap out of the Exec.' She certainly needs longer than a year in this country to prove herself to me. Can't prevent jealousy from creeping into my voice.

'So what if I have?'

'So, what if we checked on all that Red Letters stuff you fed us? What if you were just some nobody from the outback, some – oh shit, I don't know – some imposter. It's been done before.'

Must recapture discussion while she's reeling from accusation. Take the plunge and announce my intentions to use hui as a platform for a set of demands any reasonable revolutionary would agree to.

The race issue: Convince her that government must make reparations here. Still remember with fondness my Anthropology field trip to Ruatoria. Offered rotten corn, which I declined, but joined in all other festivities. Maori not as uptight as Pakeha. No intellectual leaders as such, but am convinced they have things to teach us.

I suggest lobbying Education Department for White Paper on maraes at all secondary schools. Diana in agreement. Do not inform her I acquired idea from Meg, whose mother (headmistress of large

Waikato co-ed) invited local tribe to build marae at her school. Meg also told me that during the Christmas break she was party to special house-cleansing ceremony, complete with tohunga and elders. Maoris certainly know how to be ceremonial, I'll give them that. Not that it did said house-owner any good. According to Meg, who has begun to manifest a decidedly mordant take on life (which leaves me uncomfortable: politicians need immeasurable reserves of optimism to deal with the shit they have to put up with from unsympathetic masses), he died of a heart attack soon afterwards.

Back to hui.

International aid: My position well broadcast. Am coming less and less to favour such terms as 'undeveloped' and 'poor' nations. Too pejorative. Diana accuses me of resorting to euphemism to cover my back, concerned a liberal such as myself will sweep poverty under carpet. I object hotly. In the end, we both agree that First World economy must be made responsible for parlous state of Third World.

Diana brings Fanon in at this point, another 'must read' book, she tells me. 'One per cent aid!' Scornful. Mannishly places hands in pockets and jingles change.

'What's the problem?'

'It's pure tokenism. The US has got the World Bank by the balls. They couldn't give a stuff about national pledges.'

A fierce southerly gets up, bringing hell to bear on the loose tiles in our chimney. Permit myself a moment of distraction. Diana troops after me into lounge as I try to track down ominous gurgling. Must remind landlord to check roof before we have a major disaster on our hands. 'What would you suggest, then?'

As if preparing for major thrust, my sparring partner suddenly strips off her jersey, which I see is worked in corny cable pattern, throws it carelessly into my armchair. 'Allow colonised peoples to own the means of production.' Tosses hair from wild eyes.

I force my mind away from the parlous state of roof.

'And tip these big multinationals out of Asia and Latin America. The US is behind all of them,' she spits out.

'How do you propose to do that?' *Here we go.*

'You know me – I agree with Fanon that violence will be necessary. No one wants bloodshed,' which is a whopper: Fahey would be in element if state of war declared, 'but,' she charges on, 'there are times when justice has to come out of the barrel of a gun.'

So we're back to the revolution. I dislike that kind of rhetoric. Cheap to say, and impossible to deliver.

Another symphony begins outside in the trees, which creak and moan like a herd of cows in labour. Wonder briefly how many branches I'll have to negotiate in my constitutional tomorrow morning. Imagine the furrows out on the harbour all capped with white; wish I could be out there, tossing on a matchstick of a fishing-boat instead of having to deal with this storm in the sitting room.

We then come to blows over education. Those Latin troublemakers Fahey worships are thinking through their feet if they dream we can shake up the system. For one thing, we're burdened with a mass of local PTAs all manned by IQ-deficient individuals who wouldn't know a radical thought if they fell over one.

Diana takes issue, which is putting it mildly. 'I loathe the liberal position!' she explodes. 'It's a cop-out.'

Yours truly urges calm reflection. 'Look, I'm all for change, but education in this country is totally bogged down with inertia. We'd never make any progress.' Don't let on I have plot up my sleeve for disrupting same.

'What about *the little red school book?*'

What about it indeed. There's some more sloppy thinking for you. I don't know why she has such a bee in bonnet over this. Perhaps a nasty school experience? Low grades for papers at Sydney? Who knows what academic men have disillusioned her.

In the end, we agree to a trade-off. Pretend to hand over summit discussion of education. Christ knows what she'll do with it: my plot will have to be pretty good to claw it back later. Make the supreme sacrifice in return for her not standing in our way when it comes to the youth lobby. We must speak to government with *one voice*.

Evening concludes with Meg bursting into room with an offer of toast and cocoa. Both of us look thankful. Diana takes herself home, Meg and I manage to engage in meaningful conversation before

Steph turns up on way home from library, hair blown about and wet as ropes, stockings clinging to legs.

Reading this month
the little red school book by Soren Hansen and Jesper Jensen
Diana carries this one around in her jeans, yet I still can't fathom why it's so damned important. The authors tell the reader that youth clubs are a form of control. (Girls' Life Brigade, Scouts, Junior Red Cross, etc. To tell the truth, all aforesaid are members of National Youth Board, and potential funding for hui.)

Well and good. Privately, I've never been a fan of Scouts, but then what do authors do? They advocate groups for school students! Suggest they meet twice a week at school and have talks, discussions, pop sessions, films and other forms of entertainment. (!) Absurd. Always thought Denmark and Sweden taking the wrong direction; this book does nothing to change that.

How the hell do kids know what they want in third form? Remember Mum refusing to allow us to choose from Sunday cake plate till we were quite old. 'You know you want me to choose, Henry,' she used to say. The only thing was, every Sunday tea she made me eat honey-crunch, which I hated. She was right, though. Authors are dreaming if they think they're going to produce revolutionary school kids.

Rest of book full of warnings on University Entrance (an intimidation of sixth-formers), drugs, sex, abortion, diseases. 'Marks are a means of power,' they thunder. I'll say. And thank God for that. There are too many goats at university already.

Speaking of which, tertiary education does need urgent work. Full of feminist students and old male lecturers masquerading as young bulls. Take Gerry Parsons. Mentions Marcuse's liberation in words that might have come from teen pop culture:
There's been this Great Refusal against global establishment. It's where things are at now, guys. Chicks too, Marcuse urges you to break with the familiar.

And so on, ad nauseam. Some members of the older generation cause great embarrassment in their attempts to prove how switched on they are. Rubbish. No one can be seen through more effortlessly than an old man attempting to be 'switched on.'

One of my Geography profs has delivered same lecture for last twenty years. Notes wafer thin with age. *Au contraire*, young people sit up when their leaders think outside the pitch. I like to feel, along with Marcuse, that intellectuals such as myself have rare aptitude for sniffing out the familiar, stripping away the sham, and ruthlessly breaking from its prison.

Am less certain when Marcuse praises the sexual revolution. As far as I can see, spending too much time fucking during term is bad for anyone's study programme. Work first, play later. Nothing wrong per se with sex in daytime. In fact, have had some exciting encounters in broad daylight. (Heard the other day that working class more likely to make love with light switched off. Will scrutinise sexual habits carefully from now on.) *But*, intellectual projects must continue to take priority.

The man is doubtless romanticising the drug culture, something I've never got into. You can find yourself in bed with anyone when you're high, and that, I find, doesn't altogether suit me these days. My eye's become more discriminating with age. Rooting around on the floor with some shop-girl at a party is all very well.

Personal Diary, Vol. 5, 1972
June
The first day of winter, damp and cheerless. Meg and I made love. Frustrating experience, as she was clearly a virgin. Asked if the earth moved, except she seemed to have no idea what I was talking about. Referred her to Hemingway. (*For Whom the Bell Tolls*, if my memory serves me correctly.)

She had a prominent mons and pubic hair in shape of *loveheart*. Extraordinary. Most common arrangement, according to my reading is the delta formation or V. Does this mean she could be highly sexed?

Immediately afterwards, wrote a poem:

A season of saffron
smoulders on the hills.

Bright-tongued firebirds
flash across
the slopes
and flaunt their gold-brushed feathers
in the late cool brilliance
of the sun.

Like the onomatopoeia. Steph did too. A further creation, not shared with Steph, found its way onto Meg's pillow shortly after. Well, she does remind me of a native.

In the meantime, Steph has moved in. Trouble in her flat. Bad timing perhaps, nonetheless, a challenge to juggle two women at once. She insisted there be no rivals, so Meg and I have become inventive. Earlier this evening, it was a lecture theatre in Law Dept.

I led her up the back steps of the theatre. Very dark, she clutching the back of my jersey as we went. Squeezed down behind the last tier of seats. The warm timbers creaked above, arching like some vast boat.

I floated forward with the tide. 'Meg, Meg.'

Abruptly, she rolled over.

'Lie still a moment, won't you!'

'The floor hurt my back.'

'No, it didn't. You enjoyed it.'

'Won't Steph be worried? It's late.'

Could feel my calm ebbing away. 'You go home first and I'll go for a walk in the gardens. Trust me, Steph won't think anything.'

Despite the risks of discovery, reconnaissance of new sites for sex adds much to its pleasure. Temporarily mislaid my green notebook, but no matter. Hands full at present.

Reading this month

The Art of Loving by Eric Fromm

Have had this forced upon me by Steph. Directed to the slim section at back on practice of love. I think she was impressed by Fromm's emphasis on discipline and faith, qualities Steph has in tiresome abundance when it comes to playing her cello and hanging on to me. Not that I wish she'd turn her attentions elsewhere. I need, yes, need her love. For those rare moments when I feel lost, she's there to remind me of who I am and where we're going.

Personally, have difficulties with an expression like 'love'. Most intellectuals I'm into consider it's an impossible word in today's society. Men and sex: yes. Men and love: nothing more than a white elephant. When it comes to their cocks, look at all the males who are only too ready to favour their animal instincts over that debilitating condition known as being in love. I'm no different. Only trouble is, sex more often than not turns into an alienating experience where, if you don't watch out, you can wake up with total memory loss. Note to self: nothing ventured.

Risks aside, unlike Eric Fromm, who still believes in love, I *embrace* post-coital loneliness. I suspect it's what drives me along. Men are monads, always will be.

On Wednesday had dinner with the olds, and Dad, who's begun work on some other interminably long project, suddenly reared up on elbows and pronounced, 'The human condition is one of quiet desperation.' Stunned. Never heard him admit to this before. Then he got up from table and went to listen to a record in lounge. Most disconcerting. Wonder if trouble in store with him and Mum. Mum acted unsurprised, so perhaps it's been going on for some time. Garth indifferent, chewed noisily on steak. But this is precisely where I take issue with Fromm. Loneliness, separation, desperation are inevitable. *But the moments of their experience pass.* That is what women are for. Mum's menopause just getting in way.

To conclude, Fromm out of focus. Misses real challenge, which is not to look down. *Ever.*

Personal Diary, Vol. 5, 1972
June/July

Consequently, I have been unable to tell Meg that I love her, which is what I know she's been waiting for. We talk about it in terms of a meaningful relationship. The best I can offer at present. A passionate woman, yet hard to kick into life. Send her away to study *The Joy of Sex* and Desmond Morris again, but she returns with mournful face and no orgasm. Do I prefer her passion that stops short, or Steph's abbreviated comes?

Hui planning and travel dominate these two months. More rain than usual: trees keep up a continuous drip, clothes hang damp on line. Even clean washing pongs.

Travel thing sprung out of nowhere; will have to reneg on rent next month unless Dad offers to come up with the extra. Spent a small sum on driving up north with Diana; another whack on three-day trip to Sydney in July. A relief to leave the rain behind, although we did hit a tropical storm our first day in Australia.

Even now this entry looks odd: Ballantyne and Fahey hive off to Ninety Mile Beach, thence to Sydney. Here's what actually happened.

A development forum came up unexpectedly at the University of New South Wales, and Corso voted to pay fare, insisting my presence was vital. Gratifying, if not exactly well timed as was just dusting self down and calming Steph after northern trip with Diana. However, rapidly decided the forum was unmissable, especially seeing it could well strengthen my hand at hui. So, dug into my own pocket and found enough for Steph to accompany me stand-by. Then, blow me if Fahey doesn't invite herself and Lou Waters along! Doubtless challenged by my aspersions on the Red Letters, which we'd only just begun to discuss sanely at Ninety Mile Beach. Probably she was still smarting from her Jessie affair, too.

I must say, though, Diana and I did have a useful time up north. Shitting myself over our last hui conversation and the many key areas on which we'd disagreed, I'd taken it into my head to spend a few days with her in more productive debate. It was not long after her break-up with that wretched pancake-maker, and it occurred to me that on the rebound, she could be vulnerable enough to make some compromises over the summit.

Neither Meg nor Steph saw it that way.

Meg looked miserable when I informed her of travel plans; apologised for her poor performance in bed. Steph turned into raging fury and refused to have sex. I couldn't get them to see that sometimes personal choices have to be put aside for more strategic interests.

Despite our history of opposition, Fahey and I managed to spend a day or so in Northland in amicable discussion; self came home relaxed and convinced that summit would be in better shape. Made a note to contact her avatar, Josh Rideau, when I had the chance.

And then the invitation arrived from Australia, with no choice but to go. This time, felt Steph needed attention. Meg seemed capable of waiting; a mature quality in a lover which I admire.

Coincidentally, Diana and Lou Waters turned up at the airport, heading to Sydney on the same flight as ours. Diana insisted Lou would be attending the forum, which pissed me off, actually, as I'd already decided Waters was impossibly doctrinaire. Hah! Wait till Aussie Corso heard me cut her down to size.

While mind harmlessly occupied thinking of political matters as we all waited in departure lounge, Steph's gaze travelling suspiciously between Fahey and myself. Really, nothing significant in the fucking sense had gone on between us at Ninety Mile, so once more Steph cavilling at nothing. Still, attempted to keep my horns in at Sydney, which as it turned out was a good thing; I needed all my resources once I met Fahey's mystery man from the Red Letters, Josh Rideau.

Looking back, the Sydney fiasco makes me shudder. Worse, I returned to Wellington less convinced than ever that Fahey under control. Pointless going into detail, except to say that Rideau and I ended our brief association with a rather physical kind of conflict. Our last dinner in Sydney culminated in a contemptuous Rideau tossing a sugar bowl over my head. All the truisms I've refused to entertain about Australians came home to roost. He behaved like an ignorant lout, and I told him so. We spent considerable time insulting each other's forebears, and by God, despite the lurking sugar crumbs, I came off best. (Steph told me so as soon as we climbed on to plane.)

Meanwhile, Fahey and Waters decided to stay on a few days longer. I was eternally grateful they didn't show up for the return flight, because would have tipped my wine over both of them. Neither stood up for me. Waters managed to secure an alliance with a group of leftie Fijians at the forum; Fahey too far gone down path of radical politics to come to my aid with Josh Rideau. As Rideau banging on about radical politics and Kiwi conservatism, caught Fahey exchanging an amused glance with the pressed-tin ceiling. Rideau's current fuck no help either. So much for an alliance between the sexes. Christ, deeply regret taking Fahey into confidence over hui.

To cap it all off, Hamish now informs me she's behind this new military training weekend taking place shortly. Irresponsible bitch. Anyway, where would they find the weapons? And can you imagine the skinny Arthur Meyer or Lou Waters brandishing an assault rifle in anyone's face? Weapons and violent revolution are for Third World countries where life is cheap. I cannot support a military takeover of the state unless all democratic means exhausted, and that by no means the case in NZ. Besides, Fahey's ruining our hui credibility.

Late July, post-forum UNSW

Turn up at Otaki for the military training exercise. Based on the if-you-can't-beat-'em-join-'em rationale. Owing more to the dreariness of proceedings than any master plan on my part, I suggest a noisy interruption of the military training ballot. If the Australians can do it, so can we. Find myself in cahoots with Fahey, who evinces new respect for self. Unfortunately unable to follow through; prematurely depart the Crockford while Diana left hiding in toilets. Oh well, a man can do only so much.

Unsure whether my next move was wise. Persuaded Arthur Meyer to lift one of the White Paper drafts from the Education Department. To tell the truth, ever since Sydney, Fahey has been giving me a headache.

May have temporarily lost nerve. Called Meyer in a panic and asked him to break into the department for me. Fortunately, my credibility still high, with said document quickly finding its way into my filing cupboard. Meyer thoroughly reliable in that way, though we were both disappointed no mention made of break-in in press. Sat down at once to see how I could best use it to advance the demands of the hui on government.

So far, so good. Unfortunately, bloody document only resided in Garden View Road files for two weeks. Came to take notes one brutally freezing morning when frost had hacked away at cinerarias outside window, only to discover it was missing. Turned flat upside down all day, but to no avail. Steph a nervous wreck; Meg withdrew sullenly into bedroom. Forced to come to unwelcome conclusion that it had been stolen, by persons unknown. Nasty feeling to have one's home broken into by thieves; must change locks as soon as we've boosted kitty reserves.

No prizes for guessing who's the chief suspect. All my suspicions come back to Diana Fahey. I know it seems impossible: we're still allies, after a fashion, working together on this hui, for God's sake, but the stealth of the whole thing has her signature all over it.

We have a futile phone conversation, during which I confess to the theft and subsequent loss of the paper. Diana full of false sympathy, feel I get nowhere. Must assert leadership before she destroys everything we've been building.

Sense my frustration focusing on her announcement of a further military training weekend. She would make an excellent Red Guard. Narrow-minded, doctrinaire and bloody dangerous. Decide to tackle her head on. A difficult discussion, which went something like this:

Myself. 'Ah, Diana, I hear you have announced more resistance training.'

She, aggressive, 'So what if I have?'

'Well, the hui committee is concerned you may be undermining what we're trying to do.'

'That's nonsense. I'm simply giving it more clout.'

'I can't see how running yet another weekend on the use of firearms could possibly give the hui more clout.' Refrain from mentioning the disastrous outcome for self of the last one.

She responds by giving me a tiresome lecture on the need for armed struggle, a lecture deeply reminiscent of Rideau's a fortnight ago.

'You see,' she concludes, 'in the long run, deaths from the revolution will be far less than the suffering of the people now.'

As I said to Rideau in Sydney, I've always found that reasoning pure bullshit, but refrain from saying so again now. Patiently, I take Fahey back over the terms of our agreement. She can play around with the education question, I'll lead the summit lobby of government. I cunningly suggest that should the government fail to recognise the hui's remits, something more confrontational might be called for, but we were a long way from that at present. I can see that this prospect attracts her. Will need to keep on offering these sops if I'm not to lose her totally.

The meeting ends with nothing agreed, except that Steph and I will not attend Diana's latest weekend project. We part with her grim reference to Brecht (is there a revolutionary connection here? *Check.*): 'He who laughs has not yet heard the terrible news.' Christ. She's become a real worry. And I'm still convinced it was her who stole my White Paper. Would Rideau have put her up to this? I wonder. If so, what's his game?

5 August 1972   Copy to file *Correspondence: Hui*

Hans Batchelor,
National Youth Board,
P.O. Box 449,
Wellington

Dear Hans,
Our organising committee is making excellent progress. We have made contact with successful applicants and informed them of our general expectations and a number of administrative matters. The catering and booking arrangements are in hand. Various committee members are now at work preparing background papers.

There is, however, a more delicate matter we need to discuss. I believe you have met Diana Fahey. A friend of hers, Lou Waters, told me you both were at that stir on The Terrace recently. Clearly she's a charismatic woman with much talent, and from my own experience of her work, I can see she'd have a lot to contribute to the radical lobby.

Unfortunately, it's the exact nature of her radical politics that's in question. She wishes to sweep a number of remits through the hui that would throw this country's education system into a spin. She displays an irrational attachment to Paulo Freire and Ivan Illich. Are you familiar with these writers? Both happen to be revolutionary dreamers who believe we should 'deschool' society: a position quite unsuited to the New Zealand context. It's likely, of course, that Fahey will not find a clear mandate, but I'm taking this opportunity to inform the NYB of her intentions.

Another point: I have a suspicion, and it's not much more at present, that Ms Fahey is capable of quite dangerous forms of sabotage. Prefer not to go into details: trust me on this one. She'll have to be watched.

Did you ever know Rick Shaw at our old alma mater? He's a rising star with TV News these days. I'm about to press the flesh and see if we can't get him to cover the hui. A camera on site in Takaka would be just the thing.

Keep in touch,

Henry Ballantyne,

Chairman, Hui Committee

Personal Diary, Vol. 5, 1972

August

Big surprise this month turned out to be the launch of a new party called Values. Unimpressed by name, which suggests genuine alternative to two-party system. Complete phonies. Consider their emasculation of mawkish Labour ideology to be a danger.

One of their front-men an irritating person, with skin pulled so tight on face that he resembles a monkey. Earnest, ignorant mouthing of leftie positions. Atrociously lacking in solid intellectual groundwork. A cheap pull. Sadly, it's working. More than your usual numbers of women and beardless youths dance attendance.

Am tempted to grow a beard myself to avoid being mistaken for one of their leaders. Which actually happened, during recent lunchtime session in town. Furious with the encounter, as was Steph.

A journalist from the *Evening Post* drinking with cronies at table came over to us. Have taken to reading *Guardian* and other responsible foreign papers over sandwiches and beer once a week with Steph.

Staff treat us with respect as they sense, and am not exaggerating here, our role as young intelligentsia of city. Said journalist accosted me with the following howler: 'I say, aren't you Sonny Edwards, the Values man? Can you give us a comment on where your values will take the new party?'

Myself, frosty: 'Values have precisely *no* values. They couldn't lead a country town into a cocked hat.'

No resemblance to Edwards *whatsoever*. Journo slunk back to table. Steph and I downed beer and left.

When Values Party announces a meeting in Island Bay I go again, this time armed with well-thought-through objections. Hall packed; almost one thousand fans. If hui had half of this support I'd begin to feel our pressure on government could have some bite. Raining outside; wind making a fearful racket. Speaker's weak voice fails to carry beyond halfway down hall. Minions scuttle on to address breakdown in sound system, which now begins to boom like an international airport. When calm is restored, I catch the following pearls.

'Ladies and gentlemen, fellow voters, the meeting you are attending this evening is one of historical importance.'

Historical importance, my arse.

'Men and women across the country are disillusioned by the fruitless war of attrition waged every election by National and Labour candidates.' Edwards surveys us excitedly. 'Main party politicians are lucky to address a hundred people. Why are people streaming in to listen to the Values Party?'

He gives a nod and at once a giant screen shoots down in front of stage, almost toppling him off platform. Gives audience a reassuring smile, waves his hand and we are then subjected to small film, clearly low-budget job, on the party. They have obviously co-opted format of *Movietone News*. Unsteady soundtrack unwinds to sound of Douglas Lilburn playing some complicated pastoral, well beyond, I'd wager, 99.9% of audience. Accompanied by well-modulated voiceover (yes, I have to give them that) as we follow a geriatric cyclist biking around New Zealand. Inane observations on the endangered environment, excessive affluence, lack of humanity in urban centres etc. Naive beyond belief, but it's exerting a powerful tug on audience, who lean forward, eager for question time.

Leap to my feet as screen disappears into the flies. 'Mr Edwards, could you tell us who your financial backers are?' That ought to sort him out.

Pay no attention to the rumble building all around me. Values supporters do not like my insinuation that their values may be driven by commercial vested interests.

'Our support,' answers Sonny Edwards sharply, 'comes from concerned people everywhere. Small people like you and me.' Sonny directs a scowl at me and hurtles on. 'I dislike, sir, the implicit nastiness of your question. Values is against corporate monopoly, just as we do not support those pressure groups who manipulate parties on the eve of an election.' A very emphatic finish. This time, no doubt about his glare.

Values must know of my work on politics and development issues. After all, I am widely published. I suppose they think they can strangle us by stealing our ideas. Let's hope they choke on it. Meanwhile, am jabbed in armpit by missionary-attired woman: untidy grey bun, grotesquely inflated waist. Who admonishes frostily, 'Some of us have come a long way to hear Mr Edwards, young man. How about remembering your manners and letting him speak!'

Sit down fuming, reflect on the threat to every decent pressure group that Edwards presents. If we're not careful, as well as doing us out of a job, Values will stuff up the chance of lobbying government for good. Give that man half a chance and he'll scuttle the protest movement faster than a rat up a pole. Wait till I weed those pensioners out of Bird and Bush. Then we'll see.

Arrive home, still raining, in bleak mood. Steph sawing away at cello in sunroom and Meg disappearing out the door wrapped in all-weather mac.

'Where the hell are you going?'

'Walk.' She is equally rude, a practice that seems to be increasing of late.

'Well, don't make a noise when you come in. I'm stuffed.'

Recline on bed and consider the ingratitude of the young woman I have rescued from the provinces and a likely career as a machinist or a teacher of crafts at polytech. Who still can't come. At least I don't think she does. It's hopeless. Steph breathing down neck over suspected infidelity, and feel getting it up regularly for two women with hui looming a bit much. May have to give one of them the push.

Last thing before my nose sinks insensible into pillow is that Fahey didn't attend Values meeting. I suppose she knew they were just a pack of Luddite young conservatives. Clever her.

Personal Diary, Vol. 5, 1972
October/November

Eventful two months, as expected. First up was death of well-known poet in October, James K. Baxter. Sad to watch the man drive himself into grave like that. A total wreck at end. Last few years, whenever I saw him, obvious to all he was courting disaster. Thin, sporting a hacking cough. Once I called him for advice on an ex-commune charge of his called Anne, who'd decided to crash at Garden View Road. And I mean crash. As far as I could tell, she never washed, spent all her waking hours wrapped in a blanket. For first time, thought Meg's padlock a sensible idea. House began to smell like a tip.

Jim gets on the phone and in that withered voice of his says, 'Let her shit on the carpet if she wants.' Horrified. I'm not having a commune dweller shitting on my carpet, I don't care how disturbed she is. In the end, Anne packed up and went. Certainly got no encouragement from me. Even Meg, who has somewhere in her possession an aged clipping on 'The Art of James Baxter', uncertain how to be kind. 'At moments like that,' I told her, 'kindness is a waste of oxygen. What Anne needs is a shrink and a drying-out house, not a student flat where people actually want to get on with their lives and make a difference to this country.'

Will miss reading the occasional outpouring from Baxter. My favourite, the poem about high-country loner watching sunset. Domestic quarrel over vegetable patch a close second. Blue-collar dad and repressed, conservative mum definitely a working-class scenario. With my vastly different background (parents very upper-middle class) I can nevertheless identify with the rigidity of the lives of that generation. What is it about women that incites habitual frustration in the male? Baxter rescued us from complacency and fear of dirt. In principle.

Next, to early November hui, which proved a challenge. Must admit, greater than anticipated. Failure to read Steph correctly a shock. Our sudden break-up probably responsible for her rebellion. As for Diana, her complete turnaround at hui, hand in glove with Batchelor (not surprised he's out for my blood – will have to temporarily forgo our drinking sessions), seemed a bizarre way to jump, even for her, although it does indicate that my misgivings were correct. Note to self: refuse to work closely with people of suspect background, supported by even more criminally inclined troublemakers.

Steph's disloyalty, however, totally unexpected. Up till the hui, I'm convinced she had been my closest ally. A serious blow, which even I had difficulty rationalising. All well now, but it took a while and drained my energy.

Meg's support, despite padlock on door, again gratifying.

Here follows verbatim record from Takaka notebook.

Sky overcast with cumulus on arrival. Rain in the air; all along coast waves displayed in untidy cross-hatch. Had been looking forward to trips to Goat Bay and Totaranui. Hope for good weather after hui. If brochure correct, Takaka area worth investigating.

Rest of delegates due to arrive late afternoon. Noticed that Steph and Meg making no effort to get on. Steph chewing nervously on hair, Meg taking off for yet another of her moody walks, so I was left to make up beds.

At dusk, mozzies attacked, landing on any exposed flesh they can find. Retreated into sleeping bag to avoid their insect whine. Dad would be in his element.

Rose early before girls to make breakfast. Three piles of food to one side of the bench marked 'S', 'H' and 'E'. Must have been remnants of Steph's attempts to calculate daily food rations: packet of tea, cubes of butter, weighed allowances of muesli, four slices of wholemeal bread packaged in Gladwrap.

Experienced moment of genuine fellow feeling for political leaders who, at the end of the day, are responsible for a meeting's success or failure. Too much charm and the audience suspects secret agendas. A confession of weakness and the man is a hypocrite, or undependable. An excess of direction can lead to accusations of domineering and manipulation. I know. I've seen it myself. Rehearsed strategies for rest of day.

Fahey arrived next in battered bus sloganed over with 'Ban the Bomb' and 'Out of Vietnam Now' in faded colours. One of the cooks (name Anton) had driven a group of them down, stores packed into back of vehicle, along with several marijuana plants in pots! I inspected and then, eyeballing Diana, informed the cluster of cheerful travellers that my summit was not going to be another dope-smoking hippy gathering.

'Not a problem, Henry.' Diana put more effort than usual into placating me. 'Cooks always keep to themselves. And these people here,' a cheery arm waved responsibly, 'will do the same. They're such brilliant cooks I couldn't resist them. Anton does a mean bolognese.'

'Okay. But keep a low profile. I don't want my delegates distracted.'

By 10 p.m. 120 delegates, drawn from all over the country, had arrived. Carpenters, farmers, school teachers, journalists, a housewife, shop assistants, students and apprentices stood holding their satchel of background papers and summit schedules, expectantly looking to us for leadership. It was a wonderful moment. Looking back, the best. Also present were representatives from Nga Tamatoa. Delighted about that. We need Maori youth to give our platform more clout.

Delegates crowded into cabins, cautiously made friends. I think in awe of the giant task the committee has entrusted to them. Faithful to our democratic aims, Steph had attempted to mix delegates from different social backgrounds. Naturally, she'd made a stab at their likely standing, thus there were some dismal cabin atmospheres that first night, but by the following evening most of the disaffected had relocated. Rooming parties went on into early morning. Regret to say some of delegates could be seen fraternising with the cooks. Most, however, earnest young people determined not to allow their minds to be fogged by abusive substances. Level of engagement with issues exhilarating.

For the next three days hui buzzed with productive activity. Meg and I on high. Four areas of interest: Education, Development, International Politics, Environment. Delegates chose at least one area and attended daily workshops. Evenings free for socialising and for the committed to lobby controversial remits. Euphoria and co-operation ruled. Cooks in perpetual good humour, served pots of steaming tasty food day and night. Anton's bolognese as piquant as Diana promised. On Tuesday evening Meg caught taking plate of leftovers back to cabin. Steph's anxiety about protein allocation thankfully appeared to have faded.

Huddles of people met spontaneously over meals to work on submissions. Afternoon plenary sessions orderly, co-operative. It looked as if aspirations to use gathering as platform to twist government's arm being realised!

Every morning Steph and Diana drove down to Takaka to send press release of progress to Wellington. A team of cameramen and journalists due to arrive day before hui concluded.

Things couldn't have been going better. My workshop reached unanimous agreement on most of issues tabled: Vietnam War, Arab/Israeli conflict, United States imperialism in Latin America. Took a risk and allocated Meg the Development workshop. Hear she did tolerably well. Workshop managed to secure support for higher prices for Pacific Island fruit imports. Well done, Meg!

Fahey, despite ongoing doubts, got stuck into Education. Major scrap centred on a group of teacher tearaways demanding abolition of School Certificate and University Entrance. During heated debate and name-calling they backed down. If trouble were to come from Diana, it would be with those rebels, who seemed largely to be a gang of immature attention-seekers.

Things still critical; couldn't relax my grip for a moment.

Have had good news from Steph about Environment. Uncertain initially about hand-picking her for job of chair, but all reports were glowing. Apparently the workshop ranged as widely as others: pollution, urban expansion, the marketing of hemp, tourism, logging in beech forests and land ownership all considered. Good. Government won't know what's hit them. Perhaps underestimated her grip?

One afternoon session impressed by stunning-looking woman enrolled at Lincoln College studying sheep breeding. Went by name of Bridget and worshipped by Matthew, student from Auckland. Bridget had obviously been reading Environment briefing papers prepared by Steph.

'It is true,' she began sternly, an Amazon leading a herd of awe-struck savages, 'that we are blind to the spoliation of our planet. It is also true that the greed of multinational corporations is stretching the ecosystem beyond its natural limits.'

Watched as Matthew regarded Amazon with mouth open.

'While we must give scientific research its due, we must equally attend to the negative implications of technology.'

If Matthew opened mouth any wider, a gob of spit would drop on his jeans. He sprang to his feet. 'I cannot agree more with the need to tread a delicate path between the ills and benefits of science. I wish to support my associate and would, Mr Chairman, therefore put forward the following remit . . .' And so on.

Amazon shot him look of melting gratitude.

Later in the day noticed the two walking along beach, heading towards honeycomb rocks at far end of camping grounds. Reflected that the Amazon would shortly grind Matthew to powder.

Trouble finally showed its hand in our final hui committee meeting. Only two days before I met with Rick Shaw, who would be interviewing me for *Hotspot*, weekly national news programme. Interview to include live footage from final day's workshops and plenary.

In exuberant mood. 'So far, it's been fantastic,' I said to the committee, keeping niggling anxiety about the missing White Paper to myself. Meg looked daggers at Diana; Steph avoided looking at anyone. 'Better than I thought. We're looking good for Shaw's slot.'

I looked around. 'Well – Diana? Meg? What do you think?'

Meg, moodiness forgotten, right behind me. 'I agree. All our workshops have made huge progress. We do need to be sure we can direct the cameras on the day. The last thing we want on television is Anton and his bus.'

A playful Diana jogged her foot. 'Come on, he's not that bad. It won't hurt to have a touch of the sixties. No, I'm more worried about what's happening in our workshop.'

'In Education?' We all looked at her. Trouble there again. I knew it.

'Don't worry. I didn't recommend dismantling the whole institution.'

Felt momentary relief.

'But I did argue that if workers can organise themselves into unions and fight for change, so can school kids and teachers.'

'Students,' I interrupted gently.

'Yes. And I quoted *the little red school book*: "Teachers are dogs on leads too."'

Shit. What next?

'Well,' said Diana, 'most of my motions were defeated before they could be ratified.'

Struggled to say nothing alienating. 'And?'

'I warn you Henry, I'm not done yet.'

Christ, what did that mean? Could feel eyebrows accelerating under fringe, which I forgot to get Steph to cut before hui. Consequently, may look shaggy on *Hotspot*.

'A few of us have been meeting in closed session. We've got something to bring before the final plenary.'

'Well, can't we know what it is?'

'Sorry, it's confidential.'

'But damn it, Diana, you're part of the committee. You can't do this.'

Diana reminded me of our agreement – in general terms, since there were others present. Then she got up and walked out. Long silence, during which I worried all over again over White Paper disaster.

Meg began polishing glasses. 'I don't think we should be too worried, Henry. There's no sign of disaffection. Not one.'

She turned to look at Steph. 'Have you heard anything?'

Steph gazed into space ruminatively. 'No,' she said at last. Never seen her so preoccupied. Something was up, I knew it was. I couldn't put my finger on what, exactly, and no time to worm it out of her with ground about to collapse around us.

Imperative to keep several steps ahead. Neither Steph nor Meg politically sophisticated enough to be au fait with this delicate level of strategy. Whole burden for success of hui had fallen on my shoulders.

Walked up and down, mind turning over possible scenes: the exhaustive planning turning to shameful public humiliation; interim defeat followed by unseemly clawing back of ground already won; heading Fahey and rebels off at pass through some clever pre-emptive strike yet to be thought up. Possibilities all grim, but some bleaker than others. 'I'm going for a wander,' I said. 'You two need to put your ears to the ground. Network. Lobby those we know support us. See you in about an hour.'

Meg made off towards the other cabins, loyal as ever. Felt surge of relief. Steph remained pensive, then disappeared. Did not expect great show from her.

Returned refreshed from my walk. 'Where's Diana?'

'In Takaka.'

'Damn. What's she doing?'

'Everyone's gone off drinking. Diana followed them.'

'I suppose the rest of you haven't found out a thing.'

Silence. Steph got up and embraced me. 'Don't worry.'

'I do worry! She could be provoking a riot in the pub right now.' Disengaged myself and strode across floor.

'What are we going to do, then?' she asked.

'Simple.' I flashed my teeth. 'We're going to forestall any resolutions the final plenary may make until the summit is over.'

'What?'

'It's brilliant. A wonder it didn't occur to me before.'

'But you can't – that's undemocratic!'

'How could we get away with it? What about the media?' objected Meg.

'That's just it: they're arriving tomorrow. We'll fob them off. Give them a summary of our resolutions so far. Only a few sticky ones, in any case. This way, the press gets the idea that we're healthily divided.

'Of course. Of course,' soothed Steph. 'But I still don't see how you can go and ratify another set of resolutions when everyone's left. It contradicts everything you've said you stand for. I thought you wanted to give young people a voice in national politics. You're turning your back on them!'

'How are you going to get away with it?' asked Meg.

'We're going to run out of time. Something will come up. Then I'll put the suggestion that the plenary give the steering committee a mandate . . .'

'We're the organisers, not a *steering committee*.'

'Precisely! We'll slip the name change in when they're worrying about an issue they'll never agree on. I don't know. Let's say, abortion.' I waited for Steph to protest, but she said nothing. 'While the room is divided, and quite frankly, it always will be when it comes to destroying life . . .' I looked significantly across the cabin. Steph's most recent period very late, I happen to know. Suspected foul play, but decided not to pursue. Personally deeply disapprove of women assuming sole ownership of body during pregnancy. Childbearing a way of eliminating insufficiently professionalised women. Desmond Morris would bear me out.

I continued. 'I'll just assume the name without announcing it. Our new designation will *legitimately* entitle us to claim representational power.' Could see Steph troubled, weighing options. 'Look, right now I need your confidence in me. Meg?'

'They're not that stupid. They won't be easily fooled.'

'You've got to trust me on this, both of you,' I said. 'I've got the feeling it will all turn out fine.'

'What should we do, then?'

'Just support me in delaying the passage of remits through the plenary. And I really mean support,' turning in Steph's direction. 'We can't have anyone backing out at the last minute.'

A noisy banging on door and Diana fell into room, giggling.

'For Christ's sake, what have you been up to?'

'Interrogating the natives, like you said.'

'What a bloody time to get pissed! You'd better go and sleep it off. We've got a heavy day tomorrow and I need you sober.'

'Well? What happened?' said Steph.

'You'll find out soon enough.'

'If you don't tell me,' I said as menacingly as I could manage, 'you'll regret it.'

Diana sucked in her lips. Couldn't help noticing the premature lines around mouth.

'It's too late,' she smiled.

'Too late for what?'

'Some of us wrote our own press release and sent it out two hours ago. It'll be PA'd tomorrow morning. By the time the cameras get to you, Rick Shaw will have all the dirt he needs.'

Jesus Christ, I thought it was going too well.

Fahey began announcing our doom. '*New Zealand's first youth conference in chaos. Ballantyne unable to unify the masses. Delegates going home in tears.* Can't you see how the media will run it? *Taxpayers' money spent on wilful adolescents.* The government will laugh at you.'

'*Us. Us*, Fahey.' I lost it. Steph held me back, otherwise I think I would have launched into Diana then and there, and to hell with the consequences. 'You're in this too!' I yelled. I knew the veins on my neck were standing out in ugly cords, but had got quite beyond reason.

'I don't have your reputation,' she replied calmly. Then she added, 'My goals are different from yours.'

Chilled. What did she mean? Had always assumed, despite that meeting with the Red Letters, that Fahey a law unto self and that her Sydney contacts were simply to frighten the shit out of us. Now wonder if Rideau and Red Letters are not all sworn to my downfall. Disturbing thought.

Meg shrugged, pulled out typewriter from under one of bunks. 'What the hell are you doing?'

'We're going to have to draft *something* for tomorrow. Well – aren't we?'

For once I had no words. Stormed outside.

At ten o'clock next morning two deep-blue rental cars pulled up outside cabins. Three men squeezed inside our room. On wrong side of door, very young woman in ridiculously tight skirt stood guard over various television paraphernalia. Assigned Diana bureaucratic task to distract her. Well, I had to do something to keep her out of trouble. Gave me a look, but complied. Five minutes later, Meg and Steph exited and took themselves off to Takaka with a set of careful instructions. Next, I led television crew in direction of school's assembly hall.

As per instructions, girls made straight for PA office. To my great relief, Meg later told me the threatened press release had not been sent. Two youths of dubious appearance had turned up just before they were due to close the night before, and passed a piece of paper over the counter. It was handwritten, and the clerk put it aside for someone to check out the next morning. Steph able to inform them it had been submitted in error, that the official conference press release would be issued later today.

They brought the unauthorised release back with them. It was bad. *Urgent*, it read. *Highest Priority*:

> Today in Takaka, the first-ever youth convention to be held in this country betrayed its deep divisions, divisions that organisers Henry Ballantyne, Steph Jackson and Meg Shepherd have been anxious to suppress.

Fahey's name was missing. Naturally.

> Before this convention began, there was a rare opportunity for youth to debate and air their differences. Sadly, the organisers have sabotaged that opportunity and confirmed the suspicion of most of us that politics works hand in glove with corruption.

Our credibility as a mouthpiece for youth nearly incinerated! Couldn't believe we had the luck to intercept it. Declared state of war with Fahey.

Meanwhile, after assessing assembly hall for filming of final plenary, made way towards beach and cameras. Rick Shaw intended playing up theme of natural environment and youth. Suspect he would like another Woodstock. Shaw's personal lifestyle irresponsible, his drinking habits well known in the city. A few months back, following brilliant interview with French ambassador on butter imports to Europe, he was arrested after driving around Parliament on the pavement. Needs careful leading. Not always open to suggestion.

Raised my hands in sweeping motion as if distributing a vast, wholesome picnic. Have been told before the movement looks convincing. Dismissed Steph and Meg with a brief nod. Rick and I joined Matthew and Tim, two of the hui's most vocal participants and my most loyal supporters, trailed by attentive film crew. Camera closed in on Matthew, Tim and myself in earnest conversation, the waves of Golden Bay bubbling and swirling around our calves. Rick rolled up his trousers to join us for a final take.

Paid no attention to Steph and Meg, now joined, I saw from the corner of my eye, by Diana. All regarded me balefully from upper slopes of beach. None of them could be trusted to appear on *Hotspot*. Meg too partisan, Steph doesn't know right hand from left, Diana a traitor and would sell me down drain.

Did not let the threat of a botched plenary cut into my enjoyment of this moment in front of cameras. Sun poured down on us, water cold and refreshing.

Final session indeed a close call, with Fahey smuggling Batchelor into hall intending to call my bluff. Not that it worked. Batchelor skedaddled, leaving Fahey gaping like stunned mullet. Steph's ploy more testing because so bloody unexpected. A shop girl from Tokoroa! What was she thinking when she invented that maverick twaddle?

Situation eventually righted itself without yours truly so much as lifting a finger. Knew I could count on Rick for a perfect shot of capitulating plenary. What is that expression? Rolling with the punches?

December

Just returned from short trip away with Meg and Steph. Misguided, probably, and sex didn't work out as anticipated, but head feels fresh and have plenty of plans to occupy self over summer. Steph off to Solomons to do fieldwork. Seems to be spending most of time interviewing virile young Solomon Islanders with greased bodies.

Gradually piecing together the story of National's demise in election a month ago. Clever Labour for campaign advertising strategy. Particularly liked the irony of: *When it comes to building a house there is only one thing they* [young couple and child wearing disappointed looks] *can afford to do. Dream.*

Rental accommodation undoubtedly on increase. In my capacity as Students' Association Housing Officer some years back I remember visiting immigrant family living in dire accommodation. Cramped, steamy quarters. Took along old ex-Ballantyne family Zip frying pan. Minus a leg, but they were grateful to have it. Urban lifestyle inevitable if we continue on current economic growth path, both of which I welcome. Trick is, to manage all this growth *intelligently* through rebuilding city spaces. (A pleasant memory of a loft encounter in Greenwich Village floats into mind as I write this.) By all means, shift shabby factories to outer reaches. And put more effort into making apartment living desirable. Prefer a cosy bachelor pad over a three-bedroom bungalow any day; most of our generation feel the same. Personally, find the notion of house in the suburbs remote from culturally stimulating events repellent. If Labour grimly stick to this dream no matter what, they could be in trouble further down track.

Meg came home one afternoon all excited after having seen their 'Preserving Time' poster. Babbling about an ecosystem in a preserving jar. Presume because her Agee containers contribute to kitchen storage, though how this can be connected to what a political party is doing I have no idea. Our accord, which reached a high at the hui, now wearing off. Her mind persists in making unexpected connections. There must be a strong tendency towards chaos in her head, that's all I can say, and thank God I'm no longer sleeping with her. Too eccentric by half.

Fahey encountered on street shortly before Christmas, looking worse for wear. An uncomfortable Batchelor trailed her by several paces. Fail to comprehend what he sees in the woman, who still only wears trousers, although now without the Mao beret. I suppose he knows she was a lesbian in another life. Spare a moment of conjecture about what has happened to Lou Waters. She was very taken with Fahey, but no concern of mine.

Have observed desertions before, as well as sudden reversals in political allegiance, although Fahey's mutation into right-winger has me mystified and still, I must confess, alarmed. Will specifically instruct Hamish to warn NZUSA to be on their guard. Normally dislike their doctrinaire form of politics, but betrayal of me at hui and subsequent alliance with Batchelor has my alarm bells ringing. What will Red Letters think of her now? Or does she only make selective reports?

Collective level of paranoia in nation recently risen steeply. Wouldn't surprise me if Muldoon were to blame, but undoubtedly is being egged on by Americans. Visited American ambassador recently (some sycophantic connection going way back between her and my parents). We breakfasted on waffles and maple syrup, handmade in ornate silver waffle-iron. She was too anxious by half to gauge my opinion of communist sentiment among youth.

'Madam Ambassador,' I said, 'if there is a disaffection among New Zealand's young people, it is because their betters are setting them a poor example.'

'I beg your pardon?'

Ambassador stung at implication.

'Well, if you look at only the most recent examples of negotiating conflict in Asia and Latin America, New Zealanders can be forgiven for seeing a mighty power riding roughshod over local culture and politics.'

Waffle-iron snaps shut. I am lucky not to be turned out on my ear, but Americans too polite to go for full-frontal attack in social situations. Instead, she gives me a particularly greasy rasher of bacon and pretends not to notice as it splashes all over my shirt. Dexterity at breakfast for me usually a tricky affair. Swallow humiliation.

Comfort myself with having made my point, notwithstanding.

Wonder temporarily if Diana in league with the Americans, but dismiss idea as moonshine. Discernment for the politician a troublesome thing.

Personal Diary, Vol. 6, 1973
January

Currently having a major rethink about degree and future career. Failed hui sure to be the cause. I wonder: would formal study of the mind and cognitive processes avoid similar faux pas in future? Can hear Peter Berger throwing fits. Unavoidable. His soft research into group dynamics failed me at the key moment. I looked through plenty of bloody keyholes, but it didn't seem to draw political success any closer. A more sophisticated, not to mention reliable, radar required to enable correct discernment of character. Ability to plumb motive and predict which way punters will jump are life-saving skills in my line of business.

I must say, would have been spared a lot of trouble if I'd had access to Fahey's conversations with Batchelor. It can't all have been pillow-talk.

Yes, undoubtedly owing to cock-ups at hui, now obliged to revisit tedious questions on meaning of life and the pattern of emotive behaviour. Unprepared for the defection of both my right and left flanks. Not even a hint of Fahey's alliance with Batchelor prior to that final plenary. As for Steph's unique brand of deviance and game-playing: it doesn't bear thinking about.

Remember: worrying's a waste of time. Just because Berger can't cut the mustard, doesn't mean to say I won't find another approach. There'll be new methods around somewhere. And they'll be a damn sight less sentimental than that whingeing on about 'spirit and the inner man' they produce in English departments.

My contempt for the kind of stuff passing for an education in the humanities these days reached its peak during a conversation with Steph (Meg absent in Cambridge) about whether the soul exists and, if so, in what form.

The two of us had had a nasty encounter at the Mt Vic Four

Square, where we'd gone to do flat shopping for the weekend. Arrived just as the shop was closing, and the bastard calmly continued packing away his bananas as if we weren't even there. Steph tried the diplomatic approach, but totally useless. He couldn't give a stuff that we needed supplies for weekend and that it was against our principles to patronise dairies. Felt like pelting him with rotten fruit and shop sweepings stuffed into fruit crate. Thought better of it. Steph particularly upset. Been quite fragile lately; would like to make up with her after catastrophe of hui, but not quite ready to forgive all. Decided to put kid gloves on and listen sympathetically.

When she'd recovered, she began worrying about the grocer's lack of humanity, for God's sake. I mean, some individuals are on the side of the dead from the time they first open their eyes. On the way home the conversation went something like this:

'Henry?'

'Mmm?'

The Concert Programme was on. I was tapping out Mozart's Horn Concerto on the steering wheel of Mum's car.

'Do you think we have souls?'

'What?'

'You know what I mean. The soul. The essence of a person.'

'Christ, I don't know. I don't think so. What made you ask?'

'The grocer. I don't think he had one.'

'*Good Lord*, I'm an intellectual! I don't believe in things you can't prove rationally.' I sat, shoulders back, sucking in gusts of air. 'And neither should you. You're an intellectual. You should behave like one.'

Silence for a few minutes. Then she was off again.

'You can't prove feelings, either, but everyone has them.'

'Yes, but you can see the *effects* of feelings. Feelings move us to action sooner or later. How can what you call a soul be more than that? It's just a trumped-up word for feeling, decked out in religious jargon.'

Mozart was winding up to a magnificent conclusion. 'How about letting me listen to this?' Pause. 'Now that's soul,' I said, purring. 'Not your kind. Soul's just a word for a fortuitous grouping of atoms and molecules. Nothing more.'

'Genius, you mean?'

'Yes, I suppose. But it all boils down to a lucky mix of genes and environment. It certainly doesn't last beyond death. That's too infantile. You live, and then you die. Mozart, Shakespeare, Einstein – they don't live on in some spirit world. Their work might, but their atoms have gone.' I looked over at her. 'Fuck! Their cells were probably part of Hitler's! Soul as beauty? That's just shit.'

We need more rational dissection of sentimental 'truths.' Am reminded of *Harrad Experiment.* Its courage, its hacking away at conformity. Those students took nothing for granted: asked questions about everything. 'Everything is permitted, nothing forbidden,' someone once said, don't remember who now. Today, in the seventies, those same sceptical powers of observation can be brought to bear on the muzzy world of the soul. Steph's weak grasp of harsh material realities, I am convinced, allowed her to fabricate a whole life of deception. Culminating in that Janet Seed game that saved her bacon (and ours, I admit it, but for different reasons). Contra Steph, intellectuals must be unafraid to think and express iconoclastic values that go *against the grain*, that ruthlessly locate personal morality (i.e. psychology) in a material world. Steph betrayed me, and herself, because she'd spent her life in a cupboard, so to speak. Her soul wasn't inviting her to somehow 'become' Janet Seed and so be more authentic. No, it was out of fear and bad faith that she turned into a shop assistant from Tokoroa. Bookshop, my arse. While lacking in earlier malleability, post-hui Steph still reminded me of permanent arriviste in foreign country. Easily knocked by upheavals; held back by anxiety. Death to all literati who mumble about the soul. Pure hogwash.

In that weary frame of mind, still mulling over what to do about sex life – a right desert at present, downed coffee, then caught train to Petone, bus to Days Bay. Need my allowance increased – all these drinking sessions in the city are draining my capital. Dad will be sure to oblige. He's recently been made a professor on the strength of his new book on fruitflies, and his old days of despair seem to have sunk without trace. *Drosophila*. Nice name. Almost wish I'd stayed with Zoo.

Arrived home to greet old flatmates, Veronica and Thomas. She is expecting, stomach so swollen you can see her belly-button, which protrudes like a sultana through her clothes. Disconcerting, pregnancy. Don't wish to see Steph go down that path. *When* we get back together. You never know what having a sprog is going to do to you. Mum very disfigured from Garth and me: unsightly veins all down one leg. Other darker things are rumoured, but Thomas will certainly refrain from whispering them in my ear. He's as cocky as ever and his head still displays the same residual amount of hair. Junior lecturer in 18th-century literature at Auckland. Specialising in Pope, as per usual, and Dryden, whom I've never read, although I seem to remember Steph declaiming his poetry to me one evening when I was feeling particularly exhausted.

Conversation with guests went something like this:

'Oh, hello, Thomas, Veronica. Surprise, surprise.'

'Hasn't it been a long time?' gushes Veronica, 'and look at me now!' Strokes belly with both hands.

I politely avert gaze. Steph stares avidly.

'Ahem!' I say. 'Well, how about staying for a coffee? We've just boiled the jug.'

'Mmm, great beans,' exclaims Thomas, plunging his beak into packet. 'What's the blend?'

'Blend?' I ask blankly. Apart from aborted Four Square expedition recently, Steph does our shopping, consequently am happy to remain in ignorance about same. Obviously, Thomas believes the Great Cultural Leap Forward in New Zealand will be spearheaded by an obsession with comestibles.

'Kilimanjaro or Tanganyika?' he persists. 'Come on, Henry, don't play games.'

The women have moved into the lounge. It looks as if we will have to slog it out.

I apply a swift slash to the jugular. 'Well, Thomas, some think, others cook.' Soften the blow. 'To tell you the truth, I leave that sort of thing up to Steph.'

Guests depart soon afterwards. Not soon enough for me. Steph is looking dewy-eyed and I can see will need reacquainting with our original pact – *when* we get back together: no ties, no long-term commitment; pure sexual and intellectual pleasure.

March

To return to degree. Spent the holidays dissecting the purpose of study. Exhausted, and perplexed at shifts occurring in thinking. What's happened to my belief in equal opportunity? Good question. Suppose numerous others like myself face disillusion sooner or later. Only, I'm damn well not going to give in and drop out, like Runcie. Or throw a psycho fit like Steph.

Stupidity of peers deeply frustrating, to which one final solution remains: give them elitist education. That hui proved you can bend over backwards to promote informed and intelligent debate, and still end up with omelette on your shirt. Christ, who thought I'd be on the same side as our Old Boys' Club? How ironic that I've come round to supporting the kind of club lingo that used to make me want to vomit, although have no intention of going to one of their bloody race meets. Can't see Steph togged up in hat and high-heels, either.

In point of fact, I've given the elitist position a great deal of thought. Old Guard couldn't hold a candle to the mental complexities I've put myself through lately. In brief, my thinking is as follows:

> Autonomous colleges of learning must be set up, with the right to select on the basis of intellect alone. The education system needs to be *more* tiered, not less. If the above sounds like a revival of monasticism, it bloody well is. Only in select colleges on the lookout for gifted, innovative young men (well, mostly) will there be room for new ideas to germinate. Democracy *opposes* non-conformism, while pretending not to.

As for what young people in Wellington are feeling now, post-hui, it's been all downhill in my opinion. Intellectual debate has fallen right off, student vigilance is torpid again after the past six years of focus and activism. 1968 was a fiery year in Europe, with protests in every main city, but we had our hour here in New Zealand. I like to think of the 1972 hui as reflecting the crest of awareness in our youth, where the cream of a society struggling to keep up with international trends slogged it out in critical debate and discussion (some of the time).

Sadly, self-interested politics, mostly to do with gender as far as I can see, have since come to polarise student body, detracting attention from key questions of economics and role of state. Meg Shepherd's interest in feminism growing by the day. She's extended her list of frog thinkers to include Simone de Beauvoir, whose only claim to memorability as far as I'm concerned is to have screwed Sartre. When I put forward the argument that the other *is* the antagonist, am met with frosty glare.

Personal Diary, Vol. 7, 1974
August

Norman Kirk died this month: whole country falls into mourning. Kirk, the last of the old-style Labour politicians claimed by the work-ing class. Not a fan of his style myself – too much moral seriousness over minor matters; the real problems (intellectual laziness, for one) never addressed. Yet couldn't ignore the reservoirs of feeling present at funeral. Maori especially demonstrative.

Makes one think about the nature of greatness. What is it exactly that leads to a desire to bask in one's own charisma? I had that and lost it at Takaka. Sea of attentive faces and then the Freedom Song. Magnificent.

For some reason am reminded of the parable drummed into me in Divinity. 'Ballantyne,' brayed McKenzie in Oxford vowels – the idiot still insists on robins perching on snow-covered boughs; we get the fag-end of the British Christmas card trade out here – 'explain to the class why the woman with an issue touched the hem of the garment of Christ.'

'Excuse me, sir, I didn't catch that.'

'An *issue*, Ballantyne, a *menstrual* issue.'

God have mercy, how was I to know? Class erupted. Could think of no worthy riposte.

'It's a parable of *power*, Henry. Of power passing from One who is worthy to one who is not.'

Just so: the masses want a man who will put himself in the line of fire and then let them touch him.

September

Find myself coming at the question of who owns what with new interest. Notorious Kiwi economist, who shall remain nameless, paranoid about overseas ownership. Was in same boat myself. Recall a heated exchange with old beau (or should that be belle?) of Diana's over a bottle of South African wine. Lucky not to have wound up with claw marks all down my face. I always knew that pancake parlour was a front.

Even when you had to pay twice as much for a pair of homemade trousers from Kirkcaldie's, I used to go on about how we should support local industries. Until, that is, I heard how said Kiwi economist recently came to an undignified end. You wouldn't catch me dropping valuable papers all over a gorse-covered hillside. Spectacular. Half the neighbourhood turned out to watch, while detectives thrashed away at bushes with their truncheons.

So what if said economist now a wealthy man with eclectic collection of curios and rugs? Furnishings spied one evening by Hamish, who has become the youngest Treasury boffin on record and, so he says, a discreet fan of the man's. Who obviously earned his African knick-knacks and Bokhara rugs or what have you doing time in New York. Impossible to see said treasures as fruit of a long spying relationship with Russia. Brigadier Gilbert has watched one James Bond too many.

And Hamish had better look out or he'll be accused of being another of those government-department reds by Muldoon.

Tide of opinion now on the turn, must keep up. Let's skittle those fusty protection clauses! Bemused at own disloyalty – may even find myself advocating hobnobbing with US, Madam Ambassador notwithstanding. To tell the truth, am exhilarated by prospects of opening this backwards-looking little country up to the buzz of international commerce.

October

Decide eventually, after lengthy discussions with Hamish, to combine Economics with Psychology. Have a hunch union will be lethal. Why not assess human capacities for growth and tie them to global capital? No reason to turn my back on social activism. Psychology could only benefit the way we address politics now. Incisive urban planning bound to be enhanced by more accurate measurement of individual potential for – let's see, transformation. Yes. In fact why didn't I think of the expression before?

Word opens enormous possibilities. Can envisage a future where architects, town planners, economists and psychologists, funded by investments from multinationals, will join forces to create the ideal environment.

Another brainwave brews . . . Let's marry *The Harrad Experiment* with Harvey Cox's secular city. Cox happens to be an American somewhat hung up about religion, who argues that anonymity is liberating. Couldn't agree more. Mystery, ritual: as the man implies, these are fascist and bourgeois experiences. Out they go! I liked this: *We are free to use the switchboard without being victimised by its infinite possibilities.*

We simply need to immunise ourselves against those who serve us, who see our public faces. Who wants to share their life story with a checkout girl? I could help people prepare to deal with the effects of urbanisation. I could run weekend seminars, help people embrace their public personas. Sex without love is a creative survival ethic. At least my opinion of sex hasn't changed!

Mobility, anonymity, profanity, amorality: these qualities can be celebrated and discussed by citizens *transformed* through their new freedom. Into what, one may ask? Gods, according to Cox. Unhappily, term for me invokes dead-end humanities liberalism and my conversation with Steph about soul. Still, am prepared to flirt with idea that we secularise god. Wonder what Steph would have to say after her god – her mother's, more likely (What's got into that woman? She used to be so switched on) – led her to tell lies at Takaka.

Herd mentality, the very thing I'm fighting against at university, will slow people from seeing the beauty of this marriage proposal, but with time and enthusiastic public face (my own), they'll come round.

We need a different *Howl*. Here's mine:

Howl After Ginsberg

Liberate the captives,
Throw off the antiquated
names until the city
grows to a terrible new
ark, without fear or soul
ploughing dark into light
on the watered furrows of the world.

December

Small handwritten invite to new art show arrived in post yesterday.
Pinned it on flat noticeboard:

> The Shed invites Henry Ballantyne and Steph Jackson
> to an exhibition of *objets trouvés* by Meg Shepherd.
> 12 December at 5 p.m.
> RSVP to The Shed Gallery, Wharf One

New flatmate impressed with the terminology and wants to
come with us. After a trail of disasters in the flatmate department,
Steph and I finally found two who please us. One, an ex-St Cuth's
girl, father in large Auckland law firm, mother a pianist with Auckland Sinfonia. Rebecca Radway. Confident intellectually, prodigious
reader of French and German, will have to watch my step. She
enthuses over a frog by the name of Foucault, who has apparently
rewritten the whole of European history.

'Steph,' announces Rebecca, 'the order of things is up for grabs.
Take nothing for granted.'

One evening we were sitting around fire melting slices of cheese
(*raclette*, informed flatmate) to eat with potatoes.

Steph naturally mystified by her remarks.

'People sort objects into groups according to a *system*, a *man-
made* one.' Smearing yellow over a lump of crusty potato. The woman
has an annoying habit of over-emphasis.

'And?' asks Steph innocently.

'Well, if it's *constructed* it can be *changed*. You know, the whole
health system is built on a way of seeing the human body.'

She is warming to her theme, and I surreptitiously examine the remaining potato.

'Change the way you understand the body,' she intones, seizing the potato right out of my hand, 'and you can change the way you deal with illness.'

'That surely doesn't mean you're in favour of getting rid of doctors,' I interrupt, annoyed. I've heard about a radical fringe in the health lobby. Osteopaths and homoeopaths, for instance. Mad as meat-axes.

'No, not at all.' Rebecca eyes me speculatively.

Beautiful face and bosom. Cashmere cardigan, Steph tells me.

'I agree with you, Henry. Government can be pressured for reform from *within*. Foucault just shows us how we can *organise* reform, that's all.'

Reluctantly agree to peruse Foucault if he's in library, which I doubt.

You know, one can't venture outside these days without tripping over some noxious French phrase or other. Frankly consider Europe more tyrannical than US at present, with sibylline exports designed to stump everyone. I don't believe for a moment that Shepherd coined the *objets trouvés* phrase plastered all over the invite; she must have heard it in conversation with a frog-lover.

I duly RSVP, Steph's artistic background to blame for our curiosity. The evening an eye-opener. Met at door to The Shed, a conversion of a wharf storehouse, by none other than Lou Waters. Invited to consume slice of tasty cake. Apparently, part of the exhibition. Close up, the cake a replica of New Zealand: North and South Islands in snowy profile. Two red sugared jubes stuck into icing, one on each island, labelled Tokoroa and Takaka respectively. Began to feel apprehensive: what else would the artist have up her sleeve? We soon found out.

One wall completely covered with dark velvet cloth upon which was appliquéd a woman – presumably, despite brown skin, the Virgin Mary. Enigmatically titled *The Crown I Wear is my Own*. Strange: Meg never expressed Catholic sympathies to me. Virgin's hands and feet appeared to be bleeding roses, clouds of stars filled upper reaches of work. Oddly touching, if discomforting viewing for a secularist such as myself. Down the whole length of the room ran a row of tables, the kind you see in hostel dining rooms. On them stood a number of suitcases, each one cut in half by a railway line made from painted matchsticks.

'*Main Trunk*,' hissed our new flatmate, who was stealing along behind us.

'Huh!' I said. 'Well, she certainly spent enough time going back to Cambridge.' Suddenly realised my efforts to subvert Meg with non-conformist holiday reading had failed. For in one case spread-eagling the tracks, I saw a display of books filled with what looked from a distance like scribble, although couldn't be sure. Their lurid covers were edged, Steph told me later, with blanket-stitch and French knots. Clueless, till Steph informed me when we were cleaning our teeth before bed, that Shepherd had actually stolen and Xeroxed some of my correspondence for this exhibit. *The Harrad Experiment* and *The Naked Ape* had found a sensationalist cover artist who had gone to some trouble to make their contents even more salacious than they really were! At least she read them. Too late to make a fuss now, but that woman proved to be one more bloody expensive investment that came to nothing.

Another case had been filled with embroidered samplers. One, called *The Happy City*, featured tiny figures made out of a silky material. A final exhibit in the *Case* series contained a model of Meg's mother's house, complete with frosted-glass front door and umbrella tree. Delicate work. She really is a skilled craftswoman.

Above our heads spun a model of a planetarium. All in favour of astronomy: the night sky a favourite place of mine. Shepherd's sky tilted towards astrology and the occult, I fear. Gigantic figures of the zodiac suspended from ceiling, made from papier mâché and then painted. Next, a glittering Milky Way full of sequin and mica stars surmounted by a silently turning planet. Sense this was the dramatic centrepiece. Resembled crystal, probably perspex with clever lighting. One surface bore the image of a split-open heart pierced by a seed whose husk supported a corona of leaves. Label on wall read: *Klepto Girl, Star of the Dawn*. Meaningless to me, despite the crowds of curious viewers who clustered underneath the perspex and peered into its luminous depths.

At that point, Steph had another psychotic episode, claiming that Meg had stolen her *idea*.

'What the hell do you mean?' Anxious to hush her up. Gallery exceptionally crowded.

'The morning star! That was my idea!' Steph getting more hysterical by the minute. 'Don't you even remember the Black Virgin? You don't, Henry, do you?'

For the first time in my life I felt thick as a plank. Was this what I had to look forward to? Left her temporarily on floor to view the remainder of the exhibits. Quite frankly, all getting too much.

Last straw was the ties. Shepherd had taken them from my wardrobe – my ties! – and nonchalantly turned them into a patchwork bedspread. Wondered where that grey one had disappeared to; accused Garth of helping himself to it. She must have stolen them when Steph and I were away – no idea when. Should have taken more notice of her padlock. Considered remonstrating with her, but got caught in crowd and found myself in front of Batchelor, who was wandering around exhibition as if lost without Fahey, who'd flown off to Australia six months ago.

'Hello there, Hans,' I said. It was the first time we'd exchanged words in over a year. 'How's it going with the NYB?'

'We've had a parting of the ways. Disagreements about funding. They're for the chop, anyway.' Batchelor, who had had too many wines, was ogling Steph, now sobbing into her handkerchief.

'Meaning?' Amazing how quickly you can become out of touch. It's only been a year, and already pressure-group politics seems like another life.

'The government's losing interest in funding youth organisations. Says they're full of radicals out to make trouble.'

'So they are, Hans.'

Batchelor stared at me in amazement. 'Christ, Ballantyne, what's happened to you?'

'The political struggle's elsewhere now, Hans. It's all technology and economics. Follow capital. You can't go wrong there.'

The party-dependent Batchelor retaliated in the only way he knew. 'I see Lou Waters cut you a piece of cake from the top of the South Island,' he sneered.

I swallowed my humiliation. Waters had dished me up the cake bearing the red Takaka jube. Under Shepherd's instructions, no doubt.

Gathered up flatmates and departed without having greeted Meg, who had been surrounded by admiring group of spectators all evening.

Cablecar back to Kelburn, quick cup of coffee before beginning Christmas reading programme. Flat quiet; Steph's lamp shone out cheerfully from bedroom.

Steph's story

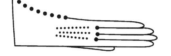

When Henry Ballantyne and I fell in love, we promised each other three things: an intellectually stimulating relationship, time for our own lives, and fidelity. I got the first two, but not the third. Back then, Henry's numinous presence somehow justified the wounding infidelities, but never lessened my feelings for him.

When we first met, with his clean hair flicked out of his eyes and cheeks polished pink by the air, he reminded me of an ambassador from a bright water globe, or a star fallen to earth and still burning. He'd stayed behind to lobby the abstainers at an SRC, of whom I was one.

I wasn't surprised by what happened. In fact, I'd been expecting it. The Jackson family is full of apocryphal narratives of betrayal, mostly of women by men, Lydia told me tartly, as she continued to put up with Teddy's habitual flirting.

Just because my mother had some remote connection with Katherine Mansfield did not signify to me that we were doomed to be short-changed by the men in our lives. It simply lay in the nature of things. Biology predisposed men to pursue the life of nomads, and women to repair the ruined walls they left behind.

How Henry and I finally fell apart is another story. In this one, you will read how my mother's warning came true; and how I learned to be a repairer of walls between my lover and the wrecked friendships he left in his burning wake.

Of course Lydia had far less to worry about than I did. My father rarely got *involved* with his other women. I think by the time they reached their fifties Teddy had become worn out with the demands of his temperamental house clients and spent most of his weekends – when he wasn't drawing plans – walking Socks along the beach. They'd lived in New Brighton for years, where I'd take the ferry home every year to see them, Lydia making amazing fat-rich dishes from *The Moosewood Cookbook*, and Teddy pestering me to come and see his latest project. My sister, who'd turned into an equestrienne, was usually off with her horses, but we'd do our annual Christmas shop together, buying records and design mags for Teddy, art books for Mother.

In my second year of university, Lydia suddenly stopped painting, held a last exhibition, and enrolled for a handful of Theology papers. Teddy, who'd never got used to her sea-changes, grumbled and ranted about the falling family income. The rest of us made encouraging noises and kept our distance. I must admit, the sight of one's mother wearing reading glasses poring over a biblical concordance was a shock. We had never been a church family and Teddy had belonged to the Communist Party almost all his life, so on both sides we were surrounded by unbelievers.

It turned out, however, that her skill did come in handy – not long after I'd begun a degree in English and Psychology. (Much to Henry's disgust, as he thought it was a hopelessly bourgeois thing to do, and I should be continuing my studies in Sociology. He was always trying to persuade his friends to abandon the arts, which he said were doomed, because they softened the mind and had nothing to say to the world.

I gave in to Henry many times, but not over that. We came to an arrangement. I would help him with his poetry, which he wrote in secret, if he would leave me in peace to study English. If he suspected that there was a huge irony in writing in private what he condemned in public, he never said and, unlike Meg Shepherd, I did not steal his diaries in an effort to find out.)

At once I began to realise that almost everything in English literature had some connection, no matter how obscure, to the Bible. Lydia and I would spend hours on the phone talking etymology, and whether some archaic word in a text by Spenser came from Latin or Old English. We both went through a craze of reading Anglo-Saxon elegies, and were fascinated by the early saints and mystics, a passion I kept away from Henry.

My story really begins with Dr Murphy, who wore orange bell-bottoms while he lectured us on the Restoration. Being an Irishman, Dr Murphy hated all forms of royalism, so he tried to paint Charles II as an effete halfwit. He seemed to forget that after the horrible zeal of the Puritans, England needed fun and games. The thing I hated most about Puritanism was Oliver Cromwell's nose. Its massive pores and squamous, flaking skin made me shudder, and clearly poets too, who under Charles's patronage came out of their country retreats and wrote outrageous lampoons, tearing every last bit of Christian seriousness to pieces. This put Dr Murphy in a contradiction. He loved bawdy theatre but hated the English, which he tried to resolve one morning by giving us a fiery lecture on solar energy.

'Never forget the power of flattery,' he said, 'the flattery of power. The Restoration was for a time the epoch of largesse and open-handedness.'

The seats were hard and my shoulder ached. I scribbled some notes.

'Charles II's court was in its way as splendid and libertine as the court of the Sun King. His poets were preoccupied with the Jacobean ruler's effulgent qualities. They used metaphors of burning suns and stars blazing through the skies.'

Effulgent. The word rolled nicely in my mouth. I saw a dull, watery English sky lit up like an old-fashioned palace of lights, and Charles, wearing a wig, dazzling the crowds below.

'*Fame runs before him as the morning star,*' pronounced Dr Murphy with his eloquent Irish diction, gathering up his gown for the last five minutes of class. 'Now this puts me in mind of that even more exquisite line, where the aristocrat, in rebellion against his king, is referred to as *day star, son of dawn.*'

The lecture concluded. People stood up and swarmed into the doorway. I sat wondering why Dryden had given the lovely name of *day star* to a traitor. Did that mean the traitor was good, depending on the faction you supported? And that words like 'corrupt' could slide to the back of the poet's dictionary without a second thought, that it was legitimate to be dazzled by one's own creation? Or was he trying to show that what can go against the law can also be beautiful?

Which would make sense to an Irishman, of course, I thought to myself. I could certainly see Dr Murphy's affection for traitorous words, especially if they were beautifully put.

And I saw all over again that poets had once been on the cutting edge of life, in politics up to their necks. What MP today would tremble if a verse or two from Henry found its way into his afternoon mail? I tried to imagine our prime minister giving a poet a stash of money and land, or the SIS phone-tapping because the owners wrote seditious poetry. Henry had been right in a way: literature had lost its bite. The struggle was elsewhere.

My lover's face used to hang before my eyes in a splendid blaze of light, illuminated even more now by those English lectures. Psychologists would say I had an idealisation problem – which must have contained some truth, but not the whole of it. Henry's ardour to live the knife-edge of politics led everyone he touched to be inspired. He was a truly talented individual, great even. His move into what is known these days as life-coaching after graduating was inexplicable, not to mention a shameful sell-out, and we were both relieved, I think, when he fell out with the counselling centre where he worked and turned to politics again. I hear he continued to work privately for years with a handful of clients when the House was not in session, but living miles away from Wellington as we do, no one's ever been able to inform me as to his eventual success as a counsellor. It still strikes me as incongruous; he would have been PM by now if he'd poured all of his talents into politics.

To return to my story. After Dr Murphy's lecture on poetry, I called Lydia in New Brighton.

'Can you check a reference for me, Mother?'

'Not another word! Why can't you use a dictionary? There must be plenty in that library of yours.'

In the background I could hear their ancient Bendix thundering its way through a load of washing.

'Please. It's important.' I waited. 'Can you find out the meaning of *day star*?'

Years ago, dusting one of Lydia's bookcases, my sister and I had found an illustrated book of legends that contained a story about a preternaturally bright star. When the Earth was exhausted, it said, and the sun had shrunk to a small reddish ball, the Day Star would descend. People would sell all they had to follow its glittering progress across the fact of the globe. There was a pen-and-ink sketch inspired by the combined visions of Milton and H. G. Wells. The star looked metallic and had just blasted a ziggurat of arrogant spirals into ruins. Tiny figures were fleeing into caverns at the bottom left of the drawing, pursued by creatures with wings. As the star's hot light spread, the story had continued, the gazers burned in their tracks, crumbling, like the tower, into sightless mounds of glass and salt.

We'd ghoulishly turned the story into a play and acted it for Teddy and Lydia, me playing growling bass notes on the cello, my sister screaming theatrically at a piece of black silk I'd taped over the sunroom window.

'*Day star?* Ah ha! I don't need a dictionary for that.' Lydia's voice became instantly more cheerful. She was ready for a theological exchange at any time of day or night. 'The day star, Steph, was an expression used in the Old Testament to describe the Son of God.'

Son of God: the hero archetype. I'd just begun reading Jung, so what Lydia was saying made good sense. It suited Henry so well, too, with that lovely head of hair he washed every morning. My clean morning star, bent over his desk, writing letter after letter, inserting the thin blue tongues of carbon paper, smoothing the white top sheet down flat, searching passionately for the analysis that would best fit the social crises we could see happening all around us.

Right now, he was gathering support for a youth summit, compiling mailing lists of potential backers in the business community and the media. He'd co-opted me on to his organising committee for the summit, and I must say I went to my first meeting feeling apprehensive, expecting the debate to be driven by unsympathetic views.

When I arrived, I found I knew no one except Diana Fahey, who'd been to our party the year before, and was now on the Exec. Henry's eyes swung around the room, caught mine.

'Ah, Steph, I'd like you to meet one of the summit applicants you might remember my inviting to assist us: Meg Shepherd. She's from Cambridge and is helping to spearhead publicity in the North Island.'

Of course I did. My memory was fiercely accurate when it came to recalling Henry's favourites. I smiled across at a plump, awkward-looking girl with glasses and rather conservative clothes. She seemed a poor choice for a spokesman, but I trusted his intuition. Undoubtedly he had his reasons.

The meeting was called to order and he began his address.

'Hi, folks! Some of you will know me. I'm Henry Ballantyne, chairman of the organising committee for the New Zealand Youth Summit. Or shall I say hui, for that's what our conference is: a political buzz session for youth; and a first, I believe, for New Zealand.'

His gaze swept us and came to rest on me. I'm important to him, I thought: he needs me . . . he needs my loyalty. Diana Fahey intimidates me, but I won't let myself be cowed by this group of people. And I won't let Henry be put down, either.

I needn't have worried. He was truly splendid.

'I'll be steering you through this next hour,' he went on. 'Two things. First up, I'd like you to meet Steph Jackson, our minute-taker. She's been with us from the beginning and you've probably spoken to her over the phone already. Second, I'm sure you all know Diana Fahey. She comes to us from Sydney, with a long history of involvement in the protest movement. Because of her experience in running student activist retreats, we've decided to co-opt her onto the organising committee.'

Henry paused, clearing his throat.

'Now, I want to say how delighted we were to select a group of such talented people. You come from a wide variety of backgrounds, but you've been selected because of your ability to be articulate about the things that matter to young people today.'

I followed the line of my lover's shoulders, the way they sloped into his back, the softness of the dark jersey slung casually around his neck, its unoccupied arms reaching all the way down his chest to the narrow belt that circled his waist. Henry was inviting us to walk the corridors of power. 'We have here some of the country's most talented youth,' he enthused. 'It's time for us to speak up.'

My lover, Henry Ballantyne, sailing out in front of them all! He began again. 'There's a new dissatisfaction on our campuses now. We're asking questions in lectures. Pressuring the administration. Things are happening in Europe and America: protests, riots, strikes and lockouts. Governments are sitting up and taking notice of us. Parents have nothing to say our generation. Their lives are a dismal failure: to us and to them.'

I scraped my hair off my face, stabbed at it with a stray hairclip, and began writing hastily.

'New Zealand can't let all this activity go by and not be involved. I remind you of Marshall McLuhan's words that we are part of a global village.'

'Hear hear,' I interjected.

He swept on. 'We, as concerned young people, need to come together and make visible representation to government. They need to know that we absolutely *reject* policies based on pragmatism and self-interest!'

There was a round of applause.

The meeting continued with practically no opposition, I observed with relief. Henry had been too well prepared, which meant we could go ahead and set up subcommittees, and dates for further planning. With no volunteers forthcoming for catering, he unexpectedly nominated me, so for the next month I laboured away at the summit's menu.

I called one of my friends to pick her brains about feeding large groups of people. Lydia and I pored over recipe books, discussing them down the phone, Teddy complaining about excessive phone costs and the drop in Lydia's earnings. Another friend had some novel suggestions, including the vital allowance of a quarter-pound of meat per person per day. This information, being the daily recommended intake of protein, she had gleaned from her sister, who was studying Domestic Science in Dunedin. The words stuck uncomfortably in my mind. I saw a row of small lumps of red marbled with white sitting in a pool of blood on a stainless steel bench, which was why in the end I went against Henry's advice and scheduled two vegetarian meals: one of baked tofu, the other a chilli rellenos.

I moved back with Henry in June. The menu planning complete, and Meg Shepherd and I making civil noises as we passed each other on the way to the bathroom, I was ready for more responsibility.

One day, I was busy chopping walnuts for a Marmite and lettuce sandwich and brooding over how I could be of more use on the hui committee when Henry abruptly walked into the kitchen.

'Break a sheep's leg, I'm hungry! What's that you're eating?'

While I made him a sandwich, he talked about the summit and the urgency of getting out the background papers so participants would have time to read them before arriving in Takaka.

We'd chosen a site in Golden Bay, for which I'd made the booking in May. I felt I'd done everything I could in the nutrition department, and wanted to stretch my wings.

'Henry, I wondered . . .'

'Yes?'

'I wondered if I could write something for the background papers. We've worked together well before on papers.'

He looked serious. 'It's a tricky business, writing a conference background paper. You have to be very precise, with no waffling, and as well informed as if you were writing an essay.'

'You know I can do that. I want to help, and you could do with another writer.' I was certainly not going to be made redundant by a new flatmate who wore conservative clothes. Meg had moved in just before I did, which made me uneasy, but I could do nothing about it. Since we were all caught up with organising the summit, we'd have to learn to get on, and for me, that above all meant keeping pace with Henry's thinking. I was confident I had more resources than Meg as far as intellect was concerned, although I was less sure about her style. Henry's tastes were occasionally unpredictable, and for the first time since we'd met I felt a kind of disquiet.

'Tell you what. There's no one writing on the environment. I don't need to emphasise how important the green question is to all of us. Why don't you do some research and come up with a briefing paper?'

'Fabulous!' I whooped. 'I'll start on it tomorrow.' I didn't like to remind him that the Jacksons had been fighting to preserve stands of trees all their lives.

'Good stuff,' enthused Henry. He walked back from the bench. 'Look, sorry I didn't warn you I'd have to be spending more time with Meg. It's only hui business, and she's cracking into the work. I haven't the heart to push her away.'

Meg Shepherd appeared ordinary enough to me. In fact, her hair was an embarrassment. She looked as if she'd just been given a razor cut – Lydia would say a rat had chewed it. I think Henry enjoyed the feel of her skin, which he said once was as smooth as custard. Apparently, they'd been to bed when she first moved in, but I forgave him that. Marking territory on the female body is almost universal among men. And he assured me it wouldn't happen again. 'She's not worth the worry, Squidges,' he said, affectionately ruffling my hair.

'She's too straight for you anyway,' I said, thinking of her wardrobe full of vastly impractical clothes. I'd taken an especial dislike to a dark blue and white striped outfit cut from mattress ticking that had been made over into a high-fashion garment, painfully showing her up as an anachronism at meetings where the rest of us were casual and not, as I suspected she was, hung up.

'Besides,' I said nastily, 'she's got fat legs.'

'Yes,' said my lover absently, 'yes, she has.'

Fat legs or not, it took strenuous efforts on my part to regulate our encounters at the flat. I attempted to engineer contact so that there was always another person present, but the odd morning would crop up when Meg and I found ourselves eating breakfast at the same time, the rest of the flat already left for the day; or we would be rostered on to dishes for the evening meal, and would largely spend the duration in polite silence except for the sloshing of the water and Meg's aggressive flick flick flick with the teatowel. It always amazed me Henry never noticed.

Except that one evening after we'd maintained a steely quiet accompaniment to the crash of dishes hitting the drainer, Henry waltzed into the kitchen and announced gaily: 'Heigh ho, girls, you'll have to take care of the chores next week too; Diana Fahey and I are heading up north for a couple of days.'

'You're going away with Diana?' I said in a daze. 'Aren't you two no-speaks at present?'

'Which is exactly why we have to spend some time together,' he insisted. 'I've got to get her alongside before the hui hits.'

Meg said nothing. Instead, she dried her hands on my teatowel and stalked off to her room. Henry raised his eyebrows and threw me a significant look. I gave him an old-fashioned one back, but the moment of intimacy didn't prevent me from feeling uneasy. Why did he make plans without ever asking me what I felt? I hated it when he cut me out; I wanted to help him more, not less. Besides, I knew that no matter how much Henry attempted to woo Diana, he would ultimately fail. I suspected she had some secret agenda, and my suspicion became fact a few weeks later when I heard her talking on the phone, here in our house after a meeting with Henry, to someone in Sydney. I didn't let on I was home. Nor did I inform anyone: the conversation was too difficult to follow, anyway, but my instincts told me Diana was plotting something really unpleasant. If we'd only known what at the time, Henry may not have become so rattled after that terrible trip to Sydney.

The trip had started out well enough. Genuinely making an effort to restore my equilibrium after his holiday with Diana, he decided I should accompany him to a development forum at the University of New South Wales. We packed in a frenzy. I tried to disguise my euphoria from Meg, but it became impossible after Henry, who'd visited Australia twice before and had a page-long list of must-sees, took over the dinner conversation with holiday stories from his family scrapbook.

'We've got to take a harbour cruise,' he'd say over coffee. 'Not on one of those bourgeois lumps of fibreglass, either. You'll love the ferries, Steph. They're delightfully old and unpretentious.'

Or, we'd be on the point of helping ourselves to the Waldorf I'd made, and he'd insist on telling us about this place in Castlereigh Street where you could get the most amazing variety of salads. 'The last time I was there,' he said, 'I sampled melon and feta. Mum's eyes popped out on stalks.'

'Why on earth?' I naively inquired, temporarily forgetting that Mrs Ballantyne's cookbook was of the dull colonial variety.

Fortunately for everyone, at that moment the telephone rang. I experienced a jab of pleasure as Meg whiffed out of the room.

We arrived in the middle of a thunderstorm. As our taxi pulled out of the flooded terminal, the rain burst like fat pellets on its windows. Our driver, who turned out to be not long in the country, with few English words and even fewer teeth, laughed at my dismay, and drove us straight towards a black sky crackling with blue and white streaks.

'Is better here!' he shouted wildly, but for the life of me I couldn't agree.

I'd optimistically packed for summer. It was so cold by the time we'd reached the YMCA that I had to beg one of the staff to let us have another heater. The downpour had chilled me dreadfully, and realising that Diana Fahey and Lou Waters were somewhere in town did not ease the misery, but drove me shivering and numb into bed. Meanwhile, Henry wore tracks in the carpet thinking of ways to discredit Lou at the forum.

Next morning was a different story. Both of us woke at the same time with the cacophonous noise of the birds in a silver stand of bottlebrush and gum trees.

While Henry rode the train out to Randwick, I walked lazily through the streets, stopping for coffee or to buy fruit. At one point I found myself in a student bookshop. I came out clutching Kate Millett's *Sexual Politics*, a couple of student publications, and an invitation to dinner that evening somewhere in Balmain. How friendly Australians were. And how cosmopolitan. After Wellington, where everyone wore jeans or sombre blacks and browns, these people dressed as if they were going to a party. So much brown skin; and such lovely colours that the women resembled bright, ambulant flowers. I passed one girl with a lime-green top and lime-green pants made out of some nubbly material: Meg would have known. How amazing that they matched! I didn't remember anything as spectacular – or as artfully constructed – in Wellington.

We caught up in the afternoon in a bar quite close to the campus. It was dirty and cramped, and matched Henry's mood. The day had not gone well for him, the mood of the conference being more radical than he was expecting, and the level of debate – angry salvoes against American and *Australian* imperialism – took him by surprise.

'Never mind,' I said, 'we've had an invitation to dinner in Balmain. I'm sure the conversation there will be excellent.'

'Balmain?' snorted Henry. 'That's where all the criminal element hang out, isn't it?'

'I don't know,' I said uncertainly. 'The woman who sold me Kate Millet's book seemed very nice.'

I wish I'd somehow managed to read the Millett before the dinner. Nell Price, the woman who'd wrapped my book, heard we were over for the forum and invited us to her home. That's what I mean by friendly: I can't imagine any of the staff at our university bookshop asking strangers for an impromptu dinner! Especially if they were Australians. Barring Diana, my prejudices informed me that they were a cultureless lot. Henry shared my opinion but pretended not to. How wrong we were!

Around six, we taxied at hellish speed through Glebe – a fascinatingly seedy area, I would have loved a closer look in daytime – and rocked to a halt outside a fenced garden. By now it was almost fully dark, the dark so complete that despite the hum of the city I felt internally blind.

When our eyes (or was it our senses?) began to connect our bodies to our surrounds, this is what we saw: a pepper tree fountaining over a crudely home-cast iron gate; inside, lit by myriad tea-lights, water splashed into a shallow concrete dish in the shape of a shell. Green lush things fought each other for the right to be noticed: it appeared someone had tried to discipline them but given up.

'God, I wonder if they turn that thing off when it rains,' remarked Henry at the dripping shell, falsely casual. He was fretting, out of his element and trying fruitlessly to anticipate Balmain style.

Nell greeted us with kisses at the door: again, not a Kiwi habit but I liked it. Her skin smelt of lemon verbena, I think, and was in better shape than mine. I cast an apprehensive glance at Henry, but he was too busy shaking hands with Roland, Nell's husband, and inspecting the paintings crowding the hall.

Nell and Roland's house was a villa in the process of being done up. Apart from brick dust covering everything, you would have hardly noticed. Nell appeared profoundly unflappable, whisking us through the kitchen (admittedly in turmoil) to a room with a massive Edwardian table running its length, a fire crackling in one corner and French doors that opened on to the garden. It was stuffed with pot plants: asparagus ferns and orchids; maybe a rubber plant as well. Oh, and pots of cyclamen clustered with candles on the table.

There must have been about ten of us; more women than men, I think, but again, it's hard to remember the details now.

'So, what's the movement like across the Tasman?' All eyes turned towards us as we sipped our beer.

'Pretty lively, thanks, Roland.'

'Sounds like we're on the same side then.'

'Yeah, pretty much.' Henry appeared not to want to go into details.

'We're organising a national conference to take some of the issues to young people,' I put in. 'Henry and I feel that if we broaden the base of youth protest, we'll have a better voice to lobby National.' I had to say something; my lover's silence was irritating, and bad mannered.

'National?' Helen, a neighbour of the Prices', looked mystified.

'Our Liberal, dear.'

'You're wasting your time, you know.' This from Helen's partner René.

'Pardon?' Henry finally rose to the challenge.

'Why you want to be lobbying government when there's going to be a Labour rout in both countries is a mystery to me,' René said.

'No one knows for sure,' Henry responded crisply. 'That's the nature of a democracy: you keep up the discussion until it's too late to make a difference. It certainly hasn't got to that in New Zealand at present, has it, Steph?'

Nell decided the political chat was not proceeding well, and turned us in a more literary direction. 'You know, Henry – it is Henry, isn't it? I'm usually very good with people's names – I've heard about one of your poets. Writes wonderfully wicked things about society. Jimmy . . . Baxter, is it? Well – '

'James K. Baxter,' put in Henry, slumping back.

Again, that damned reticence. Here we were, surrounded by interesting people with fresh ideas, and presumably different experiences, and all he could do was sit there dumbstruck. What was it Pound said about a stone dog biting the air?

'Your man plays it close to his chest, doesn't he?' Helen, sotto voce.

'Helen honey, give me a hand with the plates, will you?'

The neighbour skipped out to the kitchen. No time to probe what was wrong with Henry – perhaps he was thinking about the forum. I felt a mild pang of guilt that I wasn't being more supportive; then forgot all in the whirl of talk.

Which was unforgettable. The women all knew the current must-reads: Germaine Greer, Simone de Beauvoir, Kate Millett. In fact, they knew them backwards! De Beauvoir I had an excellent grasp of; Greer I'd found too ascerbic, but enlightening. Unfortunately for me, the talk got stuck on Millett's reading of Henry Miller, and stayed there for the duration. Neither of us had ventured into Miller: Henry's taste was never for pornography, and I hated its cruelty on principle. But these people knew *Tropic of Capricorn* as well as I could recite English poetry. As the conversation continued, I felt I'd been caught out inhabiting an intellectual tributary, tumbling around in the brackish river I'd inhabited all my life, yet for the first time catching a shocking glimpse of a fervid, hungry sea breaking just out of reach.

Nell brought in a platter of steaming rabbit cooked à la Elizabeth David, and the talk turned momentarily to French cuisine. 'I found the recipe in her *French Provincial Cooking* – you know, the one with beef and rabbit,' said Nell.

A chorus of grunts and slurps met this announcement.

'Sauce au vin du Médoc,' she enunciated emphatically. Launched on an obsession second only to her enthusiasm for Kate Millett, Nell bubbled as noisily as the stew, which was incredibly hot: she must have had it cooking for hours. 'Do you know it comes first hand from the wife of a wine grower?'

She smiled again at Roland – a little too brightly, I thought. 'It's real peasant food, darling. Forget cutting the stuff into minuscule bits: this is a hearty, vulgar stew.'

'Thank God for that,' replied her husband enigmatically.

'Perfect, Nell . . .' 'Well done . . .' 'Bloody great . . .' Compliments began to flow from our lips, as if to make up for Roland's niggardliness.

We all knew without anyone saying that we were witnessing a culinary miracle in the Antipodes. At last you could buy rabbit and cook it in the way it should be cooked. 'Vulgar' struck me as amusing when Australians and New Zealanders spent so much time trying to escape vulgarity, but then perhaps a certain uncouth was permitted in bohemian Balmain.

I fought back my distaste for meat and took a cautious sip of the gravy du Médoc. The bouquet of pork and beef and specially reared rabbit leapt like a wild beast at my tastebuds. I tore off a lump of bread stick and mopped politely.

'But I did change it a bit,' Nell added, smiling impishly at Roland.

'Do tell, Aunty Nell!' chorused the eaters rudely.

'Well, dears, instead of adding the wine to the stew and then simmering it till it fell apart, as Elizabeth David says you should, I marinated the rabbit first, seared it quickly, *then* let it simmer. What do you think?' The cook drew herself up, awaiting our approval.

Apparently no one had a further opinion on the subject of marinating except for Henry, who inquired whether rabbit was best done in red or white wine.

'Oh, red, of course, dear.' The hostess gleamed with pleasure.

At this point I swear that Nell began to caress Henry's shin with her foot under the table, but we were so many limbs packed under the Edwardian oak that it was impossible to be sure.

Henry perked up. 'Talking of food, I thought Steph and I would pay a visit to the Commonweal,' he remarked. 'They do magnificent salads there.'

Silence.

'It's hideously bourgeois, that place, mate. Been there since the ark. You know there's a photo of the Queen in the dunny?' Roland pushed back his plate and unscrewed his pipe. 'We tend to spend most of our time at the pub these days, don't we, Nell?'

Roland and Nell politely returned the table to Miller and Millett. And Lawrence and Millett. By the time our hostess served us Turkish coffee out of an ubrik – bought, she told us proudly, at a Lebanese place in Redfern – my mind was steeped and viscous with carrots and twats and cocks. The air steamed closer, containing the tang of winter, but a false winter, overlaid with the too-close warmth of the fire, now making itself felt in the trickle of sweat that dripped and dropped inside my bra.

Roland had an obsession about D. H. Lawrence. I had no idea until the Balmain dinner that Lawrence wrote 'The Woman Who Rode Away', a savage little tale about an unhappily married woman who rides into the Mexican desert and ends up being sacrificed to the sun by Indians. Years ago I came across its distillation in a *Boy's Own Paper*, where the editors had made it sound almost noble. Roland reprised the full, nastier story for our benefit.

By this time we had finally reached dessert. Which happened to be a Burbank clafoutis, brought by Annabel, Nell's closest friend, and the partner of an older man called Frank, with streaks of white in his beard.

Frank was a bookseller whose shop had been the target of police sweeps since the late sixties. 'Censorship's a bitch, Steph,' he confided to me. 'Here, help yourself to cream. Or yoghurt? Annabel makes her own.'

Roland's teeth gleamed above the candles (hand-poured, again by Nell) as 'The Woman Who Rode Away' drew to a close.

'Come on. Lawrence was just a queer,' interrupted Henry impatiently. 'Everyone knows he hated women.'

Which was true, but again, silence descended like a rebuke – sharper, this time, as if our hosts were tiring of our failure to observe nuance.

I looked quickly at Nell, who seemed unaffected by the story's darkness. Was I the only one who could bear personal witness to the erotic power of passivity?

'Heavy stuff,' commented a male voice out of the flickering shadows, and someone, Annabel I think, laughed and said that there was nothing masochistic about her. The male voice agreed.

And kept on agreeing until we stood up and made our farewells: Henry had an important day ahead of him. As for me, I wanted nothing more than to sit under the gigantic trees I'd observed from my walk yesterday in the Gardens, and smell the air. My senses felt assaulted; I needed time to repair them.

It wasn't until we were in the taxi that I realised the rehashing of Lawrence and Miller's dirtiest bits and the critique that followed had all been part of a mysterious dinner ritual of approbation and opprobrium. Rather like, I observed, drunk on Roland's good French wine, marinating and grilling rabbit. First tenderise, then summon the fire. Good cooking, like critique, always walks with one foot in hell.

That is how to learn, I thought much later: Sydney stretched me until it hurt, and then gave me pleasure, because I felt extended beyond the provincial creature I knew myself to really be. Not quite as provincial as Meg Shepherd, of course, but still.

Nonetheless, I was not convinced by Annabel's rejection of masochism. And sadism. My love for Henry acquainted me with the push-me-pull-you twins of cruelty, and I'm arrogant enough to believe that the experience contains a universal lesson.

Having discovered that Henry was genuinely worried about the forum, I made him go over his paper before we went to bed (it was well after midnight when we left Balmain!). It sounded excellent to me, and I told him so.

'Sorry to be such a wet at dinner,' he said, squeezing my hand. 'I want this to go well: if it gets into the papers it will be good publicity for us, so I can't come out of the forum looking like a fool.'

'That's nonsense. Whatever you said, it wouldn't be foolish, Henry.'

He looked at me quizzically. I'd never felt closer to him in my life.

'Anyway,' I said, 'there are more important things than censorship. Sexuality's only part of the struggle.'

'My sentiments exactly,' he replied cheerfully. His expression changed abruptly. 'Jesus, Steph, you're not going to go all hippy Woodstock on me, are you?'

'The Prices weren't hippies!'

'They were so. Hand-poured candles, I ask you. That's just the sort of thing –'

'The whole evening was a pleasure, and I'm not going to pretend otherwise, even for you.' Idealisation wears thin, once in a while.

'Bloody hell, are you with me, Steph, or not?'

Perhaps the noise I heard out of the luminous city dark was Henry grinding his teeth; perhaps it was a truck rattling as it bounced through an intersection.

'Of course I am. You know I'm right behind you in the need to think deeply about all issues.'

'Course you are,' he mocked.

'Don't.'

'Don't what?'

He knew exactly what. 'Just don't, that's all,' I said sadly.

We collapsed into unhappy sleep.

And began bickering over a similar issue the following evening with Josh Rideau and Diana.

Granted, the setting was more dismal – Josh and his girlfriend lived in a run-down Paddington apartment with no sign of impending renovations and no objects to speak of, except for an electric typewriter in the upstairs bedsit and a printing press taking up most of the space on the ground floor. A scungy, student dive that smelt of old coffee grounds and cigarettes. It struck me as odd that Diana looked so out of sorts in the company of a colleague, but she did. Not that she appeared jealous of Sandy, the girlfriend: something else was troubling her, I decided.

'So, fuck me,' said Josh as he leaned into the fridge and extracted five beers, 'the cops are still hounding Wendy Bacon.'

He hooked the opener over the caps and yanked. The beer hissed and seethed and frothed over his arm, which I couldn't help noticing was white and practically hairless.

'Can you believe it? They can't let the whole deal go.'

'What deal?' I inquired.

Josh considered me for a moment and turned sharply to Henry. 'Where on earth have you two been?' he asked contemptuously.

'You forget, Josh: Sydney news isn't Wellington news.' Diana was apparently making an effort to keep us all convivial. She would need to work hard: quietly, I found Josh Rideau vulgar, and not in the chic sense of last night.

'Yes, but you must have heard about the censorship trials,' he pressed. 'They've been going on for bloody ages.'

'We do have Patricia Bartlett to remind us of our morals in New Zealand. The less said about her kind, the better,' sniffed Henry.

I was out of the room when the sugar-bowl incident occurred. When I rushed back from the bathroom (again, grotty and underventilated, with a beard of slime gathering around the wash-basin plughole) there was Henry dusting sugar crystals out of his hair, with Josh's girlfriend and Diana looking annoyed.

'It's all very well for you to talk about intellectual purdah,' said Henry with the asp voice he does when he's really upset. 'Look at this flat! It's a bloody disgrace. And if you're so up with the play politically, where are all your books?'

Incredible, but true. Josh seemed to have none. Perhaps he

identified with the workers and did all his studying in the library. Perhaps he learnt his revolutionary theories at night classes and study groups. I didn't care by that time: all I wanted to do was bundle Henry out of the house and get us both back to Wellington in one piece. Diana could sort out her associate. Or were they lovers? She could have been bisexual: a lot of intelligent women were these days.

Who the hell cared what Rideau was to her? It was time to go home.

Rattled, and nursing more anxieties than when he had left, Henry returned to his desk to plan the youth summit. It was a tense week, recovering from the Sydney trip. I couldn't put into words how ambivalent an effect it had on me, especially when my lover couldn't stop railing at Josh Rideau, whom he suspected of being a real troublemaker. Visiting a cosmopolitan city at that time in my life moved me deeply, but, like many experiences, I pushed the tantalising memories away in an effort to assist Henry.

We attended the Otaki military training weekend in a last-ditch effort to support Diana. For reasons Henry never explained, the planned raid on the ballot turned into a humiliating debacle and she never forgave us. After that, they scrapped and hissed through every planning committee meeting.

Rage drove him to steal the White Paper. He always used to tell us how anger was a poor friend of strategy, and it looked as if he had now become painfully tangled in his own rhetoric. Poor Henry. I felt so sorry for him when he discovered someone had broken into Garden View Road and stolen the stolen paper from his files. My first thought was not of Diana, but Meg – which was right, but not quite, or at least not yet right.

In August, Sydney and the double theft finally behind us, the wind began to blow with greater warmth. I came out of the fug of worry and planning for the youth summit one day with a longing to look around me, and found sharp smells of spice infiltrating the air: the jasmine in flower outside our window. I walked across the city and up to the Gardens, where I found the earth breaking into life there too.

In the middle of my walk I had an epiphany:

The maple trees had covered themselves in pink and green shoots, the wind hummed through them like a hive of bees. Underneath the ribbed canopy of maple, bluebells and ajuga flowered together. The blue was the same as the sky, laced with streaks and gleaming with subdued light. Ajuga crept over the ground and covered the maple roots in a throw of purple and black. Under the knotted throw, worms would be chewing dirt into humus; above, wax-eyes and fantails blinked and fluttered.

Nature was so perfectly circular, I thought. Deep reached to deep: the birds reflecting themselves to the trees, reflecting themselves to the earth, reflecting itself to the sky, the rain, the clouds. Each rooted in each, each growing out of the other. Separate, but all of a piece.

It was as if a velvet hand reached up from the ground and dropped its beauty on my tongue. I saw each plant perfect in its own shape, putting out its green life into the air and welcoming me into its essence, breaking itself open. Without a sound, the speech of plants extended its alphabet of colour, vivid and magnified, and its subtly graded shadows. I felt overtaken by a wave of joy. It rushed in the fraction of a moment from my feet to the top of my head. Ruffling my hair, it left me as if I had had a mild electric shock, and passed into the atmosphere.

Nature just was. In a flash, its undemanding being had slipped in under the yoke of politics and lodged like a protective covering between my skin and the world, so that I stood on the slope above the Gardens feeling clear and unburdened.

The epiphany sped me through my research for the conference background paper on the environment. *Man lives all his life in the dark, I wrote. From day to day he fails to notice the perfect reciprocity of the natural systems of energy that engender life on this planet. We tinker with this delicate, hypersensitive system and take it beyond its limits at our peril.*

I sat in my room and thought of the world outside that I was trying to save. I saw a membrane with a million eyes, each viscous as egg-white, spinning through an alarmed sky the colour of a grape.

When I walk on the earth I can hear it breathing. I can hear its heart when the tide moves across the land, when the rain and snows fill the rivers and lakes, when they disperse into the mists of air. My pores open to the earth's breath and I become one with it. But we are afraid of our senses and fear the harmony of the breath. We retreat into our own bodies and turn them into a fortress.

I suppose I did get carried away. Henry read over my piece, then scored out the second paragraph. He instructed me to concentrate on the theme of global capitalism and the pollution engendered by multinational corporations.

'You can't use poetry to explain politics,' he snapped. 'It simply doesn't work.'

And, as if he could see inside my head: 'Just because you've been for a walk in the Gardens and it's spring doesn't mean to say you can go on about it in a paper. Aim for objectivity. And don't say *I* all the time: it turns me right off.'

'Why not?' I was mutinous this morning. My poetic sentiments had made me strong.

'It's too bloody personal. You come across as some *woman* having opinions. Reasoning isn't about "having opinions", it's about being careful.'

Later, when I tried to remember exactly why the moment had been special, I couldn't. It had gone, sucked into droplets of sweat and old cells, sloughed away and returned to the universe.

'Why does spring have such a hold over people?' Henry asked vexatiously over dinner that night.

Meg looked up guiltily from her plate. 'It makes us feel real,' she said. They'd spent the day mailing out background papers, Henry pedantically checking every detail, and she looked worn out.

Still smarting from his rudeness the day before, I said nothing.

Henry harrumphed. 'Steph?'

I wished he wouldn't always count on me when Meg's intelligence reached its limits. 'I suppose it reminds us we're all animals. You know, creatures of instinct,' I offered.

A flicker gleamed behind Meg's glasses and disappeared. It was impossible to tell what she was thinking. I wished again that this summit would be over and that Meg could vanish back to Cambridge.

'Bang on!' he exclaimed. 'That's exactly the problem. The only reason man evolved was because he learned to take his eyes off the ground. If he'd stared at nature all his life, we'd still be heaving women around by the hair!'

'But if we hadn't been able to read the seasons, we wouldn't have evolved, either. Look how those tribes in Brazil survive – by being in tune with the environment. *And* they have an amazing knowledge of rare plants! Westerners find those places impossible.' I couldn't let his opinions go unchallenged. I knew what he was leading up to and it irked me.

'Yes, yes of course,' he conceded. 'But admit it, Steph,' – Meg had dropped behind a long time ago – 'it's our *brain power* that's got us where we are; it's thought and the ability to reason. Okay, we still fuck and eat and shit and all that, but we also reason, and that makes us *naked apes*. All this stuff about instincts is fine, I couldn't agree more, but it's our minds that are crucial – which is why I'm damn well not going to have people at the hui waxing on about nature: it's bullshit.'

Of course he was right, otherwise what were we all doing studying at university? Extending human consciousness, he would say. There were times when Henry's forms of consciousness made me feel my foot had become stuck in an unpleasantly tight-fitting shoe.

'By the way, are you coming to Gillian's party?' asked Meg, who was clearing the table with Henry.

'Oh, Christ,' he said, his triumph disappearing, 'I suppose so.' He looked at me. 'Are we?'

This friend of Meg's was having an engagement party and we'd been invited. I didn't want to go, but Henry, who saw canvassing opportunities for the summit everywhere, insisted.

'You know what we think of marriage,' I said icily.

Meg's face fell. I knew she was dying for Henry to go without me.

'I've got an essay to write,' I said brightly. 'Why don't I join you later? You can do your thing with Meg and I'll drop in on my way home from the library.'

The route to Gillian Blaikie's flat took me along Upland Road and down the hill towards Norway Street. Gillian and her fiancé were renting their two-bedroom cottage from a couple in Bird and Bush. Their sloping section was one of those deliberately neglected gardens planted to encourage wildlife, which, since their departure for South America on a working holiday, had been taken over by comfrey and fennel. I'd heard that Gillian's token gesture towards environmental friendliness had been to hang a bowl of seeds and dripping on the washing line, but, as the line was low and their cat agile, hungry birds prudently kept away.

I fought my way through rotting weeds. From the back door I could see people sitting stiffly in the lounge. The record-player was on: a country and western singer back-ending a desolate tune. Henry was attempting a conversation with Lou Waters, their flagging talk monitored by a scowling Diana. Lou was doubtless recalling his trouncing of her at the Sydney forum. I wondered how Lou and Diana were getting on after the trip, where I'm certain they hadn't been more than friends. If Diana had slept with Josh, she was clearly back into lesbian mode tonight.

I wish I hadn't seen Meg next. I couldn't believe my eyes. She was sitting in the kitchen doing something at the table with Gillian, but it was what she was wearing that was so peculiar. She looked like an Indian squaw! She must have washed her hair and plaited it while it was still damp into a dozen or more small braids. She'd dyed some old nightgown red, and wore a blue and red glass necklace threaded on a leather thong, and Henry's moccasins on her feet. Well, they looked like his, although I couldn't be absolutely sure.

I stared at her for a long time, unable to restrain myself, but she seemed not to notice.

'What do you think?' she asked me shyly.

'Meg's gone native,' exclaimed Chris, the fiancé, immediately joined by Henry and Lou.

For some reason Henry looked uncomfortable with his flatmate's squaw face crowned by a quiver of braids. 'Doesn't she look a sight?' he whispered to me. 'Christ, what the hell am I doing involved with a woman like that?'

'You're not involved with her,' I reminded him. 'You're just organising the youth summit with her.'

'She looks *fat*,' he said, 'and where did she get that god-awful shift thing from?'

He put his hand in mine and let me walk him home across Aro Valley with the moon pouring its chill, beautiful light over us.

Two weeks before Gillian's wedding, my period failed to arrive. For the first time, it was over three weeks late. My breasts were swelling and tingling as if they were full of sparklers bursting to get out, and my legs ached. I went to the doctor.

Dr Schilling was known around Wellington for his radical attitude to abortion. He liked to think of himself as a bohemian, wore loose, open shirts and jeans, and took advantage of the queues of vulnerable women who visited his surgery.

'I'm going to give you something to bring your period on,' the doctor said to me as he washed his hands. 'One injection now, and the other next week. Come to my house on Saturday afternoon between two and three.'

I joined the half-dozen others who filled Dr Schilling's sitting room that Saturday. The atmosphere was so full of despair that I absented myself from our collective suffering and turned the watermark on the sitting-room ceiling into lurid swirls of colour.

A stroke here, another there. The ceiling became invaded by one of Chagall's village scenes. There, at the base of the painting, was the glass mountain. Against it an icy tree, struggling to bring its rare, glowing fruits to birth. There was the farmer with his scythe and his upside-down woman beside her upside-down house.

I'd borrowed the book on Chagall and other fantasy painters

from Lydia. I liked Rousseau's forests and Klee's odd life-forms, although the Russian was my favourite. Looking at his dream world reproduced on Dr Schilling's ceiling, I found myself so excited I could hardly breathe. Such life. So fleeting.

The beast with the blue eye knows what the green man intends, I thought. Sooner or later the green man will knock the woman who is milking the cow off her little stool. The milk will dribble into the earth. And all the lovely red, green, yellow and blue will dissolve into the blind sheets the dreamer is left holding in the morning.

'Bend over,' says Dr Schilling.

I lie upside down on the snow-white bed, thinking of milk dribbling away into the thirsty earth.

Several days later I went to Gill and Chris's wedding with a sanitary napkin between my legs and a cavity in my chest big enough to swallow the universe. Lou Waters and Meg Shepherd had each been assigned readings during the service. Ross Cameron, a musician friend of Meg's, had brought his jazz group along; Lou's mother, I heard, had come down from Greytown to do the flowers. Diana, recently returned from another training week for radical activists at Makara Beach, arrived in her pink pyjama outfit. Henry had elected to work on summit business at home, for which I was thankful.

Why, with my hang-ups about marriage and the horrors of suburbia, did I go? Gillian Blaikie and I lived completely different lives. People talk about parallel universes and, even though I abhor science fiction, I truly believe that there are millions of worlds out there, each a breath removed from the next, all co-existing uneasily, seldom colliding. The dance of the planets takes place at infinitesimal levels in infinite varieties of size. No wonder astrologers believe conjunctions to be both rare and significant.

The truth is, I went to the wedding because I was curious. How did the middle class behave when it wanted ostentation? How did it pass on its rules for display to its children? Curiosity pricked at my skin like an irritant.

So I turned up in my favourite floppy hat and a Liberty print shirt, black tights and skirt. Suitably tasteful, but I have to admit it did grate a little with the preference for bright-coloured suits, screen-printed

caftans and sixties tent dresses reconstructed out of flowered chif-
fon. A sociologist's dream, you'd think. A writer's too, but I couldn't
see the obvious.

If I'd realised I would be meeting my future husband, I may
have dressed differently, but how was I to know there was a second
conjunction written into my sky? Lydia's concordance didn't help,
either, holding my heart in thrall through a seductive chain of stellar
metaphors to Henry Ballantyne.

Labour Weekend had turned warm, with a noticeable lack of
breeze. Somewhere close by, a city gardener could be heard hammering his tomato stakes, the ringing noise of metal against the obdu-
rate clay soil violating the air, reminding us of the hard pan of earth
that ran under our city like some hostile alien being.

St Paul's was packed with guests. It was that rare kind of
wedding that assembled every imaginable shade of the political
spectrum, and held them in polite suspension for the space of an
afternoon. I imagine that if the families had had their way, none
of us hoi polloi would have been invited, but a student wedding
breaks all the rules of social convention, which was why I managed
to put up with it.

As the crowd fanned themselves until the church seemed forked
with the rough white caps of turbulent water, Lou began reading
from *The Prophet*:

Love one another, but make not a bond of love:
Let it rather be a moving sea between the shores of your souls.

Apparently Gillian had found the words of Kahlil Gibran on a
teatowel. 'Look at this,' she'd said: '*Let there be spaces in your togeth-
erness, And let the winds of the heavens dance between you.* Isn't that
romantic?'

Henry and I hated Kahlil Gibran's verse because it made love
too cheap, too accessible. It reminded Henry of the sixties, which
he rather disapproved of because they'd turned political action into
flowers and sensuality.

A lot could be forgiven with a wedding at stake; however,
privately I found it difficult to imagine the Chris we'd met at the
party as the kind of man who would succumb to *The Prophet's*

charms. If it had been me, I would have chosen the words that said: *Empty and dark shall I raise my lantern.*

1 Corinthians 13, Paul's letter to the church at Corinth on love, was given to Meg Shepherd. Her voice rose over the hatted heads of the women:

If I speak with the tongues of men and angels, and have not charity, I am become as sounding brass, or a tinkling cymbal.

I bit my tongue and strove to listen to the words. It irked that Meg could read them so beautifully. They seemed like grace-notes, echoing in the high vaulted dome of the roof, dispersing like a flock of birds. I forgot our rivalry. Everything grew light. I held my hand up to the sun and knew I could swim in my veins – they were so blue, so transparent. I left my seat and joined the birds. They were nightingales, of course, not doves, each stuck with a brutal thorn, each with a bleeding heart. I grew dizzy and dropped from the great wooden ribs that arched overhead. My body felt strangely encumbered, weighted down by a lead of grief. In the middle of these feathered creatures speaking of love, remembering their own loves, I could only be a blank, a bird with a broken wing chained to the ground. I was a woman with no memory of love, with nothing charitable to remember. As Meg stood, swaying forward a little with her sibilant body, forked tongue turning each sound into a lantern of hope waiting to be filled, nobody knew that the woman who listened to her read with the voice of an angel was bleeding and bleeding at her core.

For now we see through a glass darkly; but then face to face: now I know in part; but then shall I know even as also I am known.

What did you have to know before love came down? I wondered, as Meg's lips continued to move. What was it, casting my eyes around at the bespectacled Ross Cameron, whom I'd met at Norway Street, clarinet case by his feet, that you could see only through the dark?

Commentators later remarked that the Blaikie–Thompkins wedding was the crowning event of the decade, remembered long after confidence in the farming community had vanished. Despite Chris's reluctance, his wedding celebrations took Wellington society by storm. The following day there was an ingratiating write-up in the *Dominion*:

> An alliance of breeding and vigour . . . One of our oldest families renews its links with the land. Yesterday Miss Gillian Blaikie married Mr Christopher Thompkins at St Paul's Cathedral, cementing over one hundred years of felicitous association between the landed gentry and city financiers. The bride wore faille and carried orange blossom. Wellington throws open its doors to this distinguished couple.

Against the noise of the reception on the lawn of the parental Hutt Valley garden, *Porgy and Bess* grew notes as thick and luxurious as cream, drifting from Ross's clarinet through the crowd to where I found myself alone in a corner of the garden, looking up into the leaves of an umbrageous fig tree.

I leaned back against its trunk. It had not yet begun to flower; its fruit weeks away. I imagined the hard green nipples of growth softening into hearts, turning purple. If you slit figs the right way, you could squeeze them into a star. Drizzle them with honey and their bed of aromatic seeds became out of this world. Divine. In my hometown of Christchurch, figs were hard to come by.

Against the late afternoon sun, the veins of the leaves displayed themselves like those tiny pulsing veins you might see in the hands of a child. A sleeping child, I thought.

I stayed while the baby grand hoisted onto the terrace rocked out 'Maple Leaf Rag'. Ross took a break and offered to fetch me a wine. He seemed nice enough. I suppose all musicians grow beards. His was golden and plentiful. We stood and sipped rosé, looked at the tulips and rhododendrons, and talked about nothing, which was very restful. I found it difficult to imagine this inoffensive person behaving like Henry Miller or D. H. Lawrence, but then who really knew a man until it was too late to un-know him?

Just before I left, the flushed Mrs Gillian Thompkins threw her bouquet. For a moment it looked as if it might spin on into the arms of the waiting dark, but at its lowest point before it landed in the bush at the back of the Thompkins' property, a sprightly arm reached out to seize the sprigs of orange blossom. Mrs Rachel Blaikie winked triumphantly at her husband. Meg looked disappointed. Lou and Diana cheered insincerely and I stole off, clutching my private bouquet of jealousy and pain. The crowd, deflected momentarily from the true stars of the evening, guffawed at the sight of Gillian's mother, who'd pinned the flowers to her suit, and then milled inside for sherry and cake.

With the summit a mere week away, Gillian and Chris sent a stream of *wish you were here* postcards to Meg from a thatched hut in Noumea. Together, we packed the final mail into manila envelopes that Meg stole from the Anthropology Department's office, and carried them down the hill to the CPO to catch the midnight post. Press agencies had to be informed, television alerted. Henry bombarded local MPs with reminders of the youth summit that was about to unfold on their doorstep. I rechecked the catering arrangements, relieved to hear that the cooks and produce ordering were under control. The household hummed. Doors crashed shut endlessly. Then, on the eve of the conference, Henry called me into his office.

'Steph,' he began, stirring his hair absent-mindedly, 'I'm afraid I've got bad news for you.'

'Oh?'

'Yes, well, it's been troubling me a lot lately. And I must say I'm finding this as difficult as you are.'

Difficult? 'Not the catering. Have the cooks let us down? You know, I didn't think we could trust them.'

'It's nothing to do with the bloody cooks. Just listen to me for a moment, will you?'

Instantly I was sober. My head was pounding and my bones felt soft and frayed as if they would crumble away into chalk or old dust.

'I've been talking things over with Meg. I can't go on pretending I don't care about her. She's getting restless, talking of not coming along to meetings.'

'I thought . . . I mean . . . I thought you didn't like her.' *Like* – the word seemed so weak. Did he love her but not like her? Was that it? Like Bertha's husband in 'Bliss' – what was his name? That horribly gross Harry? Was this me, Steph Jackson, intellectual and musician, collapsing in a heap of broken notes?

'She's unusual, but I find her stimulating – she makes me see things differently and I need that, you know I do . . . Squidges?'

Squidges? I looked down at our pillows, and they suddenly seemed lifeless and mismatched, angled together like discarded toys.

'Remember Sartre and de Beauvoir? How we used to admire them because they had necessary and contingent lovers?' Henry couldn't meet my eyes, his painfully magnificent violet ones fixed grimly on the trees outside. 'We've always said that was the way intellectuals should behave. I think it's time we gave it a go.'

'You mean you want to fuck two of us at once!' I tried to sit on the ugliness and hurt that was threatening to pour out of my mouth.

'Steady on, now. You'd still be my partner. It's just that our relationship would become more open.'

'What if I don't want that kind of . . . *arrangement?*'

'Well,' said Henry calmly, as if he couldn't see how my universe had just been wasted by an apocalypse, 'let's face it, you haven't looked well lately: you could probably do with a spell from me pawing you.'

Henry was dumping me, tonight, the night before the summit. I would have to go to Takaka as if nothing has happened. I would have to politic – on his behalf – with a broken heart. Neither Meg nor Henry, as far as I knew, suspected I'd been pregnant, and now I couldn't bring myself to confess what I'd done. I would have to share a room with them at Takaka and pretend we were a happy threesome.

I regretted the failure of my intuition, those animal instincts Henry had implied were passé. I had not been smart enough. I should have known a more elaborately deceitful arrangement would have suited him better. And I thought of a nest of spiders I once tore from the top of a dock plant, exposing its clotted white fibres to the frost. The babies, almost invisible tickling specks, had crawled curiously over my hand.

I walked out of his room, away from the Gestetner, the locked correspondence cupboard and the pile of folded shirts and miserable pillows on his bed.

I sat in the dark and watched moths dancing outside the window, thinking of Bertha's fate when she saw her husband draping a stole around Miss Pearl Fulton's neck. And I felt the ghost of my disappointed illustrious Mansfield ancestor breathe knowingly on my neck. I went out into the hall and made a phone call.

'Hello, Lydia,' I said when I heard my mother's voice. 'There's this line in Dryden, something about a day star being the son of dawn. You remember? I asked you about it before. You said it came from the Bible. I think the image is more –'

'More what?'

'More complicated. Can you look it up in your concordance again?'

I heard the wind whisper in the rice-paper pages as Lydia checked the reference.

'Ah. Yes. Here it is.' Another pause. 'It's clearly a reference to the son of God . . . *When the morning stars sang together and the sons of God shouted for joy* . . . There's another one . . . in Peter, about the day star rising in our hearts. And again in Revelation: *I will give you the morning star.* Isn't that what we said?'

'Yes, but what about Satan?' I couldn't believe it. In the middle of a break-up I was conducting an exegesis of scripture, which I knew to be a text of capitalist oppression, with my mother.

'Satan?'

'I read somewhere the morning star was a false star and not to be trusted.' I had come across a suggestion recently that likened Lucifer to the star that rose with the dawn. I sat down on the floor to steady my legs.

'I don't think that's in the Bible. From a conventional point of view, the word of God is very clear about separating good and evil. You wouldn't find a morning star that stands for God and the devil at the same time. It makes for confusion, and the God of believers was not traditionally a God of confusion.'

Good and evil; approbation and opprobrium; yes, fire and water, even: familiar processes. My body knew them well, welcomed them both.

I gave up, wandered back to our bedroom, wondering how I could feel like the weight of the world and a handful of dust at the same time. How could people experience the confusion of heavy and light without an interval of time passing between them? Would they go mad?

After all, I'd lost both Henry and an unborn child in the space of a week. I was suffering unendurable pain and I was confused down to my marrow. Worse, I was convinced that Meg had no idea of Henry's abilities, his real genius for politics, and that she was an extremely self-interested woman. If something went wrong at the summit, he would have no one to stand behind him, and just knowing that troubled me deeply.

When we got to Takaka, me crushed into the back of a Ford Escort rental with the Gestetner and Henry's guitar, the tide was in at the beach. I rolled up my jeans and let the sea foam around my legs. I stared out over the water and wondered what youth had to do with this lost place at the tip of the South Island. The beach was completely deserted. It felt like the end of the earth. I watched the wind tearing the words from my mouth, sweeping them away into a heap of sand. Somehow I knew time was running out.

Henry kept referring to 'my delegates' as if the summit personally belonged to him. It began to annoy Meg, so I challenged her, incredulous, still loyal. 'Well, they *are* his delegates,' I said. 'The summit wouldn't have happened without him. Henry is far too talented for New Zealand. You must be able to see how unusual, how ahead of his time he is.'

Was I dreaming, or had Meg began to change? I racked my aching mind for literary conventions of connivance and appropriation, because they were two words that sprang into my head whenever I thought about what was happening. At times I felt Meg Shepherd was turning into Steph Jackson. As if she was insidiously stealing away my identity: the heart beating for Henry; my words of love; the way I cooked, for God's sake! I sensed myself slipping away through an unplugged wound, and it felt terrifying. There were days when

I felt so excavated I seemed to be walking above the ground, barely skimming its surface, tilting over at the faintest breeze. Nightmare territory. At other times I realised that Meg was borrowing Henry's energy and confidence. Having studied a good deal of psychology, I was fully aware that people called this behaviour 'vampirism', but I had no idea how to warn Henry without sounding mad. Now was not the time, so I held my peace.

A crowd of delegates was already gathering, massed into buses, ferries and trains, to witness the impresario at work: his hot white star, their wavering faces beneath. My mind rebelliously filled with the sight of his green notebook, his nubbed socks hugging his ankles during yet another sexual conquest. The truth was that mixed in with my pained loyalty, Henry's charm was beginning to fail. Bits of his star were breaking off and shooting across the horizon of Golden Bay. I saw them fall, hissing into the water, but pretended not to notice.

I didn't sleep well the first night. Henry was snoring. Meg had been muttering to herself for hours. The tension was building for all of us. I finally dozed and dreamed that a man with a black face and blue eyes was threatening me with a knife.

I suppose it was all the catering responsibility, but I knew I would be chopped into little pieces and scraped, dripping with my juices, into the bolognese. The aluminium stockpot with its snout handles bubbled on the bench, the cook was laughing and smoking a joint, Diana had just come from locking Meg and Henry in the cooler.

I got up to make myself a soothing drink in the camp kitchen. It was lit up like a party ship, clumps of newly arrived delegates conversing and drinking, sizing one another up. There was silence as I went over to the bench and pulled down a cup from the cupboard, vaguely aware of two pyjama-clad bodies sprawled against the sink.

'Gidday,' said one. 'I'm Tim. This is Matthew.'

At that moment something occurred to me. I was ashamed of the Jackson name: its connections with Katherine Mansfield had brought me nothing but unpleasantness. The undertow that was Meg sucking me into oblivion had whacked me around once too often.

I hesitated. What I needed was a name no one could steal. A magic name, which would keep its owner invisible.

A white furred lie rolled out of my mouth fully fledged and ready to fly.

'Hi, I'm Janet. Janet Seed.'

'Where are you from?' asked Tim, testing my credentials.

I thought again. 'Tokoroa.'

'Where?'

'Tokoroa. It's a town south of Hamilton. Blink, and it's gone.'

'Right. Well, we're both students. Matthew's at Auckland. I'm from Canterbury. What're you up to at Tok . . . Tokoroa?'

Shipwrecked on my own invention. 'Er . . . I'm helping my mother run a bookshop in town. You'd be surprised. We get more customers than you think. We've got someone who orders all of Janet Frame's books as soon as they come out.'

'Janet Frame?' The two students looked startled.

My lie gathered momentum. 'I heard about this summit at night school. Night school. I do . . . I do . . . I'm learning Japanese.'

Matthew was unimpressed. He looked me over as if I were a piece of game ready to be run to ground.

'What workshop have you enrolled for?' he leered, leaning closer and playing with a trail of my hair. I realised that surrendering the persona of organising committee member had its disadvantages.

I concentrated on measuring Milo out of the tin. 'Environment, I think.'

'Environment. Well, well. We've got things in common, Janet! That's where I'm heading for.'

'Here.' Tim had boiled the zip and filled my cup.

'Thanks. See you guys later,' I called cheerfully.

'Hey, want us to walk you back? Wait, Janet!'

Matthew began loping behind me, but Tim pulled him away.

'Come on, leave her alone. It's late. I want to turn in.'

Relieved that the greasy Matthew had not managed to put his hand on my behind, I vanished across the black wet grass.

Henry was expecting me to chair a workshop, but Matthew would have exposed me as a liar – *Why, she's just some bird from Tokoroa!* – and I wasn't ready for that. Despite my pain at deceiving Henry, I missed the first session. When Janet Seed finally turned up, the Environment workshop had already elected a replacement chair, and they were carrying on as if nothing had happened.

For some time, Henry, Meg and Diana were unaware that Steph Jackson was missing. The delegates were so eager to run things themselves that nobody thought to ask what had happened to me.

I knew I was behaving irresponsibly, that politics wasn't to be trifled with in this way, but for the first time in my life I sensed that I was, to use Meg's ridiculous expression, being 'real'. The challenge of maintaining a fictitious identity took the sting out of my lover's rejection. In fact, it gave me a whole new life to imagine, one that absorbed my self-pity and lured me down a path that would finally turn away from student politics for good.

Henry was expecting that his loyal committee would lobby for him at every turn, and I would have tried harder to do that, I suppose, from underneath the persona of Janet Seed, but one evening I found myself in too deep to give Henry what little loyalty I had left.

Things had turned bad. The committee discovered that Diana had been in league with a faction that wanted to undermine the whole summit. Henry insisted we spend the rest of the night garnering support for his leadership. Meg strode away through the grass, a phoney Olympia waving her sword; Henry disappeared to compose himself; I was left to lobby whoever I came across.

There was an hour of the day left. Many of the delegates had disappeared to the Takaka pub, the rest, after a hard day's work, looked happy to be left alone. The stars were pale dots in the mattress of the sky, the moon insipid, half awake. Against the shore the water, too, waited, brushing the sand and retreating. Caught up in the sluggish wash and hiss on the beach, the pull of divided allegiances, I stared into space.

At that moment Tim appeared, heading off along the beach.

'Hi, Janet!' he shouted, 'Want to come?'

I could have refused and talked myself out of what was happening, but it all seemed too much effort. 'Sure.'

We crunched over the damp sand, our feet leaving giant bird marks behind us. My lungs swelled with the fresh air. On the point of disappearing with a swish of wings, I heard Henry's voice booming out of a cloud just above my flight path: *Lobby! Network! I'm counting on you, Steph!*

'Oh, Lord!'

'What was that?'

'Nothing. Sorry. Er . . . how have you found the summit so far?' I asked.

'Oh, great! We need more of them. The summit organising committee have been excellent. It must have been bloody hard making something like this work. I mean, how many other conferences are there that can say they represent this country's youth?'

'Um . . .'

'Henry and Meg are two of the most inspiring people! We had this torrid session one morning over American expansionism and I really thought Henry would lose it. I mean, there was some stringent opposition. I don't know if you would know this, coming from Tokoroa,' he looked apologetically at me, 'but young people aren't just going to do this knee-jerk loyalty thing. It's not all Woodstock here, no way.'

'What do you mean?' I asked.

'We're not going to be press-ganged into thinking what we don't want to. We've got the whole range of viewpoints here at Takaka – it's amazing!' He smacked a fist at me. 'Those three people have made one hell of a hui.'

'Four,' I said.

'Four?'

'Yes. Henry Ballantyne, Diana, Meg and Steph . . . Steph Jackson.'

'I saw that name. But she's not here, is she?'

I considered. Would he ever find out? There were over a hundred of us. 'Uh, I guess not.'

'Not that it's important. Henry's the real leader, anyone can see that.'

The effort to be loyal was exhausting. I was a failure at lobbying. 'What's been going on in Education?' I asked.

'Eh?' Tim turned and looked at me. 'It's been great. That woman's bloody impressive.'

'Oh?' That was interesting. Could Henry have got the wrong idea about Diana?

Suddenly Tim forgot we were talking politics.

'I was wondering, Janet . . . would you like to go back to my cabin? It's too early for anyone to be back from town yet. We'd have it to ourselves.'

Tim's Para Rubber coat glowed like an oil-slick. I did my Janet Seed walk along beside him.

'No, sorry, I've got work to do.'

'Work?'

'Yes, I do. Some remit stuff for our workshop needs reformulating.' Tim was staring at me again. 'You know, you don't sound like someone from the sticks. Are you sure you're from Tokoroa?'

'Of course!' I could hear myself, indignant, snappish. 'My father is on the high school board of governors.'

'Well.' Tim was impressed. 'You can't stay there for the rest of your life, that's for sure.'

'Why not?'

'You should do something with your life, that's all.'

I exploded. 'But I am! I bloody well am doing something! I love the smell of the books I sell; I like knowing who's going to order what. I love going to my night classes; I love feeding the chooks, and the frost in the winter. I love my family and driving to the coast with my boyfriend. I love simple things, and *what's wrong with that?*'

Janet Seed was making me feel more alive than Steph Jackson ever did.

I left Tim gaping at his doorway. If he hadn't been so disappointed, he would have seen me open the organising committee's cabin door. Because I'd turned into a shop assistant from the country, I'd become invisible. I represented the dispossessed. Young people were urban; ailing small towns invisible. The few delegates who noticed me disappearing into Henry's cabin from time to time probably thought I was a cleaner on the campground staff.

Girls from Tokoroa, it appeared, might as well have been cleaners anyway.

Towards two in the afternoon of the final day the assembly hall began to fill with delegates. I had decided to observe the proceedings from the school stationery room, a tiny airless cupboard stuffed with musty textbooks and Gestetner cartridges. Janet Seed would surely appreciate my cramped entente with paper and pens, would understand the need to see without being seen. Let the others slog it out – I'd had enough of the moves and counter-moves, the feints and reversals. It was like some peculiar mating game. Henry and Diana, playing the mercury of politics like seductive animals. Both of them stepping towards their prey on silver feet, barely brushing the grass, now backing away, savouring the wait; now advancing, running together with cruel swiftness.

And Meg: poisonous, duplicitous Meg. Who had spent the last few months tunnelling into Henry's ideas and pretending to make them her own. I know I should have been out there protecting Henry instead of being lost in the jungle of my own dark creations, but it was too late. Janet Seed was pulling me another direction, urging me to fly, to pipe my new secret name in a language no one else could understand.

I sat on a stool, my head pressed against a class set of *School Journals* and thought of pulling books off the shelf for lonely Tokoroa readers, of setting out for Japanese lessons in the fog, my bicycle light a soft yellow cheese segmenting the mist into chunks, sending it revolving into the vast, unfriendly night at immeasurable speeds.

At just after two, the hall was almost full. Henry had not yet taken the chair, while Meg and Tim were distributing agendas. I had a terrible fear that Henry's star was about to flop into the water.

People were still talking as he pulled out the Takaka school bell and clanged it over the heads of the delegates, who were fiddling with their papers as if they were waiting for a concert to begin. I sniffed the air. It felt fresh and unruffled. If I wanted to follow the meeting, I'd have to find an agenda. Tim had left the remaining ones on a seat near the aisle, so I crept across.

'Janet! What are you doing? Come and sit with me,' commanded Tim, pounding an empty seat with a friendly hand.

'Sshh!' I grabbed a sheet, slipped back to the cupboard.

Henry's pencil was now carving splendid arcs in a space near his head. 'In its final report presented to Parliament, the conference will press for new attitudes from the government. We will demand changes in social and economic legislation, reform in the education sector, and bold new environmental policies. Our lobby will be powerful because it will be unanimous.'

There was a scatter of applause. Were the majority with him, egging him on, willing him to take control and further their demands? His gaze flashed around the room, daring resistance to gaze back.

'I repeat, we are powerful because we have *one voice*. We *will* overcome!'

The invitation to sing was completely unexpected, a masterstroke. Henry hated music. Everyone in the flat knew his guitar was a sham. He lifted his pencil in the air again and brought it down, this time a bright shaft of a conductor's baton dissolving dissonance, urging harmony and tempo. The hall leapt to its feet, shouting out the freedom song, and I sank back in my cupboard and stuck my fingers in my ears. Delighted technicians rolled the cameras around the crowd as delegates, moved to tears, sang, stamped and clapped.

'There's been nothing like it, nothing at all!' Matthew's voice rose above the clapping.

'I now declare the meeting open for questions from the floor,' announced Henry when the singing died away and the reports had been tabled.

There was a long silence.

'Am I to understand that the meeting wishes the reports be accepted as read?'

The cameras circled the front of the hall, one on Henry, the other casting among the delegates, its eye alert and poised, a nervy barometer attuned to the slightest stir.

'Well, in that case ...'

'Not so fast, Mr Chairman!' A man's voice, deep, operatic, sounded from the middle of the hall. People craned to look. Two cameras swivelled in its direction, as Henry's face floated from his tower like that of a swooning princess.

Someone stood up, someone I knew. 'I would like to move a vote of no confidence in the chair,' the man said, leaving his seat and walking down towards the front.

The delegates, dazed from the warmth of their song, were slow to respond.

'I have vital information that all delegates must hear.' He came to a halt at the foot of the stage, looked up at Henry, turned again to appeal to the audience. 'But first, I need your permission to speak.'

'Permission denied!' Henry had recovered and strode out from behind the podium to the edge of the stage to confront him. 'This is a *youth* summit. Each delegate's selection permits him to speak and have voting rights. You, Hans, have neither.'

Hans Batchelor, Henry's Youth Board adviser. What was he doing here?

'I request a dispensation from this summit to speak,' said Hans. 'I believe it is in your interests.'

Someone else stood up. 'Fellow delegates, I move we hear what this man has to say.'

Turning to the chair, Diana Fahey said, 'Henry, I'm sure I'm not the only one here who is curious to hear his *vital information*.'

I could see Meg raising her hand, trying to steady a dangerously rocking boat. 'Mr Chairman, I think the meeting should hear Mr Batchelor's credentials before allowing him to participate in our hui.'

'Hans?'

'Thank you. Delegates, my name is Hans Batchelor. I work in an advisory capacity to the National Youth Board. Three days ago one of your representatives contacted us to complain that the organising committee, headed by Henry Ballantyne, was planning to hijack the summit's report. In the light of *information acquired illegally*, they apparently intended using it to twist the government's arm over strategic education and trade policies. The NYB called an emergency meeting last night and asked me to represent its concern. You're taking them for a ride, Henry, and they don't like it.'

Startled expressions regarded Henry as he stood on the edge of the stage.

Come on, Henry, say something, I thought. My own rage at him had begun to melt. Sweat trickled down my armpits, and a golfball of regret stuck in my chest. Henry looked around the hall and his eyes fastened on Meg. They passed on to Diana, regarding him coldly, faltered, and flicked away again. He was looking for the fourth member of the committee. He was expecting at least me and Meg to support him, to speak in that terribly charged atmosphere.

Meg stood up again. Really, she had more resources than I thought. 'Fellow delegates,' she began, 'it's no secret that our financial support for the hui came from the NYB, which is government-funded. But we believed their support came *without strings*, that we had a free hand to criticise government if we chose to.'

There were laughs and catcalls from the audience. 'Mr Batchelor sits on the council's national board. He is also known in Wellington as a right-wing extremist.'

The hall grew absolutely still.

'Now I don't know who contacted Mr Batchelor, but you can be sure they were out to destroy everything the committee and *you* have worked for. I urge you not to let that happen.'

'What does he mean by "information acquired illegally"?' The question came from nowhere. I couldn't see who asked it, and I had no idea what Henry would say. Only I knew about the White Paper fiasco, and to tell the truth, I'd almost forgotten it had happened, we'd been so preoccupied.

'What about this summit report? Were you planning to "hijack" it?'

'Of course not,' snapped Henry, his diplomacy deserting him. 'How could we possibly do that?'

'I have a witness who was present when you announced those very intentions.' Diana was on her feet, glaring malevolently at Henry. 'Steph? Steph Jackson, where are you?'

The door of the stationery room opened roughly and I was hauled to my feet by one of the cooks. 'Come on, coward,' he smirked, and thrust me up the corridor and into the hall. In a daze I noticed Rick Shaw from *Hotspot* staggering in from outside on the arm of the sound technician, who was rearranging his hair and clothes. Meanwhile, I found myself staring into the probing stare of a camera.

'Fellow delegates,' urged Diana, 'allow me to introduce the fourth member of our committee, Steph Jackson. Steph was present when Henry revealed his intentions to hijack the summit. Isn't that correct, Steph?'

For a moment I forgot where I was. Spread below me were a crowd of expectant faces waiting for a royal pronouncement: *We now declare the theatres open, let the music and masques begin.* But Henry, I thought, where is Henry? I could see the furrow of a frown on Matthew's face, his hopeful folder of minutes, resolutions and background papers a witness to his faith in the summit.

'Um, I don't know what you're talking about . . .'

'That's not Steph Jackson! That's *Janet Seed*! Hey, Janet!'

Someone was calling out from the back, a gaunt frame travelling through the crowd with irreverent speed. 'Don't worry! We'll get you out of it!' Tim came bounding up to join the growing knot of people at the front.

Diana started towards us. The audience erupted into laughter. I could see the major players hesitating, uncertain how to make use of this new development.

'Look, I don't know what's going on here, but someone's made a huge mistake. This is Janet, my mate from Tokoroa. Right, Janet?'

'Er, yes. I work in a bookshop there.'

'And,' prompted Tim helpfully, 'the hui organising committee chose you to fill their quota of clerical and shop assistants. Right?'

'That's right.'

Matthew jumped up. 'I met Janet the first night we came. She was making Milo in the kitchen.'

A snicker.

'She told me she was learning Japanese at night school,' Matthew added, speaking now to the rapt group of people in front of him. 'I think I've seen her every day since. She's been in Environment with me. She's put forward motions on pesticide control and social work in small towns, haven't you, Janet?'

'Well . . . yes. Yes, I have.'

'And very good motions they were.'

Meg was staring at me in wonder. Henry had turned away from the group of people at his feet to wink across the room at Rick Shaw.

Not even Henry could figure out why my false identity had the effect of stifling Diana's plans, but it did. One moment she and I were both staring at each other across the room, fixed in perpetuity on camera, the next, she'd moved to the back of the hall and was engaged in hasty conference with Hans. Henry reckoned it was the presence of the camera, which might have invited some snoop from Australian Intelligence to investigate the ring-leader of the counter-insurgent revolt at the youth summit. 'She wouldn't have wanted that,' he said, 'because she's got some other deception to hide.'

In the chaos that followed, Diana's voice could faintly be heard calling out, 'What about the White Paper, Henry?' as she waved a document in the air. But the hubbub drowned her shouts, and the cameras temporarily abandoned us both, chasing after Hans Batchelor, for which I was utterly grateful.

Diana decided to avoid directly challenging Janet Seed. I maintain it was because my false identity hewed too closely to her own. She was the most complex individual I have ever met, her motives impossible to untangle. Somehow, she knew that I knew. So we were caught in an unlikely alliance: two fulminators spinning exotic lies in different worlds, stuck together at this one atmospheric moment by chance, yet anxious not to prolong the association, even if it meant losing face.

When the hall had resumed a rough kind of order, Diana was invited to speak. Henry could be a very fair chair when he chose.

'It was me who contacted the NYB,' she said, entreating the delegates. 'I believed the committee's motives were suspect. We also had reason to believe that Henry Ballantyne had been involved in the theft of the White Paper from the Education Department. Maybe we were wrong.'

Matthew and Tim scrambled to their feet. They had idolised Diana. Tim, who'd reported her prescient handling of the Education workshop to me, looked stricken.

A triumphant Henry mopped up the remains of the aborted mission, addressing us as if we were children who'd had a painful shock. 'You can all see how easily power corrupts. We trusted Miss Fahey with the running of the hui. We felt she was a skilled administrator, that she had a skill the rest of us lacked.'

A new Sermon on the Mount, his best yet. Even I could assent to the way Henry swept above us all like some glorious angel with radiant hair and garment. The healing touch of his words had a miraculous effect.

Growing murmurs of support for a naive committee being betrayed by a jumped-up spinster turned ambitious bureaucrat – *Miss Fahey* – swept Henry's refurbished star up into the heavens once more. He recognised the swell of support, became outraged, self-righteous: 'Diana clearly had her own agenda. I'm ashamed to think how easily she gained our trust!'

Now Meg was whispering something to him. 'In fact, Meg Shepherd just this morning intercepted a libellous message addressed to the Press Association in Wellington. It accused us of manipulating the summit and misappropriating government property.'

By this time, his leadership was confirmed. The audience groaned. 'It's most likely Miss Fahey was responsible,' he added. 'For the record, I've never met Janet Seed before. But I do seem to remember reading an excellent application from a sales assistant in the book trade who *did* live in Tokoroa.' He was warming to the idea. 'Unfortunately, Steph Jackson couldn't be with us. She's been in Wellington for the duration of the hui. So, well done, Tim,' he said, patting him fondly on the shoulder, 'You've saved us a lot of distress.' Henry threw a final look over his shoulder at Rick Shaw, and mounted the podium for the last time.

'I think,' he said, 'we can now proceed.'

The following day we arrived back in Wellington. Diana and Hans

Batchelor had left Takaka immediately after the totara-planting ceremony. Summit delegates had been invited by local residents to plant
a native tree as a token of the goodwill of young people towards the
environment. Matthew, as chair of the Environment workshop, had
been chosen for the honour, but he had unexpectedly deferred in
favour of Janet Seed.

'With a name like that,' he said, suddenly linguistically sensitive,
'we can't not choose her.'

The summit's participants were transported in buses to a site
close to Collingwood.

'Go, Janet!' Tim stood by while I bent and patted the earth
around the totara's bole.

Local photographers from Golden Bay were present to record
the event. Apart from an under-exposed photograph in the local
paper, the tree-planting event sank into history, accompanied by ragged applause from the assembled delegates and as many of Takaka
and Collingwood's residents who cared to join us.

No one knew where Diana and Hans, humbled observers of Janet
Seed's final task, were travelling to, and no one seemed to care, as the
roar of their car's engine faded into the purple smoke of the evening,
and was submerged in the din of cutlery scraping against a hundred
school plates.

The trip home for us was hardly more pleasant. Henry and Meg
didn't speak to me until the Cook Strait ferry drew in sight of the
city, when Henry said calmly, 'I suppose you want me to be grateful
for what happened.' He said nothing for a moment. 'We don't know
you, do we? What do you think a conference is? A children's game?'

'I made something up, that's all.'

'Shit! Made something up! You were supposed to be running
Environment! Lobbying for us! For our policies! And what do you
do?'

Henry turned to Meg. 'She bloody well makes something up! God,
you're as bad as Diana! Worse! At least we know what she wanted!'

My ex-lover's mouth looked as if it were full of sour things. 'I
mean, *Janet Seed*, for God's sake. What on earth could you have been
thinking of?'

He was goading me, stinging me into making a confession. His hands grasped the rail of the ferry in a fury as we swung around, sea churning, to dock. A storm of gulls rose and hung above the boat like blinding feathers. Their harsh noises were sucked further and further away, a vain squawking swept into the turbulent air. Meg had wisely disappeared below to check our bags, and I was left confronting the man I'd betrayed and still, inexplicably, loved. How could I explain something I barely understood myself?

Henry didn't wait but plunged on as if teaching me the procedures and rules of politics, as if I were still being initiated as his most loyal acolyte. 'Politics is about *truth*. It's about justice and making right changes. It's *real*. It's got nothing to do with fantasy. You could have been playing Cluedo at Takaka for all you cared!'

But it *is* Cluedo, Henry, I wanted to say. It's about knowing there's a dead body in the room and deciding whether you want to find it. It's about conniving and bargains and disloyalties. And it's about dumping people the night before a great performance and not even caring if they bleed to death in front of you. For all his worldliness, Henry had failed to recognise that one person's political truth was as freakish and made up as the next. He never probed his motives, and when he discovered something offensive it was always in someone else.

'Okay. I'm sorry,' I said. 'Anyway, if I hadn't done it, where would you be now?'

That much was true and the others knew it. Janet Seed had saved the summit from disaster. I was unaccountably sad that her brief flare in the public arena – my own star, burning its inimitable celestial script – was over.

Falling asleep that first night back in Wellington with the three of us occupying separate rooms wasn't easy. Not for me, anyway. Who knows where Meg and Henry ended up, but I insisted he let me have our old bed, at least for the time being.

I dreamt we were back in Collingwood. Except that everything was huge and lushly overgrown. The bush wore its velvet stillness like a jewel. Then a truck arrived; another, and another; a helicopter flew somewhere overhead. Gangs of men began excavating a great gash in the cover of fern and bush, ferrying away bundles of roughly trimmed saplings, straddling fallen beech with coughing chainsaws. Then I saw a little knot of people tied to trees ringing the torn clearing; others, linking arms, stared up into gigantic earthmovers that advanced, driving them back.

And then I noticed a thin tongue of greenish yellow rising like a holy column into the air not yards from where I was standing. While the saws screamed and growled and trees fell around me, I ran towards the prickled stalks of my beloved totara. Now grown so high, its top as I looked up was only just visible, but in terms of forest trees it was a baby, a juvenile.

Before I could shout out in surprise, a man whose face was completely blank – as they are in dreams sometimes – ran towards me with a chainsaw, wrestling it into life as he approached the tree. The blade sliced and snapped; chips of white and gold flew into the air. I screamed, rushed at his legs. I swear my totara made a groaning noise that reverberated mournfully throughout the valley as it crashed at last through the remaining trees in a flurry of wind, snapping branches and sawdust.

Later, after I told Lydia I'd had an abortion, she said the tree in the dream was a symbol of my lost child, and it was a sign that I was recovering – based, I suppose, on the assumption that it's better to get one's grief out into the open than repress it. She was probably right, although I couldn't help associating the butchered young tree with our valiant efforts to make the summit a success. We'd poured so much effort into its organisation – nobody more than Henry – but for what, in the end? Meg's selfishness, Diana's ambition and my personal betrayal had ensured the hui would be forgotten. Ever since, the sight of a totara makes me feel sick to the stomach.

When relations had grown less frosty, the three of us took a few days off to travel to Coromandel. It wasn't a great idea, even though I came back feeling a good deal less hostile towards Meg and more at peace with Henry.

A day or two later Henry and I were both supposed to be studying.

Meg was out shopping; Henry had made himself a coffee and gone back to work at his desk. I asked him why he thought Diana had capitulated so quickly at the end of the summit. He consulted the ceiling for a moment. I poured a drink and sat down on the edge of his bed, which I'd vacated since Takaka.

'There was a rumour that Diana was involved in an explosion in a Melbourne department store a couple of years before she came to New Zealand.'

'A *bomb?*'

'That's what we suspect. I tried to extract the information out of Rideau, but couldn't get a peep.'

'Was she, do you think?'

'I've no idea, but I dangled it in front of her nose and she didn't like it.'

'Why would that matter?' I asked.

'Because! Because I'd got something over her!' Henry impatiently got up from his desk and tweaked his trousers from his crotch.

'But what if it's not true?'

'Who cares? What matters is that she knew I'd got hold of hostile information and it scared her shitless. That sort of information,' he added, putting his head on one side thoughtfully, 'can always come in useful.'

Later in my room I reflected on the intricacies of politics and its infinitely flammable nature. One careless gesture could ignite a whole forest, with no telling which way the blaze would burn. The politician needed to be prepared for those perilous wind-shifts, which could wipe away safe ground in a moment.

One part of me conceded Henry's superior sense of the unpredictable and how to use it. He was *instinctively* quick on his feet in a way I would never be. Another part of me felt lost: a spare part that he had discarded in favour of a bespectacled girl from Cambridge who would never oppose his opinions, because she had none of her own. Or if she did, they were well hidden.

I sat down and tried to concentrate on some scales, but couldn't. My musicianship had fallen off lately. I wasn't even making high B flat, and it saddened me.

Lydia's brisk voice breezing all the way from New Brighton interrupted my gloom. 'By the way, honey, I've been doing some checking
on your day star.'

'Oh. What did you find?'

My mother cleared her throat. 'In Isaiah it refers to Lucifer as the
son of the morning who, in attempting to usurp God's exalted state,
is felled to the earth.'

'So I was right, then!'

'It looks that way, although interpretations differ. Lucifer is also
known as the shining one. Critics think this is more likely to be a
human king than an angel. Still, there are enough grounds to link
the reference to a revolt in heaven and the fall of Satan.'

'I'm right, I'm right!' I crowed.

'There's something else,' interrupted Lydia quickly.

'What?'

'The planet Venus is the day star. It's supposed to rise in the early
dawn and be extinguished before it reaches its zenith by the sun.'

I stood still. 'Does that mean that Venus and Lucifer are one and
the same?'

'I don't know. It doesn't sound right for a conservative theolo-
gian, does it?'

So I did next what any person who is troubled in their mind
does: I opened the front door and walked out into the afternoon.

Somewhere along a city street, my legs refused to go any further.
I sat in the park mutely watching pigeons with wobbling heads
pecking in the gutter.

Birdshit limed the footpath, crusting like deposits of salt on
the pohutukawa. Passers-by crunched on the mess as they hurried
along. I felt a great gulf of despair welling. There was nothing I could
do. It trembled from the height of an immensely tall building, broke,
and funnelled upwards again like a violent water spout. I was leaking
water. It poured out of my eyes and dribbled over my face. It coursed
over my chin and down my neck in ugly, unstoppable splashes. Not
a single person stopped. Not a soul noticed the titanic heavings and
gasps that doubled me over. I sat with the pigeons and sobbed. I
sobbed for the loss of my hero; the loss of the tiny bloodied cells

sucked from my young body; and because Katherine Mansfield would not let me go.

For a moment I had felt free from that image of Bertha floating to the window one last time and seeing the horribly indifferent pear tree. Janet Seed had made me come alive. Walking in the Gardens in spring and writing about the environment had connected me with a primitive raw energy. I had found treasure in things that a man like Henry couldn't even comprehend without analysing them out of existence. I imagined him taking costive garden walks, his body closed to the marvels of the world around him, his mind glued to Higher Thoughts, knowing so much, but blissfully unknowing. Henry's garden paths had maintained ends and beginnings, and labels with directions printed on them in clear, confident letters. I traitorously wanted maps that confused my senses; invitations to deviate and backtrack that let me, eyes closed, smell my way across the earth. But Janet's usefulness was over with the summit; from now on she would remain trapped forever in an imaginary cupboard, spinning around my head with her memories of Tokoroa, as doomed as an abandoned Sputnik.

With an urgent need for quiet, I began to walk away from the harbour. Wet bush shadows and the soft tufts of feathers on the throats of wild birds were slowly gathering in my head as I walked past the Carillion and the Basin Reserve, past a home for derelicts, past the dingy rows of shops cutting the suburb of Newtown in half. I veered towards Brooklyn, walking always into the sun.

An hour later I passed through the last straggle of houses that separated the fringes of Brooklyn from the bush. The pavement lost its regularity, began to weave under clumps of wild fuchsia, lemon-wood, punga and gorse. The bark on the trees had peeled back like a skin blistered by extreme heat. It curled downwards in flaccid shavings, leaving reddish-brown flecks on clumps of fern and broad-leaf. The air smelt moist. The noise of my shoes was a soft shushing whisper on the leaves that piled the side of the road. Now there was no path at all, the gutters slippery with rain and the juice of plants. The trees wrapped me in their thick stillness. I could hear no birds except my own breath whistling at the back of my throat. The pull up the hill was steep. The road thinned to a clay ribbon, wore itself out in a blind snout of a clearing. Instead of turning back, I pushed upwards. I needed to look out over things.

The broadleaf and fuchsia turned to bracken, the soporific miasma of the bush faded into the sweet musk of gorse, still flaring on the ridges as if it were spring. I felt the chill of the wind cooling my skin too fast; marked the depths of the shadows slipping towards me as the sun nicked the gap in the hills.

But I feared going down into the growing darkness below. Down in the hollows of the city, where people moved and breathed and hoped the things that kept them alive, there was already a giving way: colour fading, clarity turning to shadows. What subtle connivances were transacted between the day world and the underworld! How incessantly they shifted, one from the other.

My legs kept on moving steadily upwards. It was air I needed – air unburdened by the clamour of instructions and secret codes and sordid compromises. Up here, a person could go to sleep and wake up on a golden ladder to somewhere else.

When it began to rain, I laughed. I suppose I'd been expecting drama. Another epiphany, maybe, or Jacob's angel to wrestle with. There was merely a sudden drop in temperature and a furious downpour that froze me to the skin. Torrents of rain pelted through the clouds and hailed on the rocks. It forced runnels and streams to track across the sides of the hills, scoring huge channels. Shivering under a lone macrocarpa, I watched as the wind sucked and spat at the earth, tearing at the delicate scalps of plants, chewing up foliage and breaking the spines of tender shrubs. I was drowning in the rain's exorbitance. My body seemed to pour water like a broken sieve.

The downpour didn't last long, thank goodness – I could have been stuck out on the hills all night. As soon as the wind died, I slid down through the bush and stumbled home. Henry was at the door to meet me.

'Christ, where have you been? What happened?' He vanished and brought back a towel and his bathrobe.

'I've just had another epiphany,' I said. And I fell into his arms and laughed till I cried great gulps of tears that ran down my cheeks and splashed on my sodden clothes.

I've noticed before that Henry always rises brilliantly to a crisis. He did this time too, running me a bath, making a cup of tea and listening to my outbursts of hurt. Meg, fortunately, did not appear. I never found out whether she was home that afternoon, because we went to bed and Henry was as tender as he had ever been. We became lovers again after that. Perhaps he was tired of Meg, perhaps they'd had some falling out: he didn't tell me, but both of us were relieved when not much later she moved out to flat with one of her old friends.

As soon as her room was emptied, I cut that ridiculous padlock from her door. And when I heard her climbing the path for the last time I sat down, pulled out some of the leftover youth summit stationery, and wrote my first story, 'The Story of the Handless Maiden':

A LONG TIME AGO on the other side of the globe there lived a happy family. The miller Johannes and his wife Maria, together with their beautiful daughter Isabelle, lived in a mill-house beside a swiftly flowing stream. 'Chuck chuck,' went the race as it pulled up rushing buckets of water. 'Scree scree,' went the huge plates of stone that ground the corn. Johannes went from the wheel to the grinding stones to the bins of flour and back again. Every day he ground the finest corn in the village. His wife mixed and kneaded until the flour became loaves of bread. When she wasn't flushed from baking bread at the mill, Maria was out tending the family orchard of apples and pears that grew on the other side of the stream.

Meanwhile, Isabelle, her father's darling, sat inside and sewed. She mended the miller's trousers and sewed patches on Maria's sheets. She hemmed sacks for Johannes's flour, curtains and tablecloths for the house, and cut out little muslin gowns for the new baby her mother was expecting in the spring. In the evening, when the sewing was over, Isabelle would take out an embroidery hoop and her needle would flash over the coarse linen cloth. 'Hi-de-hi,' sang the needle, 'hi-de-hi.'

On a day when the flowers in the orchard were as thick and lovely as the stars, the Devil came visiting. He took one look at the beautiful Isabelle sitting by the window plying her needle, strode to the mill-house door, and asked to see Johannes immediately.

'That's a fine girl you have, Miller.'

'To be sure, sir, to be sure.' Johannes was a respectful fellow who saw in front of him a gentleman of some means.

'I'd like her hand in marriage,' the Devil said.

But when her father called for Isabelle, his daughter turned pale, and the miller, who loved his daughter more than anything in the world, was forced to turn her suitor away.

Not a man to be trifled with, the Devil knocked on the mill-house door three more times, but at each visit Isabelle refused to accept his declarations of love. Finally he grew angry. 'If you do not hand Isabelle over to me when I return,' he announced, 'I will take away your mill and your wife and the new baby in her womb, and I will ruin your fields and the fruit in your orchard, and I will make you the laughing-stock of the village.'

So the miller called his daughter back and said to her sadly, 'Daughter, you must marry this man. There is nothing else to be done.'

And Isabelle, wishing to please her father in all things, took his advice and prepared herself to be married.

The night before the Devil came, she bent over her embroidery. She worked and worked until the sky grew white with the dawn. When she looked up, the sun had begun climbing over the hill above the orchard. Soon the stream would be on fire with light.

She crossed to the window, murmured a prayer to the smoke-stained Virgin in the village church, and cast a piece of cloth into the day. Then she bathed and laid her wedding gown on her bed.

The Devil's horse clattered into their yard early. He was eager to be off and wasted no time in pleasantries.

'Let's begin,' he snapped.

With trembling hearts, Johannes and Maria joined the priest and the Devil in the orchard. But as the suitor reached for his beloved's hand, a strange event occurred. All at once there was a thunderous clap of sound and the Devil flew through the air. Again and again he reached out towards Isabelle, but in vain. It was as if she were surrounded by a ring of magic, greater than his.

'If I can't have the girl, then I'll have her hands,' he screamed in a rage. And he pulled out his silver-lipped axe, hurled it through the air and cut off Isabelle's hands at the wrist.

That night the inconsolable miller hanged himself in a pear tree in the orchard. Maria bound her daughter's bleeding arms in muslin remnants, saw her to bed, and sat by the fire until at last she fell asleep. Upstairs, Isabelle, no longer able to pick up her needle, paced to and fro in her room. Finally, as the unhappy night drew to a close, she crossed to her window and leaned out into the dark. She began to sing, and these were the words of her song:

> Go little cloth
> go far away,
> find me my hands
> my sewing hands,
> and my heart
> little cloth, bring them
> back to me.

And from high in the sky the piece of embroidery heard the words of the maiden and sped away across time looking for Isabelle's heart.

Now, when Isabelle saw that her days of innocence were over, she left Maria in the mill-house alone, the unborn baby still cleaving sleepily to her ribs, and set off across the fields. By evening she had reached the beginnings of a vast forest, which was set apart from the neighbouring farmland by a deep and swiftly flowing river. As she dipped her foot in the water, from the other side came a small boat, the oarsman barely visible in the disappearing light.

Indicating that she was to step aboard, the oarsman turned the craft in the direction of the far shore. As they drew near the forest, which looked black as the darkest of dreams, Isabelle saw something that had not been visible from the other side. At the foot of the trees stood an orchard surrounded with silver gates. The smell of ripe fruit was indescribable.

The boatman left her on the shore and rowed away, while Isabelle entered the silver gates that guarded the orchard and walked under laden trees until she came to a table set in the grass, upon which sat a wooden bowl full of golden fruit. Bending down until her lips touched the rim of the bowl, she ate until her hunger was satisfied.

Then she arose from the table, passed through the silver gates on the other side and crossed into the forest, which was already full of the chatter of night. Birds made predatory swoops in the branches, beasts of prey growled close to the narrow path that wound among the trees. In the distance a storm arose. Clouds thickened and boiled around the face of the moon until the way ahead became obscured by thick darkness. Above, thunder rattled the tops of the trees, lightning and rain hissed in angry combat.

Just then a stroke of lightning split the trunk of the fir beneath which she had taken shelter and struck the girl a blow on the side of the head. She remembered nothing until she woke in a small room with a bearded face bending over her. The woodcutter who had rescued her from the storm dressed her head and inspected her closely. Without saying a word, he crossed to an alcove in the room and emerged with a pair of wooden hands. He carefully strapped them to the wrists of his guest, who thanked him, picked up her bundle of things and departed.

This time the path led her back to the orchard, where again she broke her journey with a meal of the enchanted golden fruit, this evening laid out on a silver platter. And so she returned to her village and Maria with a new pair of hands and a story of a strange orchard over the river.

In due course, Maria's baby was born, and Isabelle took care of the boy until he grew old enough to return his father's mill to its former use. He was a clever fellow, and one day, when work was over, made his sister a pair of hands from beaten silver. The new hands were dextrous, renewing her skill with the needle so that once more she made clothes for the family and fine furnishings for their home.

Over the years, Maria grew old and frail and thought more often of Johannes and their love for each other, which had been blasted by the Devil's cruelty. She called her daughter to her and whispered faintly in her ear, 'Daughter, fetch me some fruit from your orchard over the water, for I have a mind to die with its scent in my face.'

So Isabelle obeyed her mother and crossed to the orchard with the silver gates, where she found the table spread with the very piece of embroidery she had cast into the morning all those years before. On it was a single golden globe sitting in the hollow of a hand of flesh. The hand was the hand of an old woman, worn with hard work. Remembering that the orchard was a benign place, Isabelle did not hesitate but picked up the fruit from the hollow of flesh, whereupon the hand vanished. She returned home and fed it to her mother piece by piece, watching as Maria drew away from her, calling her husband's name.

When Isabelle woke the following day, she found that she had grown two pink hands, as small and perfect as a baby's. Throughout that spring the hands continued to grow until, towards autumn, when the smell of ripe things filled the air, Isabelle turned to her brother and said, 'I have spent my life wandering handless in a country of giants, and now I have come into my own.'

The maiden then slipped over her head a surplice of the purest blue, kissed her brother goodbye, and went into the morning to find her Prince.

And, 'Hi-de-hi,' sang her bright flashing needle, 'hi-de-hi.'

Writing the handless maiden's tale did not rescue me from the curse of the Mansfields, for Henry certainly strayed after that, more than once. But I kept the relationship going and didn't regret it. Henry disapproved of my writing. I'm convinced the focus of imagination on the small things, and the way it takes to trackless paths, made him uncomfortable, so after showing him that one first story, I hid the rest in a box.

To this day, the appearance of the girl who lost and found her hands remains a mystery. Yes, I'd studied myth, but this story seemed to spring out of nowhere. As we both agreed, there was no logical connection between the storm on Brooklyn Hill and the story, which Jung would have said was simply an archetype for the loss of innocence. I felt no real compunction for my heroine, although she was surely more in charge of her tragic life than Bertha Young. Nor did I connect Isabelle's journey with my own. What mattered was that we had retrieved our lives together after the estrangement over the summit; our studies were going well; and Lydia had finally got rid of her concordance.

I wondered aloud whether Henry ought to be taking his politics further while I might enrol for a course in creative writing, but he merely chuckled and suggested the *School Journal* as a suitable outlet. At the time, I saw his point. Some people, we agreed, lived and wrote quaint lyrical stories for audiences willing to be deluded. The politician inhabited a larger system and lived a greater, truer story.

It came as no surprise to Henry that I fell into the first category. After all, I had Katherine Mansfield in my blood.

Diana's story

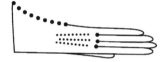

Lucky last, my father said when I was born, and he was right. I've seen, over and over in life, rivals falling before they reached the post, and in my line of business, getting there is everything. Never believe that old Buddhist rhetoric about the joy of the journey. It's bullshit.

From the time Dad saw my mat of red hair, he knew I was marked for something special. He called me Diana after his own mother, and Mum, who usually had all the say in dishing out family names, was too exhausted to disagree. Diana: Lady of the Beasts, mistress of wild things, goddess of hunter and hunted. I was in good hands. I never did get into all that goddess worship women's groups are full of now, but I certainly called on Diana when I needed her, and she never let me down. Sure, I fell into scrapes when I was young. It's the only way to learn. But I discovered how resilient I was; how I seemed to know instinctively that if you hunkered down till the crisis blew over, nothing was out of reach. If Diana is animate in any sense of the word, I like to see her as having given me a choice for my life: *Is it hunting that you want most, or would you rather be chased?* As if there were a choice. I'd always loved the sense of mastery my own body gave me, and after Jessie, I refused to surrender that to anyone. Lovers, or bosses.

My story begins in the Botanic Gardens. It was summer. Heat-wave weather, with the smell of smoke drifting over the city from the mountains. I'd run away from the hostel my parents wanted me to go to in Melbourne and come to Sydney, with a few books and clothes crammed into an old pigskin bag. The city buzzed: protest meetings and teach-ins went on all night. We took our sleeping bags, shared washrooms with the derelicts. Sometimes people would occupy an empty house for days before anyone noticed. I began camping out in the Gardens, eating fruit and reading Karl Marx, and attending one Stop the War meeting after the other.

This particular afternoon I'd got totally fed up with roughing it, and was thinking of calling home and asking my father to send me a cheque. Mosquitoes had turned my arms and legs septic. Diarrhoea was gripping my stomach so badly I could hardly stand. I knew I shouldn't have kept the chicken for so long, but I hoarded stuff up, stashing it in the station lockers, never a guarantee of good health. It must have looked excruciating – a vagrant adolescent with long, un-kempt hair and a mild case of botulism rolling around on the grass with the ibises. As I was groaning, I heard Jimi Hendrix's 'All Along the Watchtower' coming full blast from the direction of the Shade House. The usual crowd had gathered to watch an event going on just outside the main doors. I recognised almost everyone. (By then I'd made friends with a couple of dozen drop-outs and bums, includ-ing Peter and John, mad as fruit-loops, self-named after the disciples of Jesus. They wore ragged clothing and grew bird's-nest beards in which old pieces of egg and toast trembled as they spat *Fuck the war!* and *Jesus saves!* at anyone who would listen.) The atmosphere that day crackled with electricity. It felt festive, light-hearted. Peter and John wove through the crowd giving out old pamphlets left over from last week's demo, wheedling for coins. An enterprising Italian friend of mine had borrowed his father's gelato machine and was busy selling housewives coloured ices. I forgot my growling stomach; pushed my way over to stand near the pots flanking the steps. Among crimson lilies and plants bearing huge golden-spotted leaves, jugglers and tumblers and girls with painted faces showed us how the greedy multinational companies were oppressing the poor. There were clowns dressed as wealthy banana growers, American capitalists and Latin American peasants.

We took protesting seriously in those days. Here was a bunch of circus performers making us laugh at capitalism! Amazing to see you could get into the drama of politics and enjoy yourself without feeling guilty. We watched, entranced, as they went through their routine: a mix of acrobatics, placards and mime. I loved the whole show, which got a huge round of applause.

Afterwards they went through the crowd.

'Dig deep for the Red Letters, comrades!' shouted their leader, tossing the coins he'd collected into a black cap right under my nose.

Red Letters: I liked that. My head full of communist heroes, I couldn't think of a better way of bringing liberation to the masses than performances like theirs.

'Hi,' I said queasily. 'Look, I haven't got any money but I think you're doing a great job,' and then I spewed all over his sandals.

After they'd cleaned me up (not Josh, ringleader of the Red Letters – it wasn't his thing), I decided I wanted to use my socialist education and be a clown. That's how I got started with the Letters. It was amateurish, but we did get some great information from those days. I'm sure our protests were more effective because of my work, and that time we stormed an intelligence post in Melbourne was a coup.

We modelled ourselves on Soviet street-theatre troupes, making their politics more upbeat with clowns, jugglers and fire-spinners. Whenever the Letters felt the papers had smoked over the reporting of the war, for instance, we woke up the street crowd with theatre, then hit them with placards and skits about the real state of Vietnam.

Not long after the Melbourne protest, Josh and the Letters sent me to Wellington. Cunning of them. Josh knew I had the money; it clearly wasn't a question of their supporting me – he cynically knew I would go if it meant advancing the cause.

The capital of New Zealand wasn't nearly as beautiful as Sydney, and had a miserable climate I never got used to. Sydney harbour is truly the world's most beautiful. Wellingtonians go on about theirs, but it's not a patch on the sparkling water, the painted ferries, the long walks at Manly that I'd come to love. It had been a huge shock arriving in Wellington and realising the rawness of the Left there, its disorganisation and ineffectiveness. We were more awake in Sydney. That's why I'd come, an emissary from the Red Letters with training in Marx and clown school in equal measure, instructed to stir the New Zealand pot until it burned.

I took my brief very seriously. I burrowed in, made friends, gained confidences, constructed alliances with the right people. It didn't occur to me till a month into my stay to scrutinise Josh's reasons for sending me. Such as: I'd been his only rival, had threatened his authority, and so he'd exiled me to a country where people had frozen doll-sized hearts and were insufferably, falsely polite. If I had to name a national animal for New Zealand, I would have suggested the hyena, which laughs when it should be crying.

Today, I can't believe how many of my old acquaintances in New Zealand have sold themselves so cheaply. Henry Ballantyne had a stint as a life coach before becoming a grossly overweight MP who spends too much time in his constituents' beds. His relationship with Steph Jackson, the only one of his women I thought worth anything intellectually, failed after he took up politics again. Meg Shepherd, that thieving flatmate of Lou's (and yes, I admit, I did have a thing for Meg), has turned into a craft artist, with some of her work currently travelling around galleries in America. How we'd ever managed to orchestrate a youth summit together, even if it was a disaster, struck me now as impressive. Where were all the really smart minds that made it in New Zealand in the eighties and nineties? I suppose most of them were younger than us. Their mothers were probably remnants of our old women's collectives that fought for abortion, and then went out and incubated themselves in dreary suburbs.

Christ, how far I've travelled, and how subtle the workings of power now. Henry thinks he's at its nub. He doesn't seem to realise that national politics is just a lot of window-dressing for the real transactions, which go on in virtual space when he's snoring on some baa-lamb's pillow.

Not that I arrived at enlightenment overnight. Finding the location of *real* politics and putting myself there, right in its navel, took a long time. It's too dramatic to say I've been to hell and back. I've paid, big-time, though, for mistakes. Whereas Henry Ballantyne got away with his balls-ups scot-free.

Since he's still muscling into the limelight provided by the cheap press, I feel obliged to put his story right. Ideal Pacific, my old employers, are considering throwing venture capital at one of his new schemes to open up Karamea, and want whatever dirt I can dig up. That's how the corporation works: trading to their advantage on the back of dirty information. Having been given the push five years ago, I couldn't have felt more surprised when out of the blue someone from Ideal Pacific called and offered me a fixed-term contract to provide a case history of a potential investor.

Namely, the Honourable Henry Benjamin Ballantyne.

A blast from the past is the expression people use. It was, too. I put my other contracts aside and set to work.

You'd think the job would have been easy. After all, spying on people has been my life's work. As I unearth more, I can feel the past that I had willed asleep, begin to stir. It is there breathing down my neck as I scuttle through memory banks looking to retrieve old scenes buried more than thirty years ago. It is still there, laughing, as I scuttle furtively back, dragging information for Ideal Pacific onto my desk.

I remember how once it was mandatory to speak of the way politics and the personal were inextricable. Liberation meant throwing off oppressive personal habits, as well as protesting outside embassies and printing illegal newspapers. Curiously, now that these phrases have been ditched, I'm beginning to find them true again. How can people believe that privacy is a reality these days? Everything's in the public domain; Christ, you can't even fart without someone turning it into a sound byte.

I find myself working later and later. In my Ponsonby apartment, the office is packed with all this hyper-techno stuff: blue screen and halogen, terminal never down, fax and printer leads worming like spaghetti all over the floor. I do out-work for private companies and banks. Risk assessment, information retrieval, that sort of thing. Like most of my colleagues, I've become more comfortable with the engrossing dramas of cyberspace. Raking up the past is a habit I don't usually like to indulge, because the past thirty years of my life are littered with abandoned piles of luggage. I've never exhumed anything by choice.

Grave dirt! Okay, that's how it will start: Henry and I hanging out in the Wellington cemetery. Early March, 1972: a year or so after I'd arrived in the capital, so I knew a thing or two by then. First, that it was an improbable evening weather-wise – it was pouring with rain, in fact. That time of the year you'd expect overcast – after all, it was Wellington – but not rain. I hadn't even brought a jacket, while Henry was sporting this dodgy-looking duffel-coat with half the toggles missing. Apparently he'd just had a holiday in Christchurch with his girlfriend, whose parents had a delinquent dog.

I suggested decamping to his flat in Mt Victoria, but he didn't seem keen on that. We'd first met at a student meeting in favour of liberalising the abortion laws. Then we had briefly touched base at another protest, and had a drunken tumble in bed one night in November after finals, but the cemetery meeting was our first really serious exchange. (Incidentally, speaking of abortion, Henry fought like a maniac for the right to dish out free contraceptives to high-school girls. It wasn't till later that we heard about the two sixteen-year-olds he'd taken to a Coromandel bach when he was just a first-year.) Naturally, I thought our meeting that night was to be political chat followed by sex, but the fucking never eventuated, and the way the evening unfolded was probably the reason.

You have to remember that men have never rung my bells. All the same, in those exciting early years, after hiving off from Ballarat, I did occasionally make an exception. Henry was worth a try. I wanted to get inside this guy's head, find out how he thought about the world, check out his activism. It didn't take long to work out he was more of an ideas person than someone you'd want next to you in the front line, but I gave him plenty of chances. He was just that sort of man.

Since my employers are now wanting a canny appraisal of his underbelly and public face in equal measure, it's time to put words to his extraordinary successes. Particularly when it came to resurrecting himself, grinning shamelessly, after a crushing defeat in student politics. Not to mention his manipulation of me. I squirm all this time down the track that I didn't wake to him sooner, although I like to think that was because I had other things to worry about. I didn't acquire ruthless focus till my thirties.

The night in the cemetery got off to a bad start when he nagged me for not bringing my raincoat, insisting on explaining his plan to hijack the next SRC instead of going down to the rotunda. A bit of rain never hurt anyone, but I was like a homesick puppy that first year in Wellington. The slightest downpour sent me shivering for cover. I ground my teeth as water dripped down my nose and cold trails of rain wound serpent-like under my collar. The weird gothic feel to the evening – the half-crouching over broken-teeth tomb-stones; the wind driving the rain into scores of dull black rivulets coursing over crumbling plaques – only struck me later. Meg Shep-herd, I suspect, would have lapped it up.

'Henry,' I muttered, 'we'd better get inside, it's fucking freezing out here.'

He peered at me through the torrent of words. You know the language I mean – the cliques, counter-cliques, Left and Right, phonies, spies and smart politicos. Everyone significant was marked on his map. And he was as taut as a violin, his voice strangely high-pitched and throatless, not wanting to stop talking. 'That's the trouble with Australians.' He enunciated the word mockingly. 'They can't cut the mustard when it comes to a good downpour.'

Henry Ballantyne's mind could be fierce as a welding torch, but its heat covered up some singular lacks. He had only the most rudi-mentary grasp of Pacific geography and imagined that all Austra-lians knew about was flies and heat. Of course we did, but I came from inland, where the nights could freeze the snow off Santa's bum.

'Look, I'm not standing here with you in the bloody rain. Either we go somewhere else or I'm off.'

His concentration flickered. 'Oh, all right then. I suppose it would be too much for you to suggest a place?'

'What about Jessie's?' He wasn't expecting that. I might be an Australian, but I'd spent plenty of nights on the streets when he was up to his bourgeois business in Days Bay. Jessie sold cool pancakes, and she was cute, with a belly to die for, and almond-pink ears I wanted to lick with the tip of my tongue.

'Let's go,' he grunted, so we traipsed down one of those hideously endless sets of steps to the city as the rain eased and the stars set into freezing patterns above us.

'Jesus, it's full of queers,' he burst out as soon as we walked in. 'So that's your style. I must say I'm not surprised.' He cocked a malicious eye at me as we unrolled the forks from their napkins. 'I'll have honey and cinnamon with chocolate syrup on the side,' he said without looking up, as Jessie stood over us and breathed out her delicious kitchen smells. 'Yes, and make that a coffee too.'

I suppose I should have admitted to it then, but I didn't. 'Don't be ridiculous,' I said, 'I've just got a thing for pancakes.'

He shrugged. 'Well, where were we, then?'

He'd lost interest in the queer question immediately; I'm sure he didn't suspect I was lying. Men did find me attractive. My head was covered in bright red waves that dropped untidily to halfway down my back. My skin was powdery pale and I had pleasantly large green-grey eyes. Not every Aussie woman has skin like a dried fruit. Not every gay girl looks like a man, even if they do wear trousers all the time. It took me another year to get my hair cropped, and even then I regretted the loss of pulling power, which had been so handy with some of those vain and stupid males I came across at university.

'You were talking about Arthur Meyer. The protest at the Taiwanese embassy.'

'Christ, yes, that's right. Pity you weren't there to see him looking like a prick from the moment he stood up. I had to go over and rescue the situation.'

'What did you do?' I prompted.

'Snatched the bloody megaphone, of course,' he said. 'Led them to the gates myself. I got up and told them how the Taiwanese had stolen all these ancient treasures from China and ferried them across the straits.'

I looked doubtfully at his body, wondering if there'd been a fight. 'That's all?' Wondering, too, why he had to take the cultural approach. It was so elitist.

'No – shit, no. That was just to get them going – you can't feed them political stuff all the time. Young people have to be led from what they know to what they don't know. They need teaching.

They're full of ignorance here, Diana. Nothing wrong with talking Ming vases if they've got a meaningful purpose.'

He sneered, and that was the moment I really began to dislike him. His reasoning sounded too much like Josh, my old Red Letters leader. Spoken out loud in the warm steamy coffee bar, it seemed snobbish and self-interested. I didn't want Jessie to hear the contempt in his voice, or think he was my friend, so I attacked my pancakes in silence.

'What's the Left in Sydney up to these days? Apart from that weirdo woman, of course.'

Henry hadn't noticed that his duffel-coat was splashed with chocolate.

'You mean Germaine Greer? Be careful, she's a relative of mine.' A lie, but a useful one. Some lies add to your authenticity, and I knew just enough about Greer's life not to get myself into trouble.

'Shit a brick! Who would have thought a girl from Ballarat would have had such a famous connection?'

'It's a distant connection; we're not exactly close. And,' I went on patiently, 'I'm not exactly into her politics. She lacks a sound analysis.'

He seemed pleased. I suppose he thought we were on the same side when it came to errant feminists who spent more time talking about their personal lives, or the novels they'd read, instead of digging away at the roots of global oppression.

'Greer aside, the Left are more in touch there than they are in Wellington,' I added calmly.

He didn't like that, although he knew it was true that his country had the mindset of a province. After Sydney, it had been like coming to the back-end of the universe. I mean, people didn't read deeply here; they laughed at the very idea of a study group on activism. Most had no notion of the sacrifice politics required. Had they ever heard about Paulo Freire? Huey Newton and the Five? Of course not. To New Zealanders, the Black Panthers were a gang of criminals, social welfare stoodges who took tourists around Harlem on chartered buses.

The first time we'd met, I'd been able to let drop I knew the whole of *Das Kapital*, thank you very much, which was more than he'd ever read of Marx, *and* I'd met Stokeley Carmichael.

Meanwhile, my concentration was going. All I felt like doing was burying my face in Jessie's belly, but she'd paid me no notice the weeks I'd been coming. I stared glumly at her bird-slender back wrapped in a white cotton shirt so tight you could see her ribs moving up and down, listening to Henry's conclusion to the protest, which had ended with one of his friends slamming the gates on an embassy car and getting arrested.

'We made real headway that night with the press,' he gloated. 'Do you know they now make a point of calling before any march for a statement?' He'd just discovered the chocolate stain and was stealthily trying to remove it.

'What's new? Everyone's marching now,' I yawned. 'But I'm glad you've got the confidence of the press. Might make a difference when something really important comes up.'

'What do you mean?' he asked suspiciously.

'Well, I thought the arms committee was talking about a military training weekend.' One of the titbits I'd picked up from Lou Waters, a Kiwi of unusually sound analysis. Josh would have approved of her dedication. A good Red Letter always analyses while everyone else is dreaming, Josh used to tell us, and on that count he was right. Amazing they were to just miss meeting each other properly in Sydney by a matter of hours.

(Some months later, I'd accompanied Lou on the plane so she could attend the development forum at the University of New South Wales. While she networked with Pacific radicals, I caught up with Josh. It was not an unqualified success. Largely because Henry happened to have flown over to the forum too, and took it into his head to engage Josh in a nasty debate that saw the two of them getting quite physical. It has to be said that Henry definitely came off worst.)

I wonder whether, if things had been different with Josh, Lou and I would have stayed on in Australia.

I sigh. It is Henry Ballantyne's history I am being employed to write, not Lou's.

Which doesn't stop me thinking of more personal ones . . .

'Okay, okay,' Henry said that night over pancakes, the prospect of unwelcome publicity causing him to frown. 'Jesus, the last thing we want is the Right squealing to the press.'

'Or the police,' I put in.

He looked even more concerned. A police record never appealed to him, because he was always worried about his constituency: more so as he grew older and got into Parliament. Besides, a conviction would put him on a level with the attention-getter Arthur Meyer, who'd had more summonses, he told me, than I'd had sliced bread.

'Shit no,' he continued, 'that would be a disaster. I don't support the use of violence under any circumstances.'

I looked around the restaurant, which was almost empty. It being the middle of the week, they closed at 10 p.m., with Jessie pushing everyone out on the dot, slamming chairs up on tables as if she had better things to do with her evening than wait on us. All at once I was sick of Henry's company, and I think he felt the same, looking at me quizzically as if there should have been a spark, as if I had proved disappointing hunting and he didn't know why. Okay, seduction's not going to work, I thought. Anyway, he didn't turn me on.

'Hey,' I said, taking our dishes to the counter, hoping Jessie would come out from the kitchen and smile, dusting her hands off on her overalls, flushed from the heat in the room and cooking all those pancakes, 'it was good talking to you, Henry, let's do this again.'

'Yeah, sure,' he said, fastening his briefcase. 'Well, off home now, got some papers to read tonight.' He looked over my head, still puzzled at how the evening had developed, different instincts at war with each other inside him.

At least I knew what I wanted.

I went home then too, all the way back up those steps to my room on The Terrace, instead of trying to follow Jessie, as I often did. Somehow it didn't surprise me that the meeting with Henry had ended with me sitting up in bed, teeth done by eleven, reading over the instructions from Josh about student activists in case I'd missed something. There I was, propped up against a pillow that felt as if it had been stuffed with corncobs, the room musty with damp and old smoke, nursing the hots for a cook who lived in Hataitai.

I slipped into a heavy sleep and dreamed not of Jessie, but of Henry Ballantyne, who was shouting instructions for loading an automatic rifle from the end of a very long corridor.

I don't properly remember the next week, my biggest regret ever, because I got lucky. Because that cold March, with wind whipping the clouds into stony banks of grey and buckled hunks of livid metal, with gulls shrill and hungry on the wharves and a frustration in my gut so great it made me ravenous, I ran into Jessie on an impulse trip to the market. She was carrying an enormous bag of oranges and an armful of flowers: chrysanthemums, I think. In any case, they were flaming with colour, and just as we passed each other, the bag of fruit tore open and oranges rolled all over the street. Luck, I suppose it was, or synchronicity, if you're Steph Jackson. I could have invoked the gods and given my namesake the credit, but I didn't. I was still young enough to think that those sorts of gifts frequently fell out of the sky for people like me blessed with good health, a vigorous mind and parents who had treated me with that unique indulgence that comes the way of last children.

'Thanks,' she said, as I picked up the oranges and handed them to her, stupidly keeping my eyes on the pavement. *Stupidly*, when all I wanted to do was put my arms around her and smell that scent of wheaten flour and rich butter and whatever goddamn syrup she'd be making out of those oranges.

'Haven't I seen you before?'

Oh glory, she had stopped. Now she had turned around, angling her head like a curious bird. Now she was speaking to me, screwing up her face like she'd spied something delicious just out of reach.

I looked up. It was too hard to stare at the ground, which seemed to be melting beneath my feet, dissolving in a sticky torrent. 'I come to your place some nights — you know, Jessie's Pancakes,' I said, as she stared at me.

'Oh, of course you do. I've seen you there. Now I remember.' She smiled.

That's what did it — that's what gave me a memory lapse, I mean. She had eyes the colour of bitter chocolate, I swear. And the look she gave me, her lips impossibly full in a face as small as a feral pixie's, was no ordinary look, I told myself later. Didn't she feel it too, the heat that rose off our bodies so that we must have been steaming in the air, the sharp morning wind whipping around the corner of Turners and Growers while we lurched into each other's eyes?

'You came in last night with a guy.'

God, she thought Henry was my lover.

'That creep? Not likely,' I spluttered, and meant it.

We smiled dumbly at each other some more, and then when even I felt it was time to get lost, Jessie said, 'Look, ah . . .'

'Diana.'

'Yeah, well, we're not opening till later and I need to do some prepping this morning. Wanna help out?'

You bet I did. I wanted lots of things, but being as close as possible to this improbably small baker of pancakes (weren't cooks meant to be fat? This one was Thumbelina, so small I could circle her wrists with my hands and have room to spare) was what I wanted most.

The morning sun poured like a golden yolk through the fanlights as we stood in the café's kitchen. Jessie was making batter while I was trying to manipulate a juicer, surrounded by a mountain of torn fruit peel. My hands were sticky and the machine was clogged with beads of bright orange flesh. She caught me looking at her, grinned wickedly, stuck her tongue between her teeth. It made her look like a wolf, a timberwolf with a black pelt and a white furred face. I blushed. Me, lover of half the Red Letters, men and women both, my first sexual conquest when I was not much more than fifteen! Jessie made me feel like an innocent. I stood dumbly while she ran a white-floured finger along my collarbone, and then her tongue, slicking the juice from my hands and the soft part of my arms, biting at my shirt buttons. I sighed, feeling the hair stand in the soft hollow at the base of my scalp as she breathed over me.

I've forgotten the rest. What she said, what I said, what came next. I just remember waking up next morning in her bed with the smell of coffee and eggs cooking. God, I couldn't even remember getting on the bus home.

'Hi, you there, giddup,' said a voice. A steaming cup of coffee was slapped down next to me. 'Rise and shine, sweetie. I've got work to do.'

What had I expected, whistles and party hats? Her abruptness cooled me off faster than a cold shower in the bush.

'How about a good-morning kiss?' I wheedled, wanting to hold on to this moment, frightened of the prospect of spending the rest of the day in my room on The Terrace. Jessie had the pleasurable mindlessness of pancake slurry to make, which she didn't ask me to share with her today, which also meant that it was time to get back to Henry Ballantyne. In this cold toy-town I had been exiled to, even the wolves froze you out.

I couldn't concentrate on student activism at all that day, or for weeks afterwards. Jessie called the next day with another invitation to help in the kitchen. I couldn't get there fast enough. Later, in her bathroom, I inspected the love-bites around my throat while a hungry face looked back. My lover had filled me with an emptiness I hadn't known before. Not even Josh had had that effect. All my fucking had been perfunctory, I guess; I'd never had a crush on anyone. Now I spent days lying mooning on my bed, littered with papers and files and discarded underwear, staring up at the pressed-tin ceiling, waiting for the telephone to ring. I imagined Jessie's cool voice drawling into the phone, nasal and matter-of-fact, but lazy, too, living without a thought, without the dreaded analysis that every Red Letter had to have, living like a wild animal in the moment.

From the time he first knew, Henry resented my friendship with Jessie. She used to turn up around lunchtime, sweeping me off in a friend's car to a picnic with black bread and cream cheeses and salami bought on the way and stuffed into her pack. I'd leave him glowering disapprovingly in the student cafe, wedded to his briefcase and minutes. He thought her totally empty-headed and selfish. She was ruining my career as a politician, as far as he was concerned. Come to think of it, being lovers with a woman like Jessie was the best cover I've ever had, and I wish, for all sorts of reasons, it had lasted longer.

Most often we drove to Makara, where the trees were swept over into twisted shapes by the winds that rushed in from the sea, and the noise of the booming waves and wheeling birds exhilarated us both. We'd make love on some damp patch of scrub, biting lips, tasting the salt. I'd come back with burned skin and blood that boiled in my chest. My heart hammered in my ears almost constantly during that month.

Once, Henry had had enough. His surveillance antennae detected I was about to be whisked away from yet another crucial meeting on government-aid targets, so he arrived at Jessie's flat while we were still in bed. I dived into the shower as Jessie got up, spectacularly naked, to make breakfast. There was an urgent thumping on the front door. I could feel the door's angry vibrations rising up through my feet in the bathroom. The noise seemed to go on for a long time.

'Door!' I yelled, from underneath my dripping hair.

'Get it yourself!' Jessie yelled back. 'Or come and stir the bloody porridge.'

I was used to her short temper in the mornings. Henry wasn't.

'I know you're in there, Diana! Open the door, damn it, it's Ballantyne.'

Silence in the kitchen. Jessie would be stirring the porridge, methodically adding the milk and salt, stirring again, wilfully deaf to the commotion, a benign look settling over her face. I knew exactly how much she would be enjoying this.

The battering continued. My associate didn't give up easily, and had begun to pound away at the door rhythmically with his briefcase.

By now Jessie was rolling her eyes in disgust. 'Get rid of him, can't you?' she said loudly. Manners were never her strong suit.

Easier said. Any moment there would be splinters in the hall and an ugly piece of smashed panelling. I wrenched the door open. We confronted each other, Henry flushed and slightly out of breath, which was rare for him. He was very fit when he was young. And me, truculent that I'd had my privacy invaded, a little guilty I'd been planning to skip the meeting to be with Jessie. Who, naturally, made no effort to help. She simply gave Henry a scornful once-over before turning back to the stove.

'Thanks very much, Fahey. What the hell do you think you're

up to?' He strode through into the kitchen, dropping his bag onto a chair.

Jessie's breasts bobbed jauntily as she whisked a wooden spoon around the porridge pot.

The invader's eyes popped. He swallowed, following the shadows freckling her thighs.

'I don't know about you, hon, but I just can't stand lumpy porridge,' my lover said to the air.

I watched her out of the corner of my eye.

'Oh,' as if she'd just noticed him, 'and who the hell is this?'

'You've met before. In the café,' I said, frustrated with them both. 'This is my friend who makes the pancakes. Jess, Henry is in student politics.'

He flashed his most attractive smile in Jessie's direction. 'Pleased to meet you. I'm Ballantyne, Henry Ballantyne.'

Silence.

'I say, isn't that a bit risky?'

'Risky?'

Henry gestured in the direction of the stove. 'When I cook porridge, it goes everywhere. Always wear protective covering. Hah! When I cook, that is. Steph's a bloody fiend in the kitchen.'

Another silence, broken by hot plops from the saucepan.

'You know, I've always thought we don't do enough with the gay lobby,' he said brightly. 'Tell me, Jessie, what's your position on international aid?'

I fiddled with the breakfast plates. Jessie was sterner. The silence went on a long time.

Henry broke first. 'Mmmm, something smells good. What about a cup of coffee, Diana? I'm fucking parched.' He ran his eyes over the clutter on the bench. 'My God, look at this,' he blanched, holding up an empty wine bottle. 'It's South African!'

Jessie sprang. 'Like hell you'll drink our coffee,' she shouted. Her body quivered. 'I don't care who you are, just get the fuck out of my house!' She launched herself at him, spitting angrily as if she would tear the skin off his face.

They never met again, I made sure of that. Henry had this fantasy of communicating with the masses, but when it came down to it, he was useless at talking to anyone remotely ordinary. Jessie took such a dislike to him that the next time he turned up at Dixon Street for a pancake, she refused to serve him.

Briefly, politics withdrew behind a veil. My passion for engagement cooled and grew a skin, which settled in a stolid blanket over everything. Except when it came to engaging with my lover's body. Then my feelings seeped through, raw and glistening. Not yet bound, I remember thinking, into a gelatinous mass like the moulded fruit trapped unopened for years on our Ballarat pantry shelves. If we hadn't broken up, I wonder if I would have been able to stick the discipline of politics. Perhaps I should have deserted my spying right then for something more banal. Maybe we could have set up house in Makara and I could have written a novel. I'd wave Jess goodbye as she drove off for the day. There'd be a nourishing dinner waiting for her when she got back in the small hours, and we'd listen to music in the dark, floating scented candles on our outdoor fire-bath.

If only. It didn't turn out like that. For a while I continued to live totally inside a transparent sphere that gave all smells and tastes, all sensations, my lover's name. Meetings came and went. I neglected to call Josh. Lurching from day to delicious day like a drunk woman, I never thought about an end.

When one evening Jessie didn't telephone, and then the next and the next, I was gobsmacked. When I tried to call, she hung up on me; at least I suppose it was her. It could have been another amorous eater of pancakes.

You're just a choke-chained bitch, I told myself cruelly after we hadn't seen each other for a week. Get over it.

'Serve you right,' said Henry, and meant it.

Getting over first love is unforgettable, people say, and for once I could agree with popular opinion. Recovering from being dumped by Jessie took more time than I care to remember, and I don't think I've ever loved any woman with such abandon since.

When I picked up Guevara and *Das Kapital* again, I could hardly understand the language. Jessie, like Meg Shepherd, hadn't the slightest interest in politics, which had suited me fine. I used to watch her and see how real she was in her body, how her light, muscled frame came alive when we touched each other, how we shamelessly growled and nipped. That place in your mind that just *is* before you start to think about why it is: that's what we shared. She'd opened me up to a part of myself I'd never seen before, and it devastated me that she'd trotted briskly out of my life without even saying goodbye.

I was careful not to go back for pancakes again, finding another place, scummier than Jessie's, to pass the time. I tried whisky briefly, but I've never been that good with alcohol and, after vomiting into a gutter, I stuck to coffee and vile-tasting herbal teas.

As for political analysis, I went back to it with mixed feelings. It felt more like a retreat, and that was an experience I hadn't met before. Nowadays, compromise is such a part of life, your head so full of words like 'sublimation', that you know it's okay to bury yourself in work for less-than-perfect reasons. Back then, I took out my frustration on Henry Ballantyne.

He'd co-opted me onto his summit committee and all had been progressing nicely until I realised we might not end up on the same side once it actually got going. Our agendas were seriously different: who was I kidding? Okay, Josh had been particularly emphatic about shadowing potential allies, but despite Ballantyne's openness to political discussion, I wasn't as sure as I had been that Henry was open in the way Josh expected.

So one miserable evening towards the end of May, I took a taxi from The Terrace to Mt Victoria, arriving at a flat draped in darkness, apart from a small light coming from the hall. I hoped, as I marched up the path, that the light was Henry's. It would make our discussion more fraternal.

To my surprise, I encountered Meg Shepherd after pulling on the rusted doorbell. It wheezed away inside the house and, as the asthmatic chiming died away, her unmistakable chunky form appeared. Neither of us had the first clue what to say.

'Well. Meg. Hello there. Anyone home?'

'I am,' she said.

See what I mean? Meg could be like that.

'Oh. I'd hoped to be able to see Henry. Is he in, do you know?'

'I live here now,' said Meg, pushing at her glasses.

'Great.' Non-sequiturs always defeated me. 'Um, is Henry there?' I weakly repeated myself.

All of a sudden, the drifts of rain and wind turned nasty. I shivered, pulled up my coat collar.

'He might be,' Meg said evasively. 'Henry, are you here?'

And then Ballantyne, wrapped in a towelling robe, put his head around the door. I was still stranded, coat dripping, on the front steps.

'Good Lord, Diana! What the hell are you both doing? Come in out of the wet. Meg, how about a cup of coffee for our guest?'

Henry ushered me into the hall. 'I've just got out of the bath. The caliphont's been playing up and we've only this afternoon had it fixed.'

Never mind your bloody caliphont, I thought. 'Look, Henry,' I began, 'I've come to talk about the summit with you. It's about time we thrashed out our differences, don't you think? I mean, neither of us wants a showdown at the hui, do we?'

He blinked.

I sailed in. To hell with the bathrobe.

And emerged more or less intact, save the smarting from his swipe at Red Letters.

Because of Meg's presence, we were obliged to retire to Henry's office. God, he had an impressive collection of books. I spied some old favourites of mine: Ivan Illich and Paulo Freire. Freire's work really impressed me when I was young. I remember being completely bowled over when I realised the kind of sacrifices he'd made in Brazil as a young priest. I've always loathed the church – it still makes me shudder watching the old mafia back in Ballarat – but Paulo Freire made it necessary to rethink those prejudices.

Henry hadn't even read them, but could he tread water like a pro! Rationalisations rolled one after the other off his back. Except he must have known he was losing, because his composure suddenly crumpled and he accused me of being an imposter: 'some nobody from the outback' was how he put it.

Negotiations are a lot easier once one party shows their hand. He was jealous! Wait till I told Josh.

I nailed it in the lounge. Henry, distracted by the rain that leapt against the windows and howled fiendishly in the choking gutters, made too many concessions for his own good.

I swept out victorious, leaving Meg and Henry to down their cocoa and struggling to engage in conversation.

Did Henry know then that Meg had a crush on him? Or was he so obsessed with getting her into bed that he hadn't noticed her idiocy?

Not that I cared. Not really. Well, she did do something for me, but in all the time I knew her, I hadn't a clue what. Certainly not her looks, which were decidedly meagre.

That night I called Josh, the first time since Jessie; asked for his advice. He warned me to keep an eye on Henry but avoid another confrontation. And we had a long natter about military service and my theories on education, and how the two issues might be advanced – with or without armed struggle – in New Zealand.

By June, I'd begun to wake up. Too many hours spent mooning over a lover: I had to get on; the summit would be upon us before we knew it.

Late June arrived. Cold, and more cold; weeks of rain; damp on the walls; a rotting carpet of dank leaves on the path. I spent hours crouched over the one-bar heater trying to warm myself and avoid chilblains.

Henry dropped in a couple of times. Relieved that I had sharpened up my act again, out of the blue he invited me to travel north with him for a few days. Having a spell from Steph, he said. If I'd known he'd just wormed his way into Meg Shepherd's bed I might have refused. I don't know why I said yes. Wounded vanity? Perhaps. What I did know was that I wanted to punish my body until I had voided every memory of Jessie from its cells. Anywhere north seemed better than here. I could hardly wait to leave town.

We camped our way around the tip of the North Island, two

pup-tents politely close, tethered alongside country roads that were stuffed with blackberry and convolvulus and wild grasses. One morning I woke after a bad dream to the ground shaking as if it were being sheared across by giant metal blades. The blades scissored, whirred in the air, went back to tearing up the ground. Not a sound came from Henry's tent. I poked my head out of mine. Of course. A row of cows strained against the fence, huffling in curiosity. I'd forgotten what large beasts they are, how their breath steams in great clouds. I'd forgotten the awesome crunch their jaws make while chewing. Henry's muesli bowls were sitting precariously on a hacked-off macrocarpa stump, so close to the animals I could see the shadow of their ears pricking the rims of enamel. Politics, I thought wryly, shrinks the natural world. It makes real bodies and real appetites threatening and unnatural. Jessie had shown me that first. Seeing the cows reminded me all over again. I had lived in my head for too long.

No, that wasn't right either, because look how far giving into a real appetite had got me. There must be a third way: one that could knit nature and analysis. I was a political animal as well as a natural one. Surely an individual didn't have to swing from one state to the other? I just had to find the correct interlock between theory and practice.

Bircher muesli became our favourite meal during that trip: the milk cool, the chopped apple swollen with an oat-flavoured cream. We glowed with good nature and fresh food, having just enough energy to debate the future of politics without getting into a fight. A couple of times we shared the same tent: kind of pleasant, but in the sack we bored each other, which was better to admit to on the spot than have the holiday self-destruct with phoniness. Because of our accord over the sex thing, it turned into the most honest time I've ever spent with a male. So, for all those who still jeer at Ballantyne: let me tell you, he did have his approachable side.

After breakfast one morning I strolled over to the neighbouring farm. Henry stayed behind to inspect the creek, remarking on the watercress tossing in the water like lush hair, recording birdsong in his notebook. I was homesick for Ballarat and country gardens, the soft *pppprrrking* of chickens with wobbling red wattles and combs.

I missed homemade lemonade and iced tea, the jugs beaded with sweet water. Even the drone of flies, iridescent gloss on hundreds of wings filling the air with blinding sparks, made me think fondly of afternoons spent swinging in our old hammock in the orchard.

I walked briskly up the drive. Metal chips overgrown by dandelion and patches of clover crunched under my feet. The farmhouse rose up in front of me, silvered with age, very still.

Without warning, a large dog appeared out of the grass. He silently opened his mouth, slub nose wrinkling, and pulled back his lips. I remember thinking how pink his tongue was, as pink and fresh as an enormous skinned guava. How dark the pigment around his mouth, how slug-like the tongue, glittering in its dark, toothy bed. All rancorous energy harboured in the switching tail, the dog came so close I could smell his rancid, haystack breath. His coat was pure black, eerily glossy. This animal belonged to the seriously stalking breed, the ones who don't waste time in barking. Nor was there a sound from the house. It continued to stare blankly, its peeling paint dangling in shreds over the gutters.

People tell you to stand absolutely still when an aggressive dog is about to take a chunk out of your leg. It's hard work, not running. And you're not supposed to look him in the eye, either. Something about issuing a challenge, which a dog is most likely to take the wrong way. So we stood for a moment that dragged itself out on a loom of horrible details: the animal's belly crunching against the dry, untended grass, bubbles of foam collecting in the corner of its mouth. Jesus, was I scared.

I was too proud to scream or move, so it wasn't until the dog had all but sunk its teeth into my tender skin and torn it like paper that I made an unrecognisable noise, a gargling, choking noise in the back of my throat. The farm stirred.

'Rex! *Back*, boy, *back!*' With a shrill whistle, a man appeared from around the side of the house. 'Didn't you see the sign?' he demanded. 'No trespassing. Dog would have gone for you if I hadn't called him off.' His face was stubbled, unhealthy, his shirt streaked with grease, eyes hard as marbles.

'What's this?' he said, kicking the Thermos I'd dropped.

"I was going to ask if you had –'

'Had what?'

'Some milk. We're camping over the road.'

'*Milk?* Who do you bloody think we are? The bloody dairy? Cows are off, didn't you know?'

I closed my eyes and wished I was in another part of the world where the bucolic lived up to its image. Where people gave you eggs and cheese and jars of cream so thick you could stand a spoon in it.

The farmer stood there, shading his eyes, as I crossed the road and walked away. I imagined a woman to match, parched as an old seed, looking silently out of the windows, willing the world to taste the grim economy of disappointment, the brutality that had overtaken them.

'Nice walk?' Henry took another look at my face. 'My God, what's wrong? You're all white.'

We packed up and left immediately. Henry had no desire to be attacked by either a mad farmer or a mad farmer's dog.

'Where to?' he asked, for once.

'Just drive,' I said.

Ballarat haunted me that day. How could this country be paradise when it was so mean, so withered and ungenerous? Both my parents, in their different ways, had believed in the idea of beauty. My mother knew that words and nature drew on a mysterious essence that murmured at the heart of things. She would hold up the exquisite treasures of the universe for us to view, childish memories now lost in some archaic part of my body. Surf like lace along the coast road, wildflowers at Christmas, never-ending fields of wheat the colour of golden syrup. Still buried in the pages of Marx, I'd laughed at her when I was fourteen. 'You're a bloody romantic, Mum. It's escapist bullshit, all that poetry stuff.' And she would fall silent, her vegetable-stained hands vaguely fingering minuscule burrs in her silk blouse.

I'd taken the treasures of my own country for granted when I was a child. Years of politics had sealed them away from me: a necessary form of protection, I'm sure; yet now, finding how loving and losing Jessie had restored those lost strings of time, I felt strangely skinless and vulnerable.

So we came in the afternoon, Henry as troubled as me, I think, to a beach called Opononi. We pulled over to watch the wind fork the waves into drag-nets of silver and grey. A ragged overcast sky allowed knots of sun onto the bubbling water that convulsively washed and sucked at the coast. Apparently, years earlier the bay had been full of curious visitors up from Auckland to see Opo the Friendly Dolphin. They'd waded into the water to touch his gleaming sides, laughed at the fountain of spray, the snickering noises, the dolphin's fearlessness. Then one day he'd disappeared and that fleeting, spine-pricking accord between nature and human beings had vanished.

Jessie's narrow animal face looked up at me from the pools swilling with tide, and I saw that it was easier to fall in love with the rare and the beautiful, or the fey, even, than with a person in whom you saw the reflection of your own brutality. Jessie's cruelty had been for her survival. She'd had to push me away – I hadn't smelt the same as her in some way I didn't recognise. Whereas the farmer's cruelty struck me as gratuitous, a horrible act he'd willed out of indifference.

Ever after, I connected Jessie with the New Zealand countryside. I never managed to turn nature and politics into a combination that made tidy sense, but I was grateful for the trip, which allowed me to preserve the best aspects of my failed relationship without being crushed by it. Brutality outweighed love: sure, I agreed with Josh over that one; but love might yet outlive indifference. At least, I hoped so.

My holiday had restored me to hope, I thought as I lay looking up at the roof of the tent, stippled with sunlight, and that must have been worth something. I resolved I would never find myself without a reason to live.

Next door, Henry was still asleep, his face crunched into the folds of the pillow, one arm trailing on the ground.

As if he could read my mind, my companion sat up suddenly. 'What's wrong with you now?' He cracked his vertebrae experimentally, and scowled. 'Lighten up!'

'You would say that,' I said, but my heart wasn't in the mood for a fight this morning. 'Get up; the sun's splitting the rocks and I've boiled the billy.'

That was almost it, as far as Henry's and my holiday went. The day after tomorrow, we'd be leaving. But we had one final item on the agenda: a trip to Cape Reinga. Where, I learnt, Maori spirits leapt into the sea to reach the cave of the Underworld.

I can remember every detail.

Our tent that night was pitched in sight of the headland, but slightly lower, off to the east. The wind buffeted us. The air seemed full of the presence of a vivid, teeming life.

When I was younger, there'd been times when my senses had been sharp as an animal's. There were odd moments that had swung into my line of sight, demanding attention. A peculiar intensity of light, distant objects luridly magnified, smells and sounds without an origin. On those occasions the world turned into a glowing, crackling night bush in which I stalked, ears pricked. And then a curtain would fall.

It was the same now. Clouds boiled and blew continuously over the watching face of the moon. The night pressed, dense, sad and damp. I smelled the scent of crushed berries. Presences spun towards me, hesitated, hissed away with the speed of comets. If these were lost ancestors, they didn't belong to me. Or to Henry Ballantyne. A whole planetarium moved and danced and transacted out there without us. Unable to sleep, I stayed up to watch the trackless night. My companion stirred the fire once or twice, and went to bed. If he was aware of anything odd, he did not say so.

In the morning, the scream of peacocks met us. We had gone to sleep on a perfectly circular lawn that looked over the bluff out to sea. Water and light-wrapped mist filled the horizon. Gorgeous birds with proud trailing feathers strode across the grass. I suppose they belonged to someone – we never did find out. The air that morning was spare and fine, empty of the swarming presences of the night before. Now it mantled the dipping birds with an artless splendour. On a widening platform beyond, grazed a small group of sheep, the sun catching their coats as if they were on fire.

A small miracle. Ritualistic conversation seemed wrong in a place

like this. All ritual, actually, Henry said, moved at last by the specta-
cle. For surely there were no books written in any language to make
sense of what had met us. To our right, the velvet oval and the exotic
birds. On the left: the grey crumbling cliffs and the descent to the
spirit cave of the dead. It was a piercing, unexpected partnership.

Later, I saw the experience as a softening of my personal disappointment at what New Zealand was like. It reminded me that
the transactions between people and their landscapes were dances
of the most unfathomable motions. Red Letters gave us a powerful
language of analysis, but a softer part of me suspected that it left
something out. Something elusive always escaped when Josh talked
about the meaning of life. Marx, I began to think, had nothing to say
about disarming moments in the natural world like these, that left
you feeling you'd got more than you bargained for. At the time, I too
had no words to express how at Cape Reinga two worlds, Pakeha
and Maori, edged awkwardly into the Tasman together, nor my
gratitude for the chance to make a rough peace with the presences
we'd disturbed.

I thought, rather, of the morning as another dream, and we all
remember what Marx had to say about them! Imagine what he
would have said if Mrs Marx had told him about her bad dreams:
'Get over them, dear, they're only an illusion.' Or he would have
poured her an inoculating shot of laudanum syrup from the silver
chased jug on their sideboard, using the spell of one opiate to arrest
the poison of the other.

I've had plenty of leisure now to consider Marx, and you know
what? His time is over. Never mind what young people today are
reading in London squats: the man is finished and done with, and
there'll be no bringing him back, I'm sure of it.

Would Lou Waters agree, if we were to meet again?

If I hadn't run into her when I was in one of my Jessie troughs,
I'm not sure what would have happened. The dream-stoked mornings of muesli and fruit were long gone, but I hadn't wanted to
accept it was time to knuckle down to work. I'd neglected to pay

my telephone bills in order to cut myself off from Josh, who'd begun to sound impatient; I'd stopped going to lectures. Lou put me back on track, revived my interest in the mission for the Red Letters, and persuaded me to keep on at Women's VP, all in the space of a gloomy night when she ran into me weaving down Lambton Quay after one of her Corso meetings.

'Diana, what on earth are you doing here? It's pretty late for a protest, isn't it?'

In those days, people were naive enough to think politics was the only thing radicals had on their minds. If anyone had informed me that Lou Waters had had a crush on me for months, I wouldn't have believed them. Sure, we'd spent time together, but it had been strictly business as far as I was concerned. I mumbled incoherently.

A look of curiosity – no, more than that: it was compassion – crossed her face. Was this the radical from Sydney who'd scared the hell out of everyone, full of wisdom from Mao and Castro and Guevara? 'You look terrible,' she said. 'I've going to some friends round in Thorndon. Want to join me?'

Yes, as it happened, I did. We hurried around the back of Parliament up to Thorndon, where a group of radical Christians had a house overlooking the city.

Normally, any kind of Christian severely ups my blood pressure. Right or Left, they can never make up their mind which side of the fence deserves their loyalty. These days, leftie Christians are more likely to believe in trees than in Jesus Christ. Looking at recent Ideal Pacific footage of eco-activist activity, I couldn't help wondering how many of the faces were descendants of SCMers from the old days.

That evening I was in no position to argue the toss about whether violence was an acceptable form of protest, or if Jesus had really been an underground Zealot. I collapsed shakily on a chair. (I remember it vividly. It was one of those Morris Arts and Crafts chairs and it had cup-rings stained into the woodwork. Amazing what your mind recalls when the rest of the world has fallen to pieces.) Lou put a cup of scalding gumboot tea into my hand as she shooed the rest of the flat out of the kitchen.

Thank Christ for kitchen tables. We propped ourselves over a surface crusted with food (it looked as if they'd dined on banana curry for dinner), while I told her what it had been like falling in love with a woman who didn't love me back. I could see the web of squishy veins standing up on her hands, her strong and blunt-edged fingers resting quietly around the rim of the mug, and I imagined her as a vast tree with roots going down into the very core of the earth, drawing up its heat and salty-sweet minerals. She listened to me, one of the few human beings who ever did. I swear Lou Waters was sexually naive when I met her, yet she seemed able to draw on some innate wisdom about the pain of falling in love. Especially about falling in love when you were an activist, none of us supposed to have hearts. We talked and talked. About being gay, about when I'd come out and how isolated we all felt, and how politics could be bent a different way if only we could mobilise ourselves as a group.

After a couple of hours of this I felt lighter, as if the smoke that had roiled at me for weeks, clouding my sight, was leaking out of the kitchen, away from the city and my life in this elusive country.

'Tell me how you got into politics.'

By now we were meandering around Oriental Bay, watching the sunrise flood the sky with colours of vermilion, crimson and marzipan, the sound of the sea gentle against our backs.

'My parents used to have massive arguments at the dinner table about whether they were going to vote National or Labour.' Lou sighed. 'Dad would be sitting there, chewing and saying nothing, but you knew he was working up to it, because whenever he was mad his jaw would crack, and he'd throw down his cutlery and shout at us all that we were idiots, and that he couldn't stand living in a National house a moment longer. And Mum would yell back that she was sick of having a communist sympathiser in her bed, and they'd start arguing about the waterfront lockout, which happened when Dad was a student.'

We watched a bird whose feathers looked as if they had been slicked with some dark oil dive through the burnished water. A morning so still, you could almost hear the splash of the drops falling from its wings. Our feet barely touched the ground, yet I felt solid and renewed, as if breathing had suddenly become easier.

It was ridiculous. I wanted to know more about Lou than I did about Henry. From the Letters' point of view, I knew this to be a waste of time, but I couldn't help myself. I'd found a fellow traveller.

'Mum's dyed-in-the-wool right wing,' said Lou. 'I would have been proud of her if she'd been a unionist like Connie Purdue – or Rosa Luxemburg. Fat chance.'

'Hardly likely in Greytown.' Nor Ballarat either, if I was honest. I could count the number of communist women from my home town on half a hand.

A slick of lemon gelato-coloured sky was all that remained of the sunrise. Cars had begun chuffing out of garages, snorting down the steep streets to the city.

'So, what are we going to do, then?' I asked lazily, only thinking of Jessie in a muzzy, sentimental kind of way.

When Lou invited me home to meet her family in the Wairarapa, I accepted at once. She was right. It was time to move on.

'Who knows,' she said, as if she could read my mind, 'you might enjoy being away from the city.' She didn't know I'd gone up north with Henry.

I watched a lone sailboat tacking against the easterly that had got up. 'You know what gets to me? This place has no sense of loyalty.' I could see the sailor wrapped in orange leaning out over the waves. He heaved the craft around, went back to the rudder.

Lou waited for an explanation. I was having a hard time of it, but I knew there was a truth lying in wait to be said, if I could just lay my hands on it.

'In Sydney, you can see the lines that divide people. It's good, because political loyalties are out in the open. Everyone knows where they stand: for this, against that, you know?'

She looked thoughtful. How lucky for me that she didn't react all defensive, as some Kiwis would have.

'Nobody here wants to admit the power games they're up to. Everything's covered over with a mask of politeness. And that's a real disadvantage when you need muscle, because you're forced to rely on a bloody morass of self-interest. People here will support you if they like what you're saying on the day. The next time you see them, they don't want to know you.' I felt really aggrieved.

'Maybe that's true,' said Lou. 'Maybe the Left isn't as pure as we'd like to think, but you can't question everyone's motives. I've met plenty of dedicated, serious-minded people.'

'Serious-minded,' I mocked, thinking of Henry's peculiar blend of pragmatism and ideals. 'Christ, if you want decent conversation, you've got to wait till some goddamn tragedy forces out the truth!'

Now, I wonder if that hadn't been my problem with Henry all along: we'd wrangled so much because I was constantly trying to make him reveal himself. Apart from small pickings such as the jealousy thing, perhaps there wasn't anything underneath his opportunistic kind of politics. Perhaps there still isn't, no matter what he says in the press. He could be just the kind of partner that Ideal Pacific is looking for . . .

Lou and I became lovers in Sydney, of all places. Henry had been given a grant by Corso to attend a development forum. He and Steph flew to Australia on standby. I suppose after our trip north, she would have insisted on coming. I pitied her, and on the spur of the moment I decided to fund Lou. She deserved a trip away too. I'd been really pissed off to hear that Ballantyne had had her kicked off the Corso committee, because she knew more about injustice than anyone, and I was determined she be given a crack at the Sydney forum. I drew out the last of my Christmas cheque so we could travel together.

I think I fell properly in love when I watched her fastening her seatbelt. Completely irrational, and not like Jessie at all, which had been thunder and lightning and no time for reflection till too late.

While we crossed the Tasman I replayed the moment over and over, when Lou's hands cupped themselves around her waist and slipped the buckle into place with a soft plock. I almost laughed out loud. I couldn't believe I was being offered another chance at love so soon. I promised the bright waves, the turning clouds, the flight attendant who filled our drinks, that this time it would be different.

Naturally, I needed to set aside a minute for rehearsing what I would say to Josh. It hardly seemed fair to be turning up unannounced, so when our bookings were confirmed, I had dashed off a succinct cable: *Arriving Sydney day after tomorrow. Menagerie in tow. Diana.*

Too succinct, apparently. Josh flew into a temper when I introduced him to Henry on Saturday. Anyone would think I'd done it deliberately to get his back up.

'You could have warned me,' he snarled, without so much as glancing at our little group, subdued now they were on foreign soil.

I met his temper with mine. 'Nice to see you, Josh. Had a pleasant trip? Yes, Josh, thanks for asking.' Et cetera. Had he no shame?

Actually, it wasn't his lack of shame that upset me; more his apparent indifference to strategy. If Ballantyne was so important to the Letters, how come Josh was now shitting all over a possible ally?

Stupid. Like I said, it took a while. I suppose I hadn't imagined Josh would have the gall to dispatch me to my personal Siberia. In any case, I wasn't going to waste time trading insults. We had been standing outside his place in Paddington, which appeared from the street to be as much of a dive as the last one in Surrey Hills. I pushed past him into the hall, temporarily leaving the others in the courtyard, which was littered with rubbish.

'Look, Josh,' I said calmly, 'I didn't do this to catch you out. Henry's over here for a development forum and it seemed the perfect opportunity for the Letters to check him out.'

Josh pulled a crumpled packet of cigarettes from his pocket, lit one.

'Introduce him to the group; get them all round for dinner or something. We could go out after to the pub.'

Josh appeared not to attend to what I was saying. He drew in deeply, blew out with a morose *hufff*. 'They're isn't a group any more,' he said slowly. 'We've disbanded.'

'Disbanded? Since when?' I was stupid with shock. 'Why didn't you tell me?'

The smoke and the afternoon light coiled down the hall and

disappeared. I looked around for the others, who had vanished.

'You know bloody well how fragile the group was. We broke over Wendy Bacon. Well, not her exactly, but publishing our paper.'

'I didn't even realise you'd got into that side of things.' So much had happened. I felt cut off, mutilated by my exile. 'Since when has the Letters put out a paper?'

He took me downstairs, showed me the press.

'Jesus, why haven't you told me? I've been slaving away in Wellington for over a year and you didn't even think to let me know?'

'Chill out. As it happens, we only printed two issues. We ran out of money and half the group were angry about Bacon's style anyway. I still haven't paid the bloody thing off.'

Big deal, I thought. Like me, Josh had family money behind him. 'I heard she's against women-only groups.'

'So am I; they're splintering the movement. Christ, you know, I've had a gutsful of politics based on bourgeois hang-ups. We've left the workers behind. I'll tell you this for a fact: the factory workers don't give a shit about papers like *Tharunka*, and they want nothing to do with women's libbers either, especially the lesbian type.'

I remembered my charges. 'Look, Josh, I'm really sorry this has happened, but it might still be useful to sit Henry down and have a chat. Why don't we come back later? Lou's got someplace else to be, but the three of us could come. We could have a simple meal – bread and cheese even, I don't care.'

I swept up Henry and Steph and Lou and led them across the street to a pub. We downed more martinis than I could count – to hell with the expense. I left off playing the seasoned political, since they had patently been shown otherwise, which was actually relaxing – for a while. And let Henry's copious scorn waste itself until he finally grew tired of insulting the Letters and Josh Rideau, and turned his attention to the crowd of drinkers.

Lou's appointment with a couple of the forum participants from the University of the South Pacific took her over to Glebe, so she never got to sit down and talk properly to Josh, which, as I have said, was a shame. They would have found common ground, despite her commitment to radical feminism.

Instead, there were three of us who returned to Paddington around eight that evening to 'have another go at Rideau', as Henry put it. Steph had attempted to hide back at the hostel, but I had insisted she come. Henry would have been a mess without her.

It began badly. We arrived on the dot to discover Josh nowhere to be found, though he'd thoughtfully left the door open for us.

'He's gone for some beer,' I guessed, hoping there was not a less plausible reason. Such as: (1) not wanting to face up to further inter-rogation from a disappointed colleague and a Kiwi still smarting from being abandoned in the courtyard that afternoon; (2) an exciting new lover – Josh and sex had a long, excoriating partnership; (3) the formation of a new split-off organisation that I was not party to.

I tramped into the kitchen, fixed us glasses of water. Josh had made an effort with the sink: dirty dishes were stacked neatly along one side of the counter; plates, a stick of bread and some cheese on the other. A half-drunk bottle of red wine completed the still-life. He'd taken me at my word, the shyster.

'Have a look around, why don't you?'

Josh. He'd arrived with a woman and was leaning up against the door-jamb, peering at us unfocusedly.

'Hello, everyone. Goodness, what a crowd. Who's in this little *menagerie* of yours, Diana?'

'Uh, hi, Josh.' Shit, he was drunk already. 'Oh, this is Henry Ballantyne and his partner Steph Jackson. Henry's just given a paper on structural poverty in the Pacific.'

'*Structural* poverty? Well, and what are they saying at UNSW these days, Henry? Sandy and I have rather lost contact.'

'Sandy,' I said heavily.

'Yes, Sandy. Anything wrong?'

Sandy was nicer than Josh deserved. She dumped a bag of groceries on the table, greeted everyone, apologised for the state of her lover, and sat us down again.

'We turned down one of Sandy's friends to keep this appointment.'

'Shut up, Josh.'

'Serious – we missed out on a shit-hot dinner party, didn't we, Sandy?'

'Shut up, I said.'

'Diana's friends might want to know how the other half lives.' Josh sauntered to the fridge, extracted beer. 'Go on, then, you tell them.'

'No.'

'What she wants to spare you is the fucking ridiculous sight of Sydney's intelligentsia dining off Georgia O'Keefe placemats and pretending to pay homage to female sexuality.'

'What's wrong with O'Keefe?' asked Steph. 'She's a major American painter.'

I wasn't sure where Josh was going with this, but it had to be somewhere bad.

'What Josh didn't say was that we were invited to leave.'

They must be staging this for our benefit: I hadn't seen Josh so black in a long time.

'Bullshit.'

'He spent the whole time calling his hostess a phoney American imitator.'

'Jesus, Sandy, since when did radicals need to fixate on the sex organs of plants? Look at Bacon: she might not be a pure Marxist, but she doesn't waste her time on Balmain shit.'

At which point I had to intervene. 'You can't expect New Zealanders to follow every nuance of local politics, Josh.'

'You mean to tell me they haven't heard about the trials?' he asked thunderously.

Steph got up to go to the bathroom. While she was out of the room, Josh and Henry began to argue. Impossible to remember how it started, but at some point Josh stood up and tossed a bowl of sugar all over Henry.

'Christ, Josh, calm down!' shouted Sandy.

'I saw it done in a movie,' he simpered, as if making an apology.

'No you bloody haven't. Frank tipped a Caesar salad down your shirt last week. *You're* an imitator, a chicken-shit imitator!' By now Sandy was screaming and Josh was grinning drunkenly at me from the other side of the room.

How could things have got so bad?

We left Josh and Sandy to make up, and went home around 10.30. I was staying with Lou in Glebe, and we arrived back at the house almost together.

'I can't believe it; I've had a bitch of a night,' I complained. 'Sydney's full of splinter groups all intent on eating one another.'

Lou led me up the stairs, gently pulled off my clothes. Her eyes shone. She stroked my face with her hands and I heard the plock of the seatbelt, ice chinking in a glass. Something in me settled and stilled. We were all right. The rest of the world could go to hell.

'You?' I said later. 'How was your meeting?'

'Useful, I think. We're organising another forum in a year's time.'

'That's great. Where did you go for dinner?'

'Oh,' said Lou, smiling, 'I had it here with the Collective.'

'Lucky you. What did you talk about?'

'Censorship. Military service. The usual.'

'Christ, everyone's talking about censorship here. Josh and Henry had a fight over Wendy Bacon.'

'Really? The Collective said she's just into freaking people out. Have you heard of Otto Muhl?'

'I've heard the name before. Who is he?'

'He's this mad anarchist German protester who was going to cut the neck off a goose, cover it with a condom and fuck one of the women on stage.'

'Yuk.'

'Yeah. It's not my scene.'

'Nor mine.'

'Anyway, it seems that he's the hero of some of the radical groups here, and they want to bring him to Australia.'

No wonder Josh had lost his grip. No wonder he was pissed off that real politics was being smothered. What on earth was the point of attention-getting stunts like Muhl's? How would they change conditions in factories and shops?

A pity that ego had got in the way at Paddington when Josh and Henry met, because in many ways they shared exactly the same distrust of the sexual revolution. For good reason. And, as I pointed out to Lou when we were lying so close I could run my tongue from the hollow of her neck to her belly, who gives a shit about dicks and condoms anyway?

I had done my best for the cause, before I knew what had happened to the Red Letters. In fact, I kept in touch with Josh after we flew back to Wellington, and I heard soon enough that he'd found another group more committed to building Marxism in Australia.

Falling for Lou distracted me from politics briefly, but I dragged my feelings back into order, and we stayed together for three years without my making a fool of myself as I had done over Jessie. Lou likewise managed to hold on to her identity, while she looked after me as if I were a national treasure. I can't think of a single person who has cared for me better than her, or been more supportive. Since Ideal Pacific, I've become much more private about my sexuality. I occasionally think I could do with a permanent partner, but that's as far as it gets. Freedom has always been the welcome side-effect of never falling in love, and I've yet to meet anyone who can touch Lou Waters for kindness.

Josh was right about Henry. His star was on the rise, and it took all my self-control not to grind my teeth when I'd see yet another story in the press about the young student leader who was destined to be a major New Zealand statesman. He did become one, but a minor player. Amazing how the stars that burn the strongest usually implode. The pressure is just too great. I think, really, that's what happened to Henry. He received too much attention too soon, and when you put that together with a liberal mindset, his potential for doing something truly awesome dribbled away. These days, his role in Parliament is a concession, a sop to a man who had more ambition and who spent more time on strategy than any other activist I can think of.

I especially admired his planning for the disruption to the military service ballot, because I'd been convinced up till then he was always a hands-off, glove-wearing radical. (Baudelaire, Meg Shepherd told me, used to wear pink calf-skin gloves when he made love to his black mistress. Meg would say something like that. She had a peculiar obsession about gloves, which I'm certain hid the key to her character. In Henry's case, the occasions on which he actually agreed to involve himself in true grassroots action and dirty his hands were rare.) Breaking into the Crockford Building was one occasion when thought and action combined. Almost textbook in his efficiency and daring, he commanded the Working Party on Military Service as if inspired by Fidel Castro.

He broached the subject during that first dismal military training weekend, where it poured with rain the whole time and where half our participants couldn't turn up because of road slips. We sat there at Otaki staring glumly at one another while Henry and Steph made out they'd only come to speak against armed struggle. They needn't have bothered. There were no reporters to splash their maturity and youthful common sense all over the papers. Not that any of us (apart from me) even knew how to load a rifle, let alone point it in the right direction. Just because I could use a gun didn't mean the rest of us were as practical. I thought of the Letters, all of whom had studied firearms and karate, utterly committed to taking the fight against fascism and imperialism into the streets of Sydney. These people depressed with their hard-sell rhetoric that turned into hot air the moment you shoved a weapon into their hands. The only firearms we had were either grubbed from farm sheds or borrowed from pig-hunters, friends of friends. Fat lot of use we'd be in a fight.

In a mood that was distinctly grim, Ballantyne got up and waved his arms at us.

'All right then,' he said, 'it's been a terrible weekend so far. The Exec's properly cocked up this time.'

We all nodded.

'But let's not waste the day doing bugger all. Why don't we plan something real for the ballot coming up?'

'Like what?' scoffed Arthur Meyer, who'd just been released from a stretch in Mt Crawford for resisting the draft. You'd think this would have had Henry backing off as fast as his legs could take him, but if anything, he seemed to value Arthur's new experience.

I have to admit, decades later, Henry's leadership that day was magic. He did have something – courage, or quick-thinking opportunism, or simply luck on his side. He convinced Meyer that if we managed to disrupt the military service ballot there was a good chance that the government would call off the whole deal. No conscription, ever. It was better than we could do across the Tasman. I was torn between getting on the phone at once to Josh, and staying around to hear more.

'Who's willing to form a working party?' Henry trumpeted, excited at the vision we were all beginning to share.

'Diana?' he said, looking over at me, and I was in. Hooked.

'Now then,' adjusting his trousers, 'if we want to be political animals, we've got to start making real changes in our lives. Politics is a sacrificial life, as my comrade from the Red Letters will tell you. Isn't that right, Diana?'

Henry looked meaningfully at me, but I couldn't reply. We were awed by the hot sun bending towards us, melting us into runnels of wax. You had to admire his timing. It was brilliant.

'Which means using our heads,' he went on. 'Which means thinking things through properly *before* we begin.'

Around our corner of the table, the silence grew. We'd been sitting in front of a meagre lunch as Henry had begun to speak, and the sounds of our eating and drinking, of cups and spoons colliding – cheap china on metal and formica – stopped instantly.

'Okay, so we've got a tough job on our hands, but provided we do our homework, there's no reason why a select group of us can't get inside and disrupt the ballot.'

The working party chose Henry and myself to break into the building. Meyer was to provide the escape vehicle: his brother's laundry van. It surprised me that Henry had accepted such a visible role. Perhaps I'd got him wrong. I went off and dredged up an ancient map of the building from Lands and Deeds, rehearsing our strategy at his flat in Garden View Road while Steph brought us coffee in white fluted porcelain cups. Meg Shepherd, now openly one of Ballantyne's groupies, skulked in the hall trying to eavesdrop.

We decided we'd get into the building, which would probably be guarded, where one of us would set off a smoke-bomb in the toilets. After everyone had been evacuated, we'd storm the room on the top floor and disrupt the ballot. (By which Henry probably meant he planned on making a persuasive speech, but my private intention was to let off a bundle of double-happies I'd taped into cans. I been practising the timing for days – it had to be perfect.)

The day of the raid began with a thin, high sky, almost no cloud. I dressed in a suit and carried a briefcase borrowed from Meg Shepherd, which I'd filled with the cans. My plan was to visit a toy-design business on the second floor, after which I'd make for the toilets, where I would wait for Henry to lob the smoke-bomb into the men's toilets the next floor up.

It was the kind of morning that makes you believe in anything. I felt invincible, sweeping past two policemen up to the second floor, where I conducted an intelligent conversation with the manager about wooden toys. We agreed they were selling well. I gave him an address in Greytown for his Christmas catalogue, hoping Lou's father would appreciate the joke. With a sample coloured block stack and wooden doll in my case, I drifted down the corridor. When the fire alarm nearby exploded in a shrill of sound I headed for the Ladies' and waited for Henry to join me.

I waited ... and waited. Someone briskly approached and retreated. We had agreed that if one of us was caught, the other would carry out the break-in alone, so after fifteen minutes I inspected my still face in the mirror, picked up the leather case and opened the door.

Standing outside were two bulky figures. I have never felt so impotent, or so surprised. I was like a toddler, frustrated by a thicket of adult limbs and shoulders. Nothing was said. At least I didn't scream, or try to bite their hands. They hustled me downstairs, hoisting me like a captive animal to the kerb, roughly pushed me into a police car. Arthur Meyer and his laundry van were nowhere to be seen.

There was a flash. A face pressed itself against the window. A photographer held up his camera, flashed me again. Sandwiched between two uniforms, I was driven around the corner to the Taranaki Street Police Station.

Thankfully, they took neither fingerprints nor mugshot. In the company of a policewoman I was harangued by a junior detective.

'Your parents will be disappointed in you,' he accused.

'Parent,' I corrected timidly.

'Only one parent alive, then?'

'Mum died of TB when I was five.' A useful lie.

The detective cleared his throat. He flicked me another look and caught the eye of his colleague. I took heart. I knew those looks.

'Where does your dad live?'

'Greytown.' Had they noticed my accent? What if they checked? Another lie wouldn't make any difference. Besides, the Waters family was coming in handy. 'He's the school groundsman.'

'Hmmmm.' The detective considered.

'Well, young lady, if we catch you disrupting Her Majesty's Government again, we'll have to press charges, you know.'

'I'm sorry.' I heard a voice sounding appropriately abject. Nice work, Diana. But where the hell was Henry? As I signed for the receipt of my briefcase and walked out into the noise of the city, I felt outrage building inside me. Ballantyne had completely disappeared. He'd dumped me in the middle of this mess and pissed off. I briefly thought of him and Steph eating their nut roast as they stared at tonight's paper together. Of Steph, twisting her hair around a finger, shaking the paper out in surprise at my pale wax face staring from the back of a police car. 'The silly bitch,' Henry would say. 'She wasn't careful enough,' and they would both attack their puddings and slip raw sugar crystals into cups of coffee with Steph's tiny apostle spoons.

I swore I would get my revenge for his cowardice, and didn't think to wonder whether, like Josh, he'd set me up to fail because I was too smart, too brash and too full of my successes in Wellington.

Needless to say, cleaned up to make my error less humiliating, the storming of the Crockford Building will form part of the report my employers are expecting – two days to go, now – on Henry Ballantyne.

It will be followed by a terse account of his comeuppance, and will conclude with a judicious analysis of flaws, strengths and possible use-value. It would hardly be proper to openly state in the report how I determined to get my revenge for this, the worst of Henry's betrayals. Reading between the lines, however, any fool in Ideal Pacific will pick up the man's self-interest.

A well-known fact: Scorpios never forget, and never forgive.

I planned carefully. I watched and waited, and simply accepted his pathetic claims that he hadn't even got as far as throwing the smoke-bomb down before some official had wised to his disappearing up the stairs and activated the alarm system. How Ballantyne had talked his way out of the building, he never said and he wasn't asked. Meanwhile, as plans for the summit went ahead, I made sure I sat on their organising committee like some bloated spider waiting to strike. I don't think I've ever felt so utterly venomous, but just as he'd said himself, planning is everything. This time I wasn't going to mess up.

An opportunity came two weeks before we left for the South Island. Apparently Henry had bribed the unreliable Meyer to break into the Education Department and steal their draft White Paper policy for the next election. The draft actually suggested wiping the current system of assessment, and for some reason Henry thought that if he got his hands on it he could use it as a lever at the Youth summit. After the theft he went around chuckling to himself, puffed up with secretiveness and conceit.

Convinced it would make more strategic leverage in my possession, I decided to steal the stolen document from Henry myself. A day later when everyone was out at lectures, I cut through the trees, went around the back of the house and shimmied up a rickety fire-escape. From above, the back yard looked quite dismal. Next to peeling green steps stood a battered rubbish tin overflowing with garbage. The rotary clothesline creaked like an ancient windmill; faded pegs peppered the grass. I abandoned the thought of getting into Meg's room, which seemed to be hung with eccentric objects, including a tasteless crystal hanging in the window, because she always kept her door padlocked and I would have had a hell of a job breaking out again. Instead, I levered open a fanlight in Henry's bedroom, unlatched the window below and tumbled through. Adrenalin pumped through my cells. Amazing what a person will do for a cause once they believe in it absolutely, I thought.

Believe it or not, that bastard almost defeated me again. Deciding against breaking into his locked filing cupboard because I reasoned that it was the last place a guilty student leader would hide anything, I prowled all over the house. I tried to out-think him, first standing in his place, trying to get inside his petty criminal mind, and then looking at myself standing in his place. Never underestimate the trick of cracking someone's reason from the outside. It's fucking difficult.

I weighed my options, but gradually the adrenalin wore off. My mind's movements seemed slow as treacle. I fumbled the light on in Steph's room, knocked over a pottery jar. The dressing table wreathed in strings of shell and beads and two dishes of old jewellery revealed nothing. My hands grew wet with sweat, slipping on whatever I touched. Time passed as a series of hammer blows somewhere at the back of my head. I vaguely remembered the story of a criminal who'd committed a murder, then spent excruciating hours attempting to erase his fingerprints, every inch of space crying to be wiped free of the crime. They found him still going in the morning. (A prophetic scene, in more ways than one.)

This was disastrous. Time was up; I'd found nothing. As I came through the hall to the front door I cast a quick look in the kitchen. Dishes lay all over the bench, the brightly painted kitchen dresser piled high with plates and cooking implements. There was a solitary under-watered cactus on the windowsill. Above, a pair of moths fluttered on the glass. As I backed out, flushed with new shame and frustration, I saw the key rack bolted to the wall. Three slim bunches of keys dangled from plastic cup-hooks. Below them on a hook of its own, hung an antique rust-encrusted key. My gut told me it belonged to the infamous Ballantyne filing cupboard. I snatched at it, tore back down the hall, and fumbled it into the lock, fingers clumsily fat.

Of course the document was there, neatly stacked away under

E – White Paper. Thank Christ for his methodical filing system. I could have cried with relief.

Half an hour later I put on the brightest trousers in my wardrobe and sauntered into the party where Lou was waiting for me.

'How did the essay go?' she asked.

'Perfect,' I grinned, and put my arms around her. 'It just wrote itself.'

I tried not to look at Henry. The bastard had no idea I'd foxed him. He could hardly pull his face into a party expression anyway. Lou and Meg had invited all their friends to their old flatmate Gillian Blaikie's engagement party, and Henry looked dourly across the room, shuddering at Mr and soon-to-be-Mrs Noah, who stood at the door of their home counting the animals as we came inside out of the rain.

Mrs Noah's mother was there, all the way from Hawke's Bay. She wore a grey angora twinset, pearls and a Jaeger wool skirt, and smelt of whisky and expensive perfume. Meg Shepherd introduced us. Mrs Blaikie gingerly extended fingertips buffed with a nacreous pink. 'And what are you doing, Diane?'

'Diana. My name is *Diana*, D-I-A-N-A.'

Lou pinched me.

'Sorry, Mrs Noah, I mean, Blaikie. Well, at the moment I'm taking Philosophy and History.'

'Philosophy! And what do you hope to do with your degree?'

No doubt she thought everyone should be doing commerce.

'I don't know.' Then, wickedly, 'My mother used to tell me it was more important to learn to think.'

'Learning to think!' Gillian's mother had swallowed something sharp and spat it out vehemently. 'Good heavens, Diane, young women don't need to learn to think! But they *do* need to learn to present themselves,' appraising my hot-pink flowered trousers as if they were an unseemly investment.

I turned away, struggling with a huge desire to laugh wildly at all this bourgeois nonsense, and at the fact that I'd raided Henry's files and got away with it. Lou dragged me into the kitchen so we could unwrap plates of food, leaving the overdressed chook from Hawke's Bay to peck fretfully without us.

We spiked mashed egg with curry, spread it over a plate of Snax, piled chips into a dish in the shape of a crinkled leaf. The kitchen warmed up, filling with the smell of cooked savouries and coffee. Meg took down a fresh linen teatowel to polish the obligatory dust from demitasse cups and saucers, and flicked a cloth over the bench. For once we three were in total accord, leaving the two Mrs Noahs to cast delighted eyes over the satin-edged blankets and Le Creuset cookware nestled on a damask cloth in a corner of the lounge with the rest of the guests: two by two, two by two, two by two. We're all rejected animals, I thought, outside in the rain with icy water swirling around our feet. Invisible, in the dark, with the ark trembling on its rollers, tugging at the lashed ropes, ready to sail with its warmth and blaze of lights into the new world.

Henry, and Steph who'd arrived late, had disappeared when we finally emerged from the kitchen. I suppose they were as suffocated as we were by the tasteless display of greed and wealth. And by the power, too, of a kind I despised.

That night, as we lay in the dark, Lou and I tried to figure out what exactly it was that we hated.

'I can't stand engagement parties. Don't make me go to one again.'

My lover rolled over, re-tucked the sheet over the blankets. I could only just see the top of her back.

'Gill was our first flatmate.' Her voice came out of the dark. 'You feel special about friends like that, even if she has nothing in common with us.'

'What about Meg?' I asked. If Lou ever suspected I fancied Meg, with her handmade clothes and weird behaviours, she never said.

'Meg knows bugger all about politics. She's got an almighty crush on Henry and there's nothing we can do about it. I've tried to conscientise her –'

'I hate that word!' I exploded, wrenched out of the slow drift into sleep. 'The best activist keeps her speech simple. *Conscientise*: it's such an in-word, it reminds me of Ballantyne trying to keep up.'

The night grew colder. We both shivered, rolled into each other on our battered old mattress, rolled away again.

'Yes,' said Lou, 'but we weren't talking about him. He's as turned off all that materialism as we are.'

I didn't believe it. 'Crap. When push comes to shove, Ballantyne's on their side. Him and his private-school education.' The memory of an angry scene with a self-satisfied *kid* danced in front of my eyes.

Lou's breath puffed gently over my hair. 'Mmmmm,' she mumbled. 'We'll make our own ark, then.' She was brilliant at distracting me. We got the giggles, imagining our ark crowded with misfits bobbing resolutely over unfriendly seas. The moon slid sleepily across the sky. Eventually, when the windows began to lighten, we too fell asleep.

I did go to another party after that: our kind, with murkily lit rooms, shabby walls covered in posters of revolutions and Marxist heroes and endless Bob Dylan tracks. The afternoon after Gillian Blaikie's do I'd received a call from Henry, agitated, naturally, as he told me how someone had broken into his office and stolen the White Paper. Could it, by any chance, have been a person known to me? He refused to call me a thief outright. Actually, he reserved that epithet for Meg Shepherd when he discovered that she'd stolen his ties.

For a politico, here was a dilemma. Accusing one's allies rashly carried the risk of an abrupt waning of influence. Worst-case scenario: an irreparable fall from power. None of us had any compassion for losers. They were an embarrassment. God knows what would have happened if Lou and I had ended up on different sides. I'm relieved my political common sense wasn't put to the test in that way. Ballantyne still recognised me as a useful ally, his local nous for my exotic experience, so I swore on the constitution of the (defunct) Red Letters that it wasn't me or persons known to me. Moreover, in these days of Xerox machines, I demanded, hadn't he had the sense to take a copy?

'Christ, of course I didn't, Diana,' he ground out. 'That's the whole point – it had to be the original or nothing.'

'Are you sure Steph hasn't put it somewhere safe?' I asked helpfully.

'I've already asked her. She never touches my files; she'd be *persona non gratis* if she did.'

I wanted to tease him about his language, thought better of it. We parted on good terms, Ballantyne dithering between informing the police there'd been a break-in and interrogating all his potential rivals. And with me making soothing noises in his ear that sounded suspiciously like cackling.

'By the way,' he said before hanging up, 'there's going to be a stir this weekend. Want to bring Lou?'

Which was where I met Hans, when I suddenly knew what to do with the stolen White Paper.

His name was Hans Batchelor, and he was an old friend of Henry's. It was in the days when radicals and conservatives still met on the liminal zones of bohemian student flats and smoked dope together. No doubt about it, Hans was going to end up standing for mayor or something equally grandiose, but when Henry introduced us, he was a rather charming, meaty-looking man with thick dark hair and a well-proportioned face. I didn't care that he'd been a rugby fanatic, or had attended the same school as Henry. What intrigued me was that as well as working for the National Youth Board, he'd been taken on as a cadet at Foreign Affairs. Here was a man actually earning himself a leg-up into the corridors of power. Henry would be telling himself that right-wing or not, at least Batchelor would hear some of the gossip, and be nicely positioned to pass him information.

A whole lot of bells went off inside my head. I smiled quietly to myself. After we'd all taken a drag or two on the joint that was aimlessly circling the room, I sat down beside him.

'Hi, mind some company?'

Hans winked unsteadily at me. 'Are you a friend of Henry's?'

This was going to work just fine.

'We sit together on committees, see along similar lines, that sort of thing,' I said vaguely. Hans delicately pinched the roach with some tweezers and passed it to me.

'Want a puff?'

I sucked in the smoke lustily. The atmosphere in the room grew sweet in a stuffy kind of way, the fumes threatening to overwhelm me.

The pot won for a while. We stared at each other through bloodshot eyes, then launched into an unsteady discussion about the Labour Party.

'Times have changed, Diana,' chuckled Hans. 'Right might be out, but it's the way of the future.'

'What about Values?' I remembered Henry's fury about the new party.

'Pack of wankers. Totally out of touch with reality. Like that other bastard – what's his name?'

'Pardon me?' The sound in the room had begun to expand, swelling into a landscape of tortured volume shot with stabbing, electric colour. Hans's voice was a grinding saw splitting open my tender head, which made a tocking noise as it fell apart, spilling its greyish fluid to the ground.

'The fuckwit who wears a Chinese dressing-gown in public.'

'What wit . . . fuckwit?' I stumbled.

'The one who stood for Hataitai and asked for no one to vote for him. Brian someone.'

'Hataitai?' By the time I exhaled for the fifth time, I knew I was not Diana Fahey any more, not the woman who'd been abandoned by the fey Jessie, also from Hataitai, but a genius in thrall to a magnificent obsession.

'You know what, Hans?' Jimi Hendrix crashed over me, insanely loud.

Hans failed to reply. A spot on the wall to the side of his head looked as if it was about to mutate into a large insect.

'I disagree with you. If National are right for the future, they should take a leaf out of Brian's book.'

Was that a grunt from Hans? I didn't care. I was irrepressible. 'Shit, I've got a brilliant idea.'

Hans was sprawling on his back, lost in a haze of dope. I looked around the room at the blind white faces, grotesquely swollen, with greasepaint for eyes, thought, *to hell with it.*

'Let's make all candidates in the next election wear Chinese dressing-gowns. Smoking jackets, then,' I said hurriedly, catching a look at Hans's puzzled face. 'Let's call for tenders for campaign dress. You know, designers.' Meg Shepherd's face rose like a pearled mutton chop in front of me, simpered enigmatically. 'They could compete for the right to dress the politician of their choice. It'd make fan ... fan ... fantastic publicity, don't you think?'

The moments floated by in an inspired cloud, each thought more compelling than the last, until almost too late, I made a grab for sanity as it swam past. 'Look, Hans, it's obvious we've got a lot in common, do you have any plans for the rest of the evening?'

We crept out together, leaving Lou with her back to me talking shop with the Women's Collective in the hall. Yes, I felt like a bitch, but there was work to be done. When it came to politics, you needed *moral* scruples like a pain in the arse.

We hatched a plan, Hans still reeling from the pot, me clear-headed enough to know just how much to say. Then we tucked into the contents of his fridge, making plates of Welsh rarebit, without the beer. I staggered home the next morning, shamefacedly let myself in. Lou had gone shopping, so I scrubbed at my skin for an hour in the bath.

I was still scrubbing when she came home. I heard the sound of grocery bags thudding against the bench, purposeful steps heading towards the bathroom.

'Have a nice time?'

'Yes, good, thanks.' What else could I say?

It was more than I could bear, though, to be stared down by her wounded look. I shifted in the freezing water, hefted out the plug. 'Look, I'm sorry if you're upset, but it had to be done.' The water gurgled and sucked at my feet. Tears dripped down my lover's face. I felt like shit. 'I swear you'll thank me later,' I added fatuously, and reached for the towel.

Lou took off for some hours. I don't know where she went, but I was so glad to see her back that I cooked an especially nice meal and we drank the Australian wine we'd been saving.

By the time the next day rolled around, I felt a million times better, even giving myself a small pat on the back for my cunning and judicious timing. Risk, charisma, judicious hunches: I've called on them constantly in my work, and they've never let me down. At least, not for long.

Our scheme would have worked at Takaka, except I underestimated my rival's opportunism. It was his strongest suit. That, and the excited charm he let loose most effectively when his back was pressed up against ruinous defeat. Chaos brings out the best in some politicos, I've noticed it before. Josh lacked it, but another of our Red Letters claimed he needed that back-against-the-wall feeling to bring his strategies to life. I used to think powerful leaders were control freaks. I still do, but the most charismatic individuals have always been improvisers, hooked on creative last-minute responses to plans run amok. Which means bending with the storm when you know you'll get wasted if you don't.

I'm not referring to the poster heroes we stared at while we partied and swallowed our Weet-Bix in the sixties and seventies. I'm talking about people like Henry and me: small fish with big ambitions.

That's right, I did say 'Henry and me'. As I've been putting this report together, I've seen excruciatingly clearly how alike the two of us actually were. All time I was congratulating myself on my political ruthlessness, slinging off at Henry's opportunism, it was a total illusion. We were two of a kind: political animals. Our reading, our reasons, our styles were different, but the same ambition drove us. Both of us learnt when to let go; when to make peace and lie still; and when to take hold of the future and people's short memories and ride back into power.

Henry simply hasn't stayed the course as I have. Granted, I'm no longer in charge of a team of Harvard-trained geeks, but the sensitive nature of my research work assures me my world will survive, whereas Henry's is doomed. His style is too old-fashioned, being attached to sentimental notions of liberty and democracy. He's still holding forth about 'debate' and trying to get his constituents to 'lobby' the government. *Lobby*: it's such a decrepit word.

I went to Venice once in the autumn just as it turned bitterly cold and you could see the water stains of centuries on the grimy old stone. Peeling gilded porticoes and crumbling statues were everywhere, monumental in their desolation. Despotism, not democracy did for Venice, but it's the same lesson. Nothing survives, and when it dies, the best you can do is turn it into a tourist attraction. Every thick-head knows that parliamentary debate achieves nothing apart from filling the chambers with bored schoolchildren and the pockets of Wellington's service industries with the cash of our incompetent MPs. Not to mention their wives, lovers and extended families, who have saved far too many air points and acquired too much assistance with writing off their tax losses.

As you can see, I'm delaying my comments on the summit. Naturally, this is due to the fact that Ballantyne emerged less tarnished than Hans and myself.

Make no mistake: we had our hour at Takaka, along with the temporarily insane Steph Jackson, whose Janet Seed carry-on must have had Ballantyne wetting himself. I can still remember him casting around looking for support when his committee, apart from Meg, turned on him. If my voice had been as loud as Batchelor's, we might have won then, too. We might have got the summit to demand an explanation for the White Paper theft, but I couldn't make myself heard over the hysteria. I may as well have not bothered brandishing the thing. Even Henry took no notice. Bad strategy on my part. I ought to have realised that in the heat of the moment you can hold up a piece of blotting paper and incriminate the Pope. He knew I'd raided his files, in any case. His instinct told him so.

Pity about Steph's performance. Let me tell you, Henry hadn't anticipated that! Neither had we, and it goofily saved him, much to my dismay.

That's what I mean by timing. In politics, timing means seizing the moment without wrecking the future for yourself. At the summit, Ballantyne managed to do that splendidly. With the whole conference turned against him once Batchelor and I had revealed that he'd stolen the White Paper, you'd think it would have been all up, but it wasn't. I mean, how many people can cause the whole mood of a meeting to turn around, from hostility to adulation, in the space of an hour? I certainly wouldn't trust anyone who'd been planning to alter a report without my say-so. But then, I'm not everyone.

So Ballantyne won. Again. Hans and I crawled off back to Wellington in our van, and had a gruesome quarrel on the way home.

Losing Batchelor as a contact didn't hurt much. In fact, I'd finally decided to sever my connection with Josh Rideau and do things differently. His appointing me as informant on Wellington politios had taught me a lot about action groups and how they worked. I 'd got so close to bringing Henry down, but that wasn't going to impress a defunct action group in another country with problems of its own. I needed time to mull over what had happened, time to re-create myself. Information gleaned discreetly still drew me. I just had to think carefully about how to market it.

For the second time, home seemed very attractive. Ballarat began to haunt me again. I could smell all the garden smells, the cut grass and the Madonna lilies blooming next to a hedge of dew-splashed viburnum. I could see the shining jars in the pantry and a plate of burnt butter biscuits stuck with almonds and sweet sugar crumbs waiting next to cups of tea, stewed and dark. Two shadowed faces, one smooth and plump, the other stripped back to its bones, sat holding hands across the table.

I left not long after, for Australia. Lou didn't come with me this time. There were new contacts to make, and if I wanted to go solo, there was no room for my fellow traveller. In any case, she found my obsessions too wearying. In the end, I was relieved I didn't have to cart her round the country visiting the more conservative of my relatives, who would undoubtedly have given her a hard time. I didn't think she was ready for that, and I stand by my decision.

Ideal Pacific will have the report tomorrow. Meanwhile I'm left staring outside at a deserted Ponsonby street on a Sunday morning, wondering why it is that hindsight has such power to rewrite history. You can go all out when you're young and live your life in the now, but when it comes to middle age and the wisdom of retrospect, half the time what you're remembering is a story put together by a spin-doctor.

A talent I possess in spades.

I think it must have come to light when I was behind bars.

Oh – have I said? The last job I did for radical politics was when I returned to Sydney. Some of Josh's contacts wanted me to help drum up opposition to a group of fascist Yugoslavs, Ustasa. Ustasa were as anti-communist as you could get, their brutality universally resented. I heard once that their head honcho used to work behind his desk with a basketful of his enemies' eyes sitting next to him. The Australian mind balked at imagining those staring viscid jellies, which made our assignment a lot easier. Sadly, I had a bit of bad luck when a bomb plant in one of the Ustasa headquarters went wrong; consequently I got myself all over the papers again. Except that there was none of that 'poor young lady with no mother' business this time. I was sent to prison for two years.

You know, the real truth about being inside is that suddenly your life becomes so much clearer. Activism had let me down. For one thing, I never saw Josh and his friends the whole time I was at Mulawa. Lou wrote at first, with news of what her people were up to in Wellington, but I couldn't bring myself to reply. I was so sick of rhetoric. Passionate loyalties merely obstructed the real vision. The issues had to do with power, pure and simple: who had it, and how you could tap into it. Justice, self-determination, all those other bloody catch-cries: they were so much bullshit. That's when I got into the spin thing.

The sun is almost ready to break over the city. From my top storey, which boasts a niftily designed oriel window, I can see down to the shoreline. It is smoke-grey over the water, lightening all the time. My special window has entertained me for years. The curious history of the oriel used to make me smile: in my mind it was always associated with secretive upper passages and blind windows from which you could see without being seen.

Not usually a morning person, I've found that writing the report on Henry has wrought havoc on my sleeping pattern: the last few nights I've been hitting the pillow just before midnight and woken again, ragged from broken dreams, around dawn.

For once, I feel shaken. Not as you would after a disaster, when there's so much corrupt body chemistry you can't even think. What I mean is that in writing this report I'm being got at by the very part of myself I've just used to judge Henry. What if his politics are ultimately more defensible than mine? What if Parliament, despite the shit I've thrown at it, remains an option for the decent-minded?

How galling it is to think of Ballantyne as 'decent-minded'.

It doesn't make sense, either. You can't tell me that a seat in the House gives someone power; true power is the outcome of knowledge perfectly matched to outcome. I ditch the question of morality – when has it ever mattered? – and start again.

I go downstairs, light a cigarette. Predictably, I cemented my chain-smoking habit in Mulawa. If you didn't want to read, and I'd had enough of books, having a smoke filled in the time. In the half-dark, the ghosts of my old life seem to swarm closer. I wonder if Lou indulges. Smoking's had not the least effect on my skin, which after all these years is still firm. I know I shouldn't, but the habit's too hard to kick. A woman needs some stimulants in her life.

It must be growing lighter, because the smoke hangs persistently around my head like the dust rings coiled around a planet. Sainthood at last. I laugh quietly.

When was the last time I shared a laugh with someone?

Against the buttermilk walls, washed-out images begin to appear. Of Jessie, still fey, but older, with arthritic bones and mottled skin. And Lou, surrounded by a group of women, all wearing cropped, streaked hair and silver bracelets. I happen to know that Lou has recently gone to Bulgaria to teach English in a language school. I see her walking along the beach at Varna, the same beach at which those Russian leaders we used to worship spent their holidays. Does she see the irony? Does she visit the ruins of Yugoslav towns and wonder at the speed of their collapse?

Lou once represented New Zealand students at a conference in Belgrade in 1975. They toured her around villages where women proudly showed her beautiful beadwork, done in the old style, and sang unforgettable a cappella melodies that Lou said made her cry.

I would have found it unbearable, returning to a place where there had been such hope.

I light another cigarette. Outside, a gull screams. This depth of feeling doesn't make sense, even to me. Who cares now about reconstruction in eastern Europe? My provenance is the Pacific. Feelings are illusions, as unfamiliar as the lovers from my past. Quaint. Over and done. Rehabilitated.

Wait. What's this? It's Lou, taking out her camera, recording the fallen monuments, the crowded buses, the shell-wounds in city walls. Recording air thick with failed dreams and dead heroes. *Look how the people are rebuilding*, she is saying proudly to her support group back in Wellington. *Look at their courage, their inventiveness*, pointing to an orchard, recently levelled by exploding shells, now sprouting vivid spring vegetables. And to cracked window-boxes stuffed with seedlings for summer. Her dress glows with colour. I can see the light flaring on her bracelets.

The phone rings. It's my mother, still alive, hiding out in a Ballarat nursing home. After Dad died, she chose to sell up and move into one of those hideous retirement villages. And then promptly broke her hip and had to be moved into care. Because I'm in Auckland, we see each other rarely, but with the report done and a bit of a lull in clients, I can surely afford a visit.

So I fly to Melbourne. Usually I hire a car and drive home from Tullamarine, but I'm so shagged that I opt for the train.

It's useless. Even when I'm reading the *Melbourne Age*, the images keep on coming. I see a vivid image of Jessie smiling; another of Lou and me dancing at that dreadful engagement party. And waving goodbye to my father at the station in Ballarat. A whole lifetime, coiled with its secrets and its unexpected surprises, ready to unwind ahead of me. It's been years since I've wanted to remember my first relationships in New Zealand: the failed radical protest, the stretch at the infamous prison at Silverwater. Is it an incipient midlife crisis, then, all this taking stock of my past? What do Lou and Jessie want from me?

I study my nails and frown. From a distance the red looks good, a glossy tamarillo colour that deepens attractively in the light. But there is a nasty chip of white on the right index finger, threadlike cracks on the rest.

As we rattle towards Ballarat, I notice the changes since I last visited: the strip development thickening, the traffic heavier. Somehow it looks poorer than I remember. It does not feel good, coming back.

With Mum leaning on a stick, we go to a showing of *The Weeping Camel*. It wasn't my choice. Mum always was a sentimentalist – in that she reminds me of the early Meg Shepherd, before her artistic talents rescued her from a useless degree in anthropology. We sit in silence and watch the female camel ignore her baby. I've never been one to attribute feeling to animals. I know, I know – I've often seen resemblances to animals in my lovers, but never the other way around. When my cat behaves perversely, she's pure animal, without a shred of human personality. There is no damned culture of cats, no community of dogs. Such things belong to folk-tales and nursery rhymes.

I'm convinced the documentary is a set-up – a feel-good film about an obscure nomadic community angling for Best Ethnic at Cannes or whatever. An animal weeping buckets of tears because there's a violin tied around its neck? How manipulative can you get?

I do recall that not so long ago, as Mum annoyingly points out, farmers used to sing to cows to help bring their milk down. Apparently they would take transistors into the milking shed if they couldn't hold a tune. I'm still not impressed – all I can do is scoff at her. I drive home, breezily pretending I haven't just behaved badly.

Strange, what one remembers. For hours afterwards, while I am holed up in my hotel room on Chapel Street, the only frame I can drum up from *The Weeping Camel* is the shot of the young woman's hands. She ran them all over the camel's coat – soothing, stroking, comforting. They reminded me, those hands, of Lou.

If you're here for an apology, I shout, I won't give you one.

Now it's Lou who is smiling. A laughing goddess, she bends over, tongues a mystery on my forehead.

I see a farmer's dog, a grey-finned dolphin, Jessie's nose covered in spray. The images flash by faster, brighter. I see Lou, reading at a wedding. Meg Shepherd, wearing a blue and white dress, is embroidering on a cloth. Henry is there, measuring out rolled oats for muesli, Steph pouring coffee. I see myself dressed as a clown, turning somersaults in Pitt Street with the Letters. And I watch while a car drives me past Silverstream, past Paramatta, away from those gates, back into the city.

Do you believe in premonition? After all I've said, I shouldn't. Don't, normally. Except that when I arrived back in New Zealand there was a fax waiting:

> Dear Diana
>
> You may have heard about Steph Jackson's novel, *The Light-Fingered Girl*, to be launched next month in Wellington. Steph has based it on her student days in Wellington, and I dare say there are cunning references to all her friends to be found in its pages. Knowing you were an acquaintance, I have taken the liberty of adding your details to her invitation list. We do hope you will be able to join us.
>
> Kind regards
>
> Ross Cameron
>
> (Remember me? The jazz player? We met once at a wedding.)

Meg Shepherd is the first one I see.

God, she looks great. Hair a ginger-blonde, cut very short. Silver studs and a paua neckpiece. I could swear she's topped her face up with Botox, but am too polite to ask. The rest of her is black and grey – very middle-aged artist.

She stands talking to an unrecognisable Asian male. Also funkily attired but without the cosmetic enhancement – his skin is sallow and sinks into deep pocks and ugly gouges around his mouth.

'Look who's here!' exclaims Meg, drawing me into their little group. 'It's Diana Fahey. Well, I never. Come and meet Simon.'

If this is how successful artists converse, they can keep it. Meg turns out to be into numerology, consults regularly with her personal psychic and tarot reader; sells pears and preserves on the side. Inanities trip from her lips at unconscionable speed. It seems no one except me has noticed, for they are all leaning forward admiringly as, with occasional interruptions from Simon, Meg fills us in on the past thirty years.

Out of the corner of my eye I notice the Honourable Henry Ballantyne, eager to catch my attention. I pay him none. He'll keep.

I shake hands with Ross Cameron, Steph's husband. Apparently they have two children, both living in Australia. One of them, I am amused to hear, is on the dole; the other, more enterprisingly, hammering out his future at the Sydney Conservatorium. Steph, Ross confides, will be turning up shortly.

We sip our martinis. The refreshments are superior – not that I've attended many book launches, but I hadn't expected the row of spirits and the array of cocktail shakers being wielded by what appears to be an assembly of gay young men and women. Where on earth did Steph find them?

The do is taking place in the atrium of some new gallery because Meg Shepherd has apparently produced the book's cover art. The gallery is smart, coolly urban, and I am somewhat intimidated. Art has never been my thing.

Ross informs me that Meg and Steph are the best of friends, so I have no idea what happened to their old enmity. A jolt of envy hits me for people who have no gaps in their personal histories. It's a curious sensation, almost shattering, but there's little time to analyse now. People and bytes of conversation are rushing by so fast that I begin to feel hot and breathless. I tell myself it's an illusion, this sense of suffocation; that we're the only ones in the room.

'Oh,' chuckles Ross when I ask where everybody else is, 'Steph and I thought it might be nice to have a catch-up first. The rest of the guests will be along later.'

At least the savouries are circling. I hurriedly swallow a canapé, fumble in my bag for a cigarette, recollect myself in time, and head over to the bar that has been rigged in a corner of the room for a refill.

Behind me I catch the sound of Henry's already drunken burbling. 'You know what, Simon? I've had more women than you can shake a stick at, and you know what else?'

There is a frosty silence. Henry has the good sense not to continue. Someone drops a cocktail shaker, the bar clatters to life.

'The last time I imbibed a cocktail was at that awful wedding,' Ross begins cheerfully. Instead of laying into Henry, he is following me round like a yapping puppy. 'Meg's old flatmate – the empty-headed one whose name always escapes me.'

Neither of us can recall. Not that it matters. Ross is off again, as garrulous as Meg.

'I brought old Steph a strawberry dacquiri and we inspected this indecently ancient fig tree. My wife dried out yonks ago, but for a while there – you probably don't want to know this, Diana – she was Dunedin's heaviest drinker.'

I don't. I certainly haven't made this trip to listen all night to this pompous nitwit.

Henry comes trumpeting to the rescue. 'Diana,' he says, joining us at the bar and making hard work of feigning delight, 'great to catch up again. Sorry to hear about the Mulawa business. Can't have been pleasant.'

Another awkward pause. The bastard. I suppose they all know.

'True to form, Ballantyne,' I snap, poise momentarily deserting me. But I recover in an instant. Henry is huge: monstrously bulked out, his face quite liverish.

'I can't understand how you and Steph fought over him,' I say loudly to Meg, who has eased herself onto a stool next to me.

She blushes. 'He was slimmer back then. And those eyes – they were such an unusual colour I could stare at them for hours.'

Henry affects not to hear. 'So, what's cooking up in Auckland?'

'Same old same old,' I offer.

He looks expectant. 'I heard you were working for Ideal Pacific,' he says.

I suddenly realise what this is about. Henry couldn't care less about Steph's book launch. He is here to push his portfolio with Ideal.

'Come on, Henry,' I say engagingly, 'let's not talk business now. This is Steph's night. I had no idea she was a writer. Did you?'

To one side of our détente, Meg's Simon is losing control.

'Give those corporate bastards half a chance and they'll line all the artists against a wall.'

Meg is tugging at his sleeve.

'The only reason the banks and money-houses are getting behind culture these days,' persists Simon, 'is because it pays them to, in megabucks.'

How nice that Meg has a loyal fool for a partner.

Henry casts a sardonic look in my direction. I suppose they all think I've sold out. Well, they're right, and who wouldn't want to sell out? Look at them: seventies leftovers, caught in their old activist crap like stupid flies.

The rest of my rage is lost in the stampede to greet Steph, who chooses this moment to enter the room. She looks stunning. Bohemian, I guess. Hair much as she used to wear it, yet it's still strangely fashionable; black net skirt, very full; peasant blouse. Her neck is in good nick for someone our age. I'm impressed. Ross is a lucky man. Christ, I'm surrounded by beautiful women and Neanderthal men.

'Congratulations,' I murmur as she comes over. 'Not that I've been able to read the book yet, but you must be very pleased. The light-fingered girl, eh?'

Meg blushes again. Does she still have my cigarette case, I wonder, or has it been reconstructed as art?

'There's not much sense in pointing the finger, Diana. We were all thieves in our time.' Henry helps himself to a handful of pistachios.

A sanguine nodding of heads.

How can they fall for it? That phoney kind of self-knowledge must have come from his counselling days. Whatever else I've done in my life, whatever faults have turned my relationships sour, the crime of confessing in order to exculpate myself couldn't be laid at my door.

'It was just the metaphor you liked, wasn't it, Steph?' Ross Cameron again, the fumbling diplomat. I can feel my temperature building – I have to get outside or I will say something I regret.

Fortunately, the launch proper is about to begin, and the host gathers us together at the front of the crowd that has been arriving steadily while we were struggling over the past.

There is a brief speech by a woman young enough to be my daughter, remarking on the significance of the occasion. We are inspected fondly by the rest of the gathering, as if Steph's novel has turned us into domesticated pets.

A polite burst of applause, and it's all over. I remind myself to avoid such gatherings in the future, look hopefully towards an exit.

On my way out, I am accosted by a drably dressed woman. Sixties, I'd guess. She reeks of poverty, so I am quite embarrassed when she calls my name.

'Pardon?' I say coldly.

'Don't you remember me?' she says.

Hers is so unlike the beatific face in my dreams that I gasp, leap back.

We stand staring at each other while time leaps knowingly, storms an indelible tattoo at our wrists, our knees, all those intimate points we once stopped with our loving.

I move away. 'Sorry,' I say over my shoulder as I head briskly towards the waiting taxi, 'you must be mistaken. We've never met.'

'Where to, love?'

'Airport.'

It is pissing down. All I can hear is the clunk of the wipers and the hammering of Wellington rain.

'Busy day?' the driver asks conversationally.

'Yeah,' I say. I fasten my seatbelt, close my eyes.